"Who are you? V

The question drifted trem̲ from her heart.

The stranger thought of all the nowhere days and the empty, nothing nights of his life. He thought of dark alleyways, steaming jungles, two-bit hotel rooms crawling with loneliness and cockroaches—all of which had one thing in common: they were the backdrop of his carelessly lived life. He thought of endless lies, tiresome charades and his constant courting of death. He thought of the shell he'd built around his heart, a shell so hard that he could kill a man and not feel an ounce of regret.

"Believe me, Lizzie," he said quietly, "it's better if you don't know."

"Better for whom? You? Or me?"

"Better for both of us," he said, knowing that she could never grow accustomed to his hardness...but that he could grow dangerously accustomed to her softness.

Dear Reader,

If you're looking for an extra-special reading experience—something rich and memorable, something deeply emotional, something totally romantic—your search is over! For in your hands you hold one of Silhouette's extremely **Special Editions**.

Dedicated to the proposition that *not* all romances are created equal, Silhouette **Special Edition** aims to deliver the best and the brightest in women's fiction—six books each month by such stellar authors as Nora Roberts, Lynda Trent, Tracy Sinclair and Ginna Gray, along with some dazzling new writers destined to become tomorrow's romance stars.

Pick and choose among titles if you must—we hope you'll soon equate all Silhouette **Special Editions** with consistently gratifying romance reading.

And don't forget the two Silhouette *Classics* at your bookseller's each month—reissues of the most beloved Silhouette **Special Editions** and Silhouette *Intimate Moments* of yesteryear.

Today's bestsellers, tomorrow's *Classics*—that's Silhouette **Special Edition**. We hope you'll stay with us in the months to come, because month after month, we intend to become more special than ever.

From all the authors and editors of Silhouette **Special Edition**,
Warmest wishes,

Leslie Kazanjian
Senior Editor

KAREN KEAST
One Lavender Evening

Silhouette Special Edition

Published by Silhouette Books New York

America's Publisher of Contemporary Romance

For Dana, who never lets
reality get in her way.
Thanks, my friend, for sharing
your Natchitoches.

SILHOUETTE BOOKS
300 East 42nd St., New York, N.Y. 10017

ISBN: 0-373-09469-8

First Silhouette Books printing August 1988

Books by Karen Keast

Silhouette Special Edition

Once Burned . . . #435
One Lavender Evening #469

KAREN KEAST,

a nature-lover whose observant eye is evident in her writing, says if she were a season, she'd be autumn. The Louisiana resident admits to being an over-achiever, workaholic, perfectionist and introvert. Author of more than a dozen romances and two short stories, she likens writing a novel to running a marathon, noting the same determination and endurance is necessary to overcome the seeming impossibility of the task and the many obstacles along the way. Still, happily married for over two decades, she is thrilled to have the opportunity to write about the "joy, pain, exhilaration and sheer mania of love" and to be able to bring two lovers together eternally through her writing.

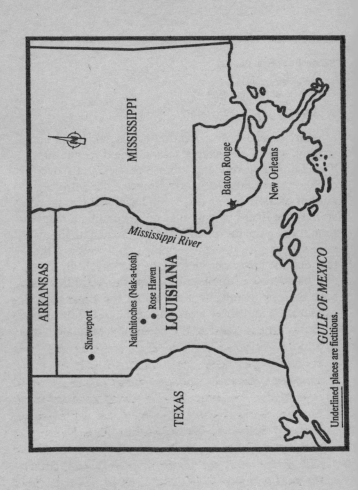

ARKANSAS

MISSISSIPPI

TEXAS

LOUISIANA

Shreveport

Natchitoches (Nak-a-tosh)

Rose Haven

Mississippi River

Baton Rouge

New Orleans

GULF OF MEXICO

Underlined places are fictitious.

Chapter One

He came out of the night. Out of the dark, rainy night. I had been going over the plantation's ledger when the storm that had threatened all day finally hit. It was a little past nine-thirty. The drawing room was hot, stifling, still. Outside, the sky was demon-black and fairly cracking open with bright bolts of wild lightning. Thunder crashed like taunted waves on the shores of heaven, and rain beat down in merciless punishment. For a reason I couldn't explain, I was apprehensive, though I had never felt so before at Rose Haven, not even after George's death. It was that prickly cold feeling that made you somehow expect the shadows on the wall to come to life and ... And what? I didn't know. And that was part of the fear. I knew only, in every bone and sinew of my body, that something was about to happen.

The old plantation house creaked under the weight of the driving rain, causing Elizabeth Jarrett to jump. A tremor of anxiety similar to that she'd been reading about slithered the length of her spine, and she cursed herself for her untamed imagination, an imagination that had been handed down as delicately as a priceless heirloom to the Jarrett women for over four generations. She likewise cursed herself for choosing this particular evening, when a storm was raging, to pick up her great-grandmother's journal. And naturally, she thought with a spicy streak of sarcasm, she would turn to the corresponding entry for that day—July seventeenth—exactly one hundred years before.

"Great timing, Professor Jarrett," she muttered, laying the journal face down on the antique peach-colored damask sofa and uncoiling her bare feet and legs from beneath her. She stood, tugged at the cuff of her white shorts and walked toward the drawing-room window. As she passed the nineteenth-century piecrust table, she noticed the clock. It read 9:37.

It was a little past nine-thirty....

"Stop it, Elizabeth Noel Jarrett," she admonished herself. She frowned. Talking to oneself was purportedly a tradition all the Jarrett women had kept alive to a greater or lesser extent. How did the old saying go? It was okay to talk to yourself as long as you didn't start answering your own questions? Well, apparently a few of her feminine ancestors had supplied their own answers. Not that history had recorded they were crazy; they hadn't been. Some of them had, however, teetered on that fine line between sanity and flakiness. Or, as her Aunt Siddie liked to say, some of the Jarrett women had met reality head-on and hadn't been all that impressed with it.

Aunt Siddie. The name brought a smile to Elizabeth's lips. It was this white-haired aunt whom she viewed as a mother, while her mother, Regan, she'd long viewed as a stranger. How odd that she'd always called her mother by her given name. How odd that she remembered seeing her only a handful of times and had only a handful of letters to represent all the times she hadn't seen her. How odd that now she would never know whether her mother talked to herself, or how she sounded when she laughed or if she was inclined to cry at a beautiful sunset. Nor would she know what her mother's last thoughts had been. Had she seen the car coming? Had she known for even a second that she was going to die? And if she had, had any of that second been devoted to regrets concerning her only child?

Elizabeth pushed the thoughts away. With her mother's recent death had gone forever the chance to know her. And how very typical of Regan Jarrett to choose to be buried in Europe, where she'd lived and played, rather than alongside the other Jarrett women at Rose Haven. In this matter, at least, Elizabeth understood her mother. She, too, had chosen to leave Rose Haven—had even fled the town of Natchitoches and the state of Louisiana—and would not be here now had her mother's death not demanded it.

She and Aunt Siddie had to decide what to do with the plantation. Elizabeth knew what *she* wanted to do with it: sell it. And for the thousandth time she wondered why she'd let Aunt Siddie talk her into living at Rose Haven for the remainder of the summer before giving her final answer.

Elizabeth sighed, knowing full well why she'd agreed. She'd never been able to refuse anything to this woman who'd tended her skinned knees, baked her favorite cookies and offered comforting excuses to a little girl who was convinced her mother stayed away because of something bad she had done. She certainly couldn't refuse her aunt anything now that her hair was growing whiter, her face more wrinkled, and her address was that of the nursing home on Keyser Street. The fact that she was now her last living relative guaranteed Siddie's sovereign power.

Elizabeth drew back the gauzy curtain at the window and stared beyond the wide porch gallery at the rain pummeling the earth. Square wooden columns painted a crisp white supported the gallery roof and were linked by intricately latticed wooden railings, also painted white. Just beyond the railings, fuchsia azaleas hugged the house and bordered the steps leading to the gallery. Across the rolling expanse of verdant lawn, two long rows of live oak trees dripping with gray Spanish moss formed a lacy green canopy that lined the approach to the stately two-storied plantation house.

These arched treetops, now dusky phantoms in the darkening night, swayed under the force of the slashing rain. Come morning, Elizabeth knew that the rose garden, for which the plantation was named, would have strewn the ground with a rainbow of fallen petals. As if to underscore her thoughts of nature's destructive power, lightning, jagged and angry, branded the sky while thunder grumbled and groaned and finally clapped loudly. So loudly that Elizabeth once more jumped . . . and again felt that eerie sense of anticipation her great-grandmother had felt a hundred years before, the night the colorful history of Rose Haven had been spawned.

Had the first Elizabeth stood at this very window?

Had she searched the darkness for some unnamed something?

Had she . . .

Elizabeth froze, her breath congealed in her throat, her eyes focused on the two-hundred-year-old live oak tree that stood alone and kinglike in the front yard. Had she seen something move? Was there a bulky shadow near the tree's massive trunk? She watched, waited, and when nothing happened, she breathed a long sigh and let the drapery fall back into place.

"Stupid," she whispered, heading again for the sofa. "You're acting incredibly stupid."

Even so, it was consoling to know there was a phone only feet away. Throughout the years, amenities such as electricity, plumbing and air-conditioning had accrued to the plantation house to which wealthy George Jarrett had brought his young bride, Elizabeth, in the early 1870s. When, twelve years later, George died unexpectedly of a heart attack one hot summer morning while tending cotton, Elizabeth, in an age when women were not known for their business acumen, had picked up the reins and continued to keep the plantation in the black. In all probability, this success alone would have been enough to earn her lasting recognition...even if she had not opened her door that fateful July seventeenth night.

Irresistibly drawn, Elizabeth crawled back into the corner of the sofa and reached once more for the age-worn journal.

The knock came at one minute after ten. My heart leaped to my throat, and a trembling began that I could not stop. Surely no one would choose to be out on such a night, so what mission ... or disaster ... had brought someone to my door? A sense of wariness, a sense of foreboding, overwhelmed me, and yet civility governed. If it were a stranger who needed my help, a night's lodging, a meal, how could I conscionably refuse him?

As Elizabeth turned the fragile, yellowed page of the journal, she recalled that this particular sentiment had led to the institution of the "stranger's room" common to

Southern plantations. The ground-floor room allowed no access to the house proper, but rather had only a single exterior door that bolted from the outside, plus barred windows, thereby making a virtual prisoner of the guest within. While Southern hospitality might demand feeding the hungry and lodging the homeless, it nevertheless reigned alongside common sense. One never knew whom one was taking in, and one was not obligated to endanger oneself or one's family.

Elizabeth read on, inhaling the moldy fragrance of time trapped in faded paper. She tried to overlook the fact that somewhere a shrub was scratching a chilling carol against the house.

Lamp in hand, my heart pounding, I opened the door. And stared at my destiny. Curiously, my apprehension and fear fled. The stranger leaned heavily against the door frame. Even slumped, he was tall, his shoulders thick, his waist and hips narrow and thin, as though they knew long hours in the saddle. His hair, plastered to his head from the rain, shone a pale blond in the dim light of my lamp, and his eyes, deep-set and brown, burned with the bright intensity of pain. He held his shoulder with his free hand. It was to this that my eyes naturally traveled, and I instantly saw the blood dripping through his fingers. I also saw the gaping gunshot wound. Even as I watched, he whispered, "Help me," and then he collapsed against me.

Elizabeth had heard the story that unfolded from that point a hundred times. It was the stuff of legends, the stuff of history, the stuff that comprised the branches of her family tree. The first Elizabeth Jarrett, using all her strength, had dragged the man the length of the veranda and into the stranger's room. There she had helped him onto the bed, removed the bullet and stayed by his side during the night. In the days and weeks that followed, she fell in love with this mystery man, whom she supposed to be a desperado who'd ridden out of the hills of the Kisatchie Forest, an area known as No Man's Land, an area notorious for men on the lam.

Coming and going in an erratic pattern, he told her little of himself, not even his name, as if wanting to protect her from who and what he was. When she discovered that she was carrying his baby, she was ecstatically happy, for her marriage had left her childless. Defying the public censure of the small, narrow-minded town, she held her head high. When the baby was three months old, Elizabeth Jarrett learned that her lover had been hanged in Arkansas for robbery. She was inconsolably bereft, and it was rumored from that time on that Elizabeth Jarrett was never quite right. Although she continued to run the plantation successfully, it was whispered that she spoke to herself and to her lover, whom she insisted frequently returned to visit her and the daughter he'd never seen. Often, she said, he would leave a single rose, which he'd pluck from the garden, as proof of his presence. Practical-minded folk insisted that she herself picked the roses, while those with a romantic turn began to believe in the ghost of the desperado-lover.

The illegitimate daughter, Rosemary Jarrett, grew up to become an internationally famous artist. She never married, though she did give birth to two illegitimate daughters, Siddie and Regan. Siddie, the elder sister by fifteen years, neither married nor had children, though she did become a renowned educator. On the other hand, Regan Jarrett evened the score for both her mother and her sister by marrying seven times. It was with husband number three, a Frenchman she divorced before Elizabeth was born, that she bore her only child. She had given the child the Jarrett name and then abandoned her to the maternal care of her sister, Siddie.

Listening to a long, quarreling peal of discontent thunder, Elizabeth raised her eyes to the portrait of the first Elizabeth Jarrett that hung above the darkened hearth. Strange. While she had spent her adulthood rebelling against the notorious "Jarrett Women"—for once she longed to be looked at singly, not in the composite picture of her ancestors—she nonetheless felt a strong affinity for this woman who was her namesake. And curiously, they looked a great deal alike—from the square though delicate angularity of their faces to the patrician tilt of their chins, from their wide, full-lashed gray eyes to their long black hair. They even had a widow's peak in common. In both cases, its prophecy had proved accurate.

As quickly as the lightning flashing outside, Elizabeth's thoughts raced backward in time to Brad Gilford, the man she'd called husband for less than two short years. In an uncanny coincidence he, too, had died of a heart attack, leaving her a widow at the tender age of twenty-five. That had been eight years ago. No, a lifetime ago, Elizabeth reflected, thankful that her memories of this man were now only warm and comfortable.

As though seeking the consoling camaraderie of one who'd shared her heartache, Elizabeth's gaze met her great-grandmother's painted one. The rain's tempo increased, the lights flickered slightly, and for a fleeting moment Elizabeth almost believed that the eyes in the portrait blinked.

"Terrific, Elizabeth," she murmured. "And I guess next you'll be seeing the ghost."

She forced her attention back to the journal.

He was heavy, and I felt his blood dampening my dress...

Thunder rumbled and rolled, and lightning charged across the sky.

... yet I somehow managed to drag him to the stranger's room ...

The lights flickered. Elizabeth, engrossed in the diary, was barely aware of it.

... where I helped him lie across the bed.

The lights flickered again. And again. Suddenly the room was pitched into both darkness and silence as the central air-conditioning ceased humming.

"Oh, good grief!" Elizabeth mumbled, waiting impatiently to see if the electricity was going to kick back on.

When it became obvious that it wasn't, she swore softly and pulled herself from the sofa. Groping, she made her way to the mahogany secretary, where for as long as she could remember matches and candles had been kept for just such an emergency. She fumbled, her fingers raking over a cut-crystal ink container and a gold-inlaid pen before finding a candle and a book of matches in a bold flash of lightning. Lighting the candle's wick, she anchored the white taper in a pewter holder. Its muted glow rippled across the room, leaving the far corners, however, crouched in darkness. In the silence, the clock abruptly began to peal. Elizabeth jumped, cursed again and counted out the hour. Ten o'clock.

The knock came at one minute after ten ...

The moment the thought occurred, she negated it.

Surely, she fumed, you're not expecting a repeat of that night a hundred years ago? That the thought had occurred as more of a question than a statement did little to settle the apprehensive feeling that had again sprung to life. Actually, the apprehension that had been palpable throughout the evening.

"Okay, Elizabeth," she said, her voice strangely eerie in the deep, almost deafening silence, "while there are those who might think your bread hasn't been fully baked, you're not exactly straitjacket material, either. Now, pull yourself together and act something in the neighborhood of your thirty-three years. Okay? Okay," she assured herself, taking a single step toward the sofa.

The tight knot in her stomach had just begun to relax, her fear to recede, when the sharp knock sounded at the door...at exactly one minute after ten o'clock.

Elizabeth whirled, a bead of hot wax plopping onto the back of her hand. It burned. But she made no effort to remove it. Instead, she listened to the sudden roaring in her ears and the incredible bashing of her heart against her ribs.

The knock came again. More boldly. More desperately? Behind it came the pounding of the rain.

Barely daring to breathe, commanding her legs to move, Elizabeth stepped forward. Her willowy, wary shadow danced on the wall in the candlelight.

At the door, she spoke—or tried to. "W-who is it?"

The empty, hollow sound of nothing answered. Then, after a few seconds, she thought she heard ragged, labored breathing. Of what? Of whom? She didn't know. And yet she knew she would open the door, for in a way she could not explain, it seemed ordained. Destined. Sanctioned by what had happened at this very door a century before.

She fought with the lock, twisted the knob in her trembling hand and pulled open the door.

The man was tall, slender, with a long-limbed, rangy build suggesting finely honed muscles. His shoulders were wide, his chest deep and heaving in a heavy, hard rhythm. He wasn't handsome—his face was too weathered, too harshly featured, too grim, for that—but neither was he unattractive. Or perhaps, Elizabeth thought absently, she was merely spellbound by his rough exterior, which suggested brawls, blue words and Saturday nights that you couldn't remember on Sunday mornings.

Jeans sheathed his legs and cupped his hips tightly and, because they were drenched, form-fittingly. In fact, every rugged inch of him was drenched. His hair, shaggy and pale blond, stuck to his forehead in uneven spikes, while his bluntly chiseled chin dripped giant drops of water. She followed the progress of one raindrop as it slid over the hollow of his throat and down into the V of the white shirt plastered to his chest. Even his eyelashes, thick and golden and fringing dark brown eyes, glistened with moisture. His eyes were his only weakness, glazed as they were with pain.

Elizabeth lowered her gaze. His right hand clutched his left arm. In the glow of the candle and in a burst of lightning, she saw the blood. It oozed through his fingers, coursed down the corded muscles of his arms like tributaries of a crimson river and pinkened his wet white shirt before puddling onto the wooden floor of the veranda.

A gunshot. She could see the raw, quarter-sized hole in the fleshy part of his arm...and suddenly she felt a little sick to her stomach. She also felt as if she had stepped back into time, or at the very least was dreaming. Or, she supposed, there was one other possibility. Maybe, unlike the other Jarrett women, she, Elizabeth Noel Jarrett, had finally managed to fall off that fine line and tumble square into insanity. Whatever—reenactment, dream or break with reality—she realized that her fear and apprehension had fled. Its flight had everything to do with the man's beseeching eyes.

"Help me," he whispered, the words choked between tight white lips.

Elizabeth had known from the beginning that she had no choice, and she fully accepted that knowledge the moment the stranger slumped forward. Acting on pure instinct, she rushed to him and propped her shoulder beneath his right arm. His weight immediately smothered her. Grimacing, she pushed her body tightly against his and, awkwardly holding the candle before her, led him along the length of the veranda. She vaguely realized she was headed for the stranger's room. This she questioned no more than she had questioned opening the door.

Thunder crackled and rain fell in thick gray sheets that were whipped into a tormented fury by the restless wind. Even though the porch was wide, Elizabeth could feel a mist of rain blowing against her bare legs. She could feel the damp floor beneath her bare feet. She could also feel her shirt growing wet from the man's soaked clothes...and wondered if some of the moistness was his blood.

The man's breathing came in a hard, ragged cadence, its bursts of warmth drifting through her shoulder-length hair to her left ear. Somehow his breath was reassuring to her. It felt real, infinitely real, in a world now constructed of shadowy fantasy.

The man groaned, presumably as pain scored his body.

"Just...a little...farther," Elizabeth managed to squeeze out from beneath the pressure of his weight.

The stranger made no response, though he let himself be guided forward.

The door to the stranger's room opened with a squeak, and Elizabeth instantly faced a new challenge. How did she, candle in one hand, heavy man in the other, negotiate the step up? She could hardly carry what felt like a couple of hundred pounds into the room. Even dragging that much weight upward was debatable.

"Step," she whispered. "You have to...help me."

The man understood, and Elizabeth could almost see him assemble his energy. Loudly sucking in air, he stepped up. She stumbled behind, almost tripping on the step. The effort to right both herself and the stranger jarred him, and he hissed between what she knew were clenched teeth.

"Sorry," she said, directing their uneven, staggering stride toward the three-quarter bed. Not even bothering to pull back the calico-quilted spread, Elizabeth, her arm sliding from his shoulder to his narrow waist, eased him down. She heard him sigh mightily as his body sank into the softness of the feather mattress. Eyes closed, he lay back, his rain-drenched head finding the bulge of the pillow, and she helped to swing his feet, shod in soaked tennis shoes, upward.

The door had closed behind them, encapsulating them in the small dark room that smelled musty and time-forgotten. The lone candle cast but a faint glow, making the objects in the spartan room—the rocker, the spindle-legged oval table by the bed, the loden-green kerosene lantern, the walnut desk, the fireplace—look like a primitive charcoal rendering of early Americana. With the air-conditioning off, the room was suffocatingly hot, and Elizabeth felt perspiration trickling between her breasts. She ignored the sweaty rivulets and turned her attention to the man lying so still on the bed.

Oh, Lord, he wasn't dying, was he? Logic told her that a gunshot wound to the arm, properly treated, probably didn't result in death. But this man had lost a lot of blood. A frightening amount of blood. And the wound had yet to be treated.

"Look," she said as she was turning to go, "you just lie here. I'm going to go call a doc—"

The man's eyes flew open, and he grabbed her wrist, his fingers manacling her so painfully that her speech skidded to a startling end.

"No!" he growled. His eyes scorched her with their intensity.

Where did he get the strength to hold her so fiercely? It was the only coherent thought that seemed capable of cutting through the maze of her mind.

Finally, in a bid for rationality, she said, "But you've been hurt. You need a doctor."

The hand tightened, his fingers digging in more deeply.

Elizabeth gasped. At the sound, at the pain pinching her face, the stranger immediately released her. Her other hand hurried to her injured wrist.

"Sorry," he whispered. The word seemed to cost him several breaths. "But . . . no doctor," he added.

If the action had bled him of strength, it in no way diminished the power in his eyes, which burned with a strangely compelling quality.

"Swear . . . it," he demanded.

"But why—"

"Swear it!"

Ultimately his eyes won. "I . . . I swear I won't call a doctor." Elizabeth saw his shoulders slump in relief. Even in the face of her promise, however, she felt obligated to point out what still remained the obvious. "Someone needs to tend to that."

The stranger nodded once. "You."

Elizabeth frowned. Prickles of panic ran wild across her body. "Me? Surely you don't expect me—"

"I'll tell you . . . what to do."

"Look," she hastened to say in what she hoped was a convincing tone, "I don't know anything about removing a bullet."

"You don't . . . have to. Clean shot. Right through." He indicated the second and smaller hole in the side of his arm. "Just . . . clean it up."

Sarcasm curled Elizabeth's lips. "Oh, is that all? You don't know how relieved I am to know that all I have to do is clean it up."

A slight twitch at the corner of his mouth hinted that, even under the circumstances, he appreciated her wry sense of humor. The faint smile vanished in a new tremor of pain. He grimaced, his lips drawn back from his teeth. Slowly he eased out a tattered breath. Elizabeth realized that some of the moisture on his face was not rain but pain-induced perspiration.

"Are you all right?" she said, knowing the question was inane but feeling compelled to ask it anyway.

"Just dandy," he said, matching her earlier sarcasm. Then he asked, "Do you have . . . any liquor?" At Elizabeth's blank look, he added, "Whiskey? Scotch? Bourbon? Anything. The more . . . the better."

Why he wanted it suddenly struck Elizabeth. "Yes. Yes, I think so."

"You'll need . . ." For a moment he said nothing more, simply lay still with his eyes closed. Elizabeth noted that the cheeks against which his honey-colored lashes fanned were as pale as a frosted autumn morning. Finally those lashes fluttered open. "You'll need . . . bandages. And sterilize . . . a thin-bladed . . . knife." At her unasked question, he answered, "To see if any . . . of my shirt . . . is in the wound."

Elizabeth groaned, grappled with a wave of nausea and raked her fingers through her jet-black hair.

He ignored her discomfort. "And a wider . . . knife." Again, Elizabeth's look posed the question. "Have to . . . cauterize . . . the wound."

Elizabeth blanched. And promised herself that she would wake up any minute now. She'd probably even laugh at the absurd dream she'd been having.

At her immobility, the stranger asked, "Maybe before...I bleed...to death?" The question effectively launched Elizabeth into action. As her hand curled around the doorknob, the stranger spoke once more. "You swore."

She turned, her eyes finding his. Though she couldn't see them clearly in the dim glow of the candle, she could feel them burning into hers with a power that forbade her to forget her vow.

"I remember," she said, the words drifting across the room's murky darkness. Again for a reason she couldn't explain, she knew she wouldn't betray him.

Back in the house, Elizabeth resorted to a picnic basket to carry everything in. By candlelight she managed to find both a small and a large knife, which she sterilized by boiling some water on the gas stove. Uncertain what else she'd need, she tossed in dishcloths and a pair of tweezers, a tube of medicated ointment and what bandages she could find— all of which Aunt Siddie had left behind when she'd moved from Rose Haven into the nursing home the year before. A nearly full bottle of whiskey had likewise been abandoned, bringing to mind the hundreds of hot toddies Aunt Siddie had served her over the years in an attempt to cure everything from the sniffles to the blues. Right now, all the whiskey had to do was dull pain.

On the way back to the stranger's room, Elizabeth prayed it would be empty, that the spell would be broken, that time would be back in its proper chronological niche. Her prayer went unanswered. As the door creaked open, a bold flash of lightning illuminated the figure on the bed. The stranger expectantly turned his head toward her.

"I found some whiskey," she said, setting the picnic basket on the small bedside table. She used the candle to light the kerosene lantern, which both brightened the room and produced stronger shadows. Blowing out the candle, she turned her attention to the liquor.

The man said nothing but struggled, grimacing, to a semi-sitting position against the bed's iron headrailing. Before the narrow neck of the whiskey bottle could clink against the glass she'd brought, he reached out and relieved her of the bottle. With a mumbled "Cheers," he brought it to his lips and swigged deeply. Elizabeth watched his Adam's apple work up and down, then watched him smear the liquid from his lips with the back of the hand that still held the bottle. He immediately took another round of swallows, clearly downing as much as possible as quickly as possible.

Elizabeth noted that his injured arm lay motionless at his side. And that his jaw, angular and strong and apparently hours away from a shave, had begun to stubble with dark brown hair. He looked... The word *wild* came to Elizabeth's mind, quickly followed by, *like a desperado who'd ridden out of the hills of the Kisatchie Forest?*

"Did you find... a knife?"

Elizabeth reined in her racing thoughts. "What?"

"Knife."

Searching through the picnic basket, she found both knives. "I boiled them in water."

"Give me the big one."

The man jerkily set the bottle down, took the knife she offered and, dragging his injured arm onto his stomach, ran the blade under his shirt sleeve. At the sound of rending cloth, a sound magnified in the silent room, Elizabeth gasped. He glanced up and smiled crookedly. "The whiskey's working. I didn't feel... a thing."

She tried to return the smile but found that she couldn't. There was something about the sight of a bloody gunshot wound—she could see where the bullet had entered and exited about three inches down and to the inside of his arm—

that dampened her sense of humor. She went back to laying out everything she'd brought with her. And wishing to God that the dream would hurry up and end before she had to do what he'd asked of her.

"Clean it out," he said. "Cauterize where it went in... and came out...then bandage it."

She glanced up, intending to speak, but words failed her at the sight of his bare chest. Somehow he'd managed to unbutton his wet shirt, pull it from his jeans and drag it off over his shoulders. Not without a heavy price, however. On a deep groan, he dropped back onto the pillow and closed his eyes, blindly wadding the shirt and using it to staunch the flow of blood from the exit wound, which was by far the bigger hole.

Taking advantage of his eyes being shut, Elizabeth lowered her gaze to the wide expanse of his chest. It shouted of a healthy strength buried deep within the muscles. She let her eyes drift downward. Tawny gold hair, thick and curly, spread like a carpet over his pectorals, tapering only to whorl around the indentation of the navel partially visible beneath the waistband of the jeans. Amid the hair hid two brown, coin-shaped nipples. There were also several dark streaks of something. Blood? Yes, blood.

She raised her eyes to find him watching her. Flustered— how long had he been watching her? Long enough to know that she was watching him?—she picked up the bottle of whiskey and handed it to him. Without a word, he took it and drew it to his lips.

As the minutes passed, a direct correlation developed between the whiskey that disappeared from the bottle and the glazed look that appeared in the stranger's eyes. A slur also staggered into his voice.

"You give...a helluva party...ma'am," he drawled, his mouth curving into a silly smile. In response to his own comment, he said, "I think I'm ... gettin' drunk."

A smile touched Elizabeth's lips, and her voice was soft when she answered, "I think, under the circumstances, that's quite all right."

Something in the tone of her voice, lacy whispers on a storm-ridden night, penetrated the drunken haze of his mind. He simply stared at her, taking in everything from the midnight-black hair that fell across her shoulders to her toes palely contrasted against the brown wooden floor. In between he noted her delicately angular face, her long bare legs, her trembling hands.

"Here," he said, shoving the bottle toward her. When she hesitated, he coaxed, "It'll help the shakin'."

She reached for the nearly empty bottle, brought it to her lips and tilted it. The whiskey that slid down her throat was fire-hot, flesh-scalding, but she was preoccupied with the knowledge that her mouth was touching exactly the spot his had. His warmth still lingered.

When she lowered the bottle, her gaze slid into his. Even though his eyes were dulled by the liquor, there was a vibrancy in them that made her feel... How? Unsettled? Yes, decidedly unsettled. And, curiously, very much alive. As if she'd been sleeping for a long while and had suddenly awakened? Yes, precisely. As if she were finally awake after a long, long sleep.

"What's your name?" he asked, shattering her thoughts like a fragile patch of ice yielding to the lightest footfall.

"Elizabeth," she answered. "Jarrett."

"Thanks, Elizabeth," he whispered. "That's just in case...I can't...thank you later."

She made one last bid. "Please let me call a doc—"

"I'm ready," he said, ignoring her plea. "Do it now."

Chapter Two

Time passed, marked not by seconds and minutes, but rather by tautened muscles, moans and ravaged whispers. My clumsiness was surpassed only by his courage, and I remember thinking, What manner of man is this who flinches not in the terrible face of pain? *Whatever he was, whoever he was, he inspired admiration. And when at last he fainted away, I felt relieved and wished that I could follow him into that blissful state of nothingness. Yet I was left behind to soak in his paleness and to breathe the heavy, cloying, sickening scent of human flesh seared in cauterization. I was left behind to wonder why this stranger had touched me so.*

Elizabeth hesitated, uncertain what to do, unwilling to do it had she known. Sensing her reticence, the stranger pulled the blood-soaked shirt from the wound and dropped it to the floor. He waited, yet still she didn't move.

"Bring...the lamp...closer," he directed. Though weak, his voice was braced with a commanding steeliness, and she, with trembling fingers, did as he bade.

By the light of the kerosene lamp, Elizabeth viewed the wound. The bullet's entry point on the outside of the arm was a small dark hole that produced a surprisingly sparse flow of blood. At least in comparison to the hole left by the bullet's powerful exit. That hole gaped open angrily, the torn flesh resembling a jagged piece of raw meat. Elizabeth swallowed back the clotted knot of nausea that jumped from her stomach to her throat. She swallowed again as bright red blood spilled from the serrated cavern in two streams that coursed downward toward the inside of his elbow.

"We're gonna be soaked...if you don't...do something."

Elizabeth grabbed a terry hand towel from the picnic basket and dabbed at the blood just as it threatened to tunnel onto the bed's coverlet. Her knuckles grazed his skin and found it warm and firm. Though he didn't visibly flinch, she felt his muscles tighten as she neared the wound. She stopped, her eyes moving to his.

"I don't want to hurt you," she said.

His eyes shone with stoicism as he replied, "That you...can't help."

Placing his hand on hers—she was instantly aware of being lost in a velvet warmth—he urged her to continue absorbing the blood. She obeyed. As if satisfied, he withdrew his hand, relinquishing the job to her. Gently, carefully, she blotted around the wound, then placed a second, protective cloth beneath his arm. That done, she again appeared at a loss.

"Take the small knife . . . and probe."

Every cell of Elizabeth's being screamed a defiant *no*. "Look, I—"

"Take the knife," he repeated.

She reached for the knife, mumbling, "Wake up, Elizabeth. Now's the time to wake up."

The knife felt cold and foreign in her hands, as if she'd never held a knife before. She gripped it tightly, afraid that if she didn't it would slip from her nerveless fingers.

"See if there's . . . any of the shirt . . . caught."

Elizabeth leaned closer, examining the injury.

"Dig," he ordered.

"But I can see—"

"You can't see."

"Yes, I—"

"Dig!" he growled, cupping her elbow and forcing her hand upward. When the knife hovered for seemingly endless seconds, he once more initiated the action. "Dammit, dig!" he said, plunging the blade into the wound. The tip disappeared, producing a new overflow of blood.

His harsh gasp filled the room, ricocheting from one startled shadow to the next.

Despite the sultry heat, Elizabeth broke out in a cold sweat.

His overbright eyes bore deeply, demandingly, into hers. "Do it!" he whispered, the torn words sounding as if they'd been wrenched from hell.

She probed, wiped the blood, probed again—all the while with her stomach churning, with her breath suspended, yet with the certain knowledge that he gave her no choice. As always when under stress, she began mumbling to herself. "I have no idea what I'm even looking for. How am I supposed to know it if I see it? Oh, God, what am I doing?"

The stranger said nothing. He simply balled both hands into fists. Perspiration poured down his already damp brow.

With each new penetration of the knife and searching twist of the blade, Elizabeth felt his pain coil deep within herself. Regardless of how much of this torture the stranger could stand, she knew she could tolerate precious little more. She had just convinced herself to quit when she saw the tiny scrap of cloth...or what she assumed a few fibers of cloth saturated with blood would look like.

"Wait," she whispered, "I think I've found something."

"Get it...out." His voice was infinitely weaker, his breath coming more quickly, more shallowly.

She glanced up, noted his paleness, then turned her attention back to the fibers.

"It'll only take a minute...." she began, but swore softly as the blade failed to capture the fabric. Instead, a river of blood swelled, sucking the threads back out of sight. She dug again. Out of the corner of her eye, she saw the man's free hand claw at the quilted coverlet with such force that two blue veins jumped into sight. He made no sound. None. Not even the sound of breathing escaped his rigidly clamped teeth. "I'm sorry," she murmured, digging yet again.

Each time the fibers eluded her clumsy attempt.

"Damn!" she swore, throwing the knife to the stand and snatching up the tweezers. She pulled the lamp closer, leaned nearer and once more set about probing.

This time the stranger's held breath hissed between gritted teeth.

"I know, I know," she muttered, working furiously. "Hang on just a minute.... Just one more minute... Just... Got it!" she cried triumphantly, holding up the minuscule fragment of cloth.

Blood smeared her fingers, but it didn't matter. In fact, nothing mattered—not the rain pounding against the roof, not the thunder trembling through the heavens, nothing—except her unlikely trophy and the increased pallor bleaching the man's face.

"Are you all right?" she asked, rushing a rag to staunch the blood.

He nodded, his nostrils flaring from his heavy breathing. Throughout it all, he'd made no verbal concession to physical agony, though it was more than obvious that the pain had taken its depleting toll.

"I got it," she said again, feeling the budding stirrings of admiration for this nameless man.

He passed his tongue across lips dry from sucking in draughts of air. "Good," he said raggedly.

She lay the tweezers down and wiped her hands on the towel.

"Heat the...blade," he whispered. "In the...lamp."

"Couldn't we just bandage it?" Elizabeth asked, recoiling at the thought of what was to follow. "Wouldn't it heal—"

The shake of his head was so slight that it was barely discernible. "Heat the...blade," he repeated, the command little more than a mouthing of the words.

She did as she was told, knowing it would do no good to argue with him and that, even if it would, he couldn't withstand an argument. Using a towel to ease the heated globe from the lantern, she adjusted the wick and thrust the blade of the larger knife into the flame.

"It'll take...a minute...to get it hot...enough," he said.

Elizabeth angled her head, finding his eyes in the dim light. His glassy eyes.

"Red-hot," he added.

She nodded, her stomach feeling suddenly hollow, like an empty reservoir.

"H-hold it . . . on each wound . . . five seconds."

She could see his strength ebbing away.

"Five seconds . . . important . . . not less."

"Five," she returned, feeling the need to reassure him.

"Swear it," he commanded for the second time that night.

She understood why he was demanding her vow. He was uncertain he'd be conscious much longer. The thought that he might slip into unconsciousness made her already empty stomach feel as if its walls might crumble at any moment.

"I promise," she whispered.

She could see him search her eyes for the degree of her commitment, then, obviously satisfied with what he saw, he closed his own eyes and lay quietly. His chest heaved in and out, calling attention to the sweat glistening from the mat of tawny hair.

It seemed to take forever for the blade to begin to turn red. The blaze, in a room that was already stifling hot, caused dewy beads of moisture to spring from Elizabeth's brow and between her breasts. The heat, combined with the high level of anxiety, produced a very real state of nausea. She breathed deeply through an open mouth in an effort to dissipate the sick feeling. The action helped only a little.

"I think it's ready," she said finally.

The stranger opened his eyes, glanced with seeming dispassion at the glowing blade and obviously agreed, for he reached back with his free hand and, fingers flexing for leverage, anchored it around a rung of the iron rail.

"Five seconds," he repeated hoarsely. "No matter what . . . I say . . . or do."

Elizabeth nodded, unable even to imagine the speed at which his heart must be beating—hers was about to jump from her chest.

He swallowed deeply, tightened his hand on the railing and nodded.

She wanted to proceed slowly—Lord, she wanted to bail out completely!—but she knew the cruelty of both. For his sake, she had to get it over with. With the knife threatening to slide from her damp palm, she stepped closer and silently prayed that she could dredge up only a quarter of this man's courage.

The moment hot metal met tender skin, the gagging smell of burning flesh permeated the room. The stranger's body went stone-rigid. He sucked in a single, giant gasp of air.

"One..." Elizabeth squeaked out, afraid that if she didn't count aloud, she'd rush the time.

The long, masculine fingers curling around the bed's iron railing grew chalky-white, while the corded muscles in his arm looked as if they would pop.

"Two..." she said, forcefully holding the knife when every instinct yelled for her to draw it away.

Sweat bathed the stranger's face and chest until his body gleamed with a coppery sheen in the dimness.

"Three..." she grated.

He growled, a low, tormented, animal-like sound.

"Four..."

His body arched from the bed...

"Five."

...then suddenly slackened and collapsed. His head lolled to the side.

Elizabeth jerked her gaze to the lifeless figure. *Lifeless.* Even though she knew that unconsciousness was a possibility, even a probability, the word brought a rush of panic, and she hastily reached over and felt for a pulse in his neck. His skin was slippery-wet with sweat and hot. She searched...searched...and suddenly found a strong beat tapping against her fingertips. She heaved a relieved sigh and, withdrawing her hand, tunneled her fingers through her hair. Her still trembling fingers. Her now blood-spattered fingers.

"Oh, God," she whispered into the silent night, not even knowing what prayer to pray. She knew only that in her exhausted emotional state, she felt the need to call out for help.

From somewhere it came. It appeared in the form of the crystal-clear realization that she had to finish everything that had yet to be done while he was still unconscious. Heating the blade again, she found the smaller bullet hole and cauterized it, again to a deliberate count of five. Once more the biting odor of burning flesh crept through the room, along with the sickly sweet scent of blood.

As if by magic the seared flesh ceased to bleed, though the skin still looked raw and implacably angry. Bandages. She needed to bandage the area as soon as possible. Laying the knife aside, she hurriedly swiped her hands down the terry hand towel and rummaged through the sack for sterilized gauze pads, which, when found, she smeared with ointment and placed across the lacerations. She then tried to anchor them by winding a roll of gauze around his upper arm. Without any assistance, the job proved frustratingly difficult.

"Darn," she whispered, unwinding the roll of gauze and preparing to start over. Raising his limp arm, she ran the roll beneath, but again, juggling arm, pads and roll, she met with far less than success. Her "darn" grew considerably stronger.

Easing to the side of the bed, she propped his arm on her knee, resting his hand, which had folded into a gentle fist, against her chest. She quickly worked at wrapping the gauze around and around his arm. As she did so, her body swayed slightly, and she became subtly aware of his thigh, hard and covered in moist denim, flush against hers and of the lax, heavy pressure of his arm balancing against her knee. She even felt swirls of crisp hair, running from wrist to elbow, slightly abrading her bare leg. And his knuckles grazed the underside of her breast with a brazenness neither would have so casually considered had he been conscious. In her leaning and twisting, she inadvertently brushed her breast again and again across his hand. She stopped only once, and that was to hastily wipe the sweat from her eyes with her shoulder.

The gauze wrapping was followed by a swath of tape, clumsily cut and clumsily applied but which nonetheless held everything in place. Easing his weighty arm from her lap, she carefully laid it back on the bed, this time without the towel beneath. He made not a single movement, uttered not a single sound.

For long moments she simply stared down at the man.

The sudden realization that her job was over, that there was nothing more for her to do, brought an instant and overwhelming weariness. It also caused a renewed, relieved trembling of her hands, which she tried to control by clasping them together. She was hot, so hot, and the smell of burned flesh and spilled blood still danced around the room to the macabre music of her stomach's churning. She suddenly once more felt as if she were going to be sick, this time in earnest.

Fleeing toward the door, she flung it open on its creaking hinges and gasped in a clean breath of rain-cooled air. Though the violence of the storm had abated, rain still peppered down steadily. The fat raindrops hitting earth and house sounded particularly loud after the silence of the small room and left her vaguely disoriented. Just the way much of the night had. The night. The stranger. She wasn't strong enough to think about either just yet.

Standing beneath the eaves of the veranda, Elizabeth thrust her shaking hands into the rain, imagining the last of the scarlet stains being washed away. Cupping her hands, she caught palmfuls of water and brought the sweet moistness to her face. She splashed it on her fevered skin, letting it flow in unchecked runnels over her cheeks and chin, down her neck and throat. The water dripped into the sweaty valley between her breasts and brought an immediate thought of the stranger's knuckles propped against that same fullness. She had no idea why the thought had come to her. It was not a sensual thought. It was simply... a thought. A thought she released as easily as she had embraced it.

Leaning back against a square column, she closed her eyes, relinquishing as much feeling as she could. Slowly her trembling lessened. Slowly her heartbeat steadied. Slowly fragrances of the summer night—the sweetness of cape jasmine, the intoxicating lure of honeysuckle, the dank smell of wet Spanish moss, the wafted purity of roses—replaced the harsher smells of blood and seared flesh. Little by little, in softly ebbing waves, the nausea receded.

She expelled a long, deep breath. In tandem, thunder rumbled gently. Opening her eyes, she watched a lazy bolt of lightning ribbon across the sky. In the measured light she saw the dark stain on her shirttail. She knew immediately what it was and stretched the fabric so that the rain filtered through, washing away the blood.

Blood.

The night.

The stranger.

Was she strong enough to think about them now? She didn't know. She honestly didn't know. And she was relieved that fate spared her from having to answer.

A moan, his moan, sailed through the night, reaching her ears and curling itself about her heart. Turning, she stepped back into the room. He lay just as she had left him, except that his uninjured arm was draped across his bare stomach. He was still unconscious or perhaps now only deeply asleep. She watched and waited, and when he didn't move or cry out again, she lowered the wick of the lantern to a hazy glow and partially propped open the door to allow in any willing, wayward wisps of a breeze. She raised the barred window, suddenly wondering if her great-grandmother had opened the window as well, or if she had believed that the nocuous night air might worsen her patient. Elizabeth let the thought slide away and quietly drew the rocker to the bedside.

Should she try to remove his wet jeans? No, she thought, though her decision had nothing to do with shyness, a fact that mildly surprised her, considering that their relationship was little more than an hour old. The truth was, she wasn't sure she could remove the jeans without his assistance. Certainly she couldn't without resorting to a wrestling match, which most assuredly would disturb his rest. And at the moment rest was far more important that the removal of wet jeans. She did untie his tennis shoes and slip them from his feet. The act evoked a tiny groan of protest, which only reinforced her decision to leave the jeans untouched.

The night was long and hot; her vigil, constant and complete. Into the silence, into the stillness made even more sweltering by the steamy rain, fell an occasional moan, a sigh, the restless rustle of man against fabric. From time to time a grimace would contort the stranger's full lips, or he would quickly jerk his head to the side as if trying to roll away from a sudden burst of agony, or he'd groan a deep, pitiful wail that knifed at Elizabeth's heart. At one such moment, as his moan ripped through night and soul, she leaned over him, using her shirttail to blot the perspiration from his brow. His breath, warm and moist, swam around her wrist. It was curiously comforting.

And he was uncomfortably hot, she recognized by the sweat dripping from his brow and chest. Looking around, she spotted the paper bag of bandaging materials. She removed what was left and, sitting back down, fanned the folded sack back and forth above him. A weak though heavenly breeze stirred amid the softly crinkling sound of paper. A sigh, which she allowed herself to believe was of contentment, seeped from his lips.

Long after her wrist ached from the constant fanning, she fanned on. And watched him. His blond hair, now dry but wildly rumpled, fluttered in the induced breeze. Even the golden, silken pelt matting his chest swayed like wind-teased wheat. She studied his chest's rise and fall, taking in bare planes, muscular ridges and the corrugated alignment of his ribs. His uninjured arm, equally dusted in tawny-brown hair, still lay across his stomach. His flat, darkly tanned stomach. Into which a navel seemingly had been thumb-punched.

Her eyes dropped lower. To the spread of lean, masculinely sculpted legs. The left jutted out at a lazy angle. A provocative angle that stretched the moist denim across thigh and belly. The waistband of the jeans had come unfastened, leaving a small V of paler skin in full view. Beneath were a series of closed metal buttons. As Elizabeth's eyes journeyed down their length, she mused that she had never so analytically studied a man before. The jeans clung to him like a second skin, with wrinkles radiating across firm, trim thighs and pointing like arrows to the bulge beneath the confining buttons. Which was solidly, uncompromisingly male. She blatantly stared . . . and realized that he was as suggestively alluring in the jeans as he would have been out of them.

Alluring?

Yes, he was alluring. Ruggedly so. And while she still wouldn't have called him handsome—not by any stretch of the imagination—she now had to admit that he had battered good looks. She also had to admit that her thoughts and feelings, both of which had stolen upon her almost unnoticed, were no longer the asensual thoughts and feelings of earlier. When she'd remembered the feel of his hand grazing her breast, the thought had been simply a thought. Now, having evolved like the infinitesimal changes of a sunset viewed at one-minute intervals, it was subtly more. Something in the way he sprawled across the bed, something in his indisputable masculinity, reminded her, as gently, as softly, as naturally as the rain now sprinkling the roof, that she was a woman.

She stopped fanning. And sat quietly as a wave of confusion washed over her. There was something more, wasn't there? He touched her in a way that transcended the sensual, in a way that called upon soul-deep feelings. She could hear, as clearly as if he had spoken, a new language falling on her ears, tugging at her senses. It was a language built on possession. She felt an inexplicable, almost ethereal, possessiveness toward this man. This man who was no more than a stranger.

Bonding? It was a logical explanation for her feelings. Sharing a traumatic event bonded people together. And what they'd just gone through had definitely been traumatic. And yet . . . And yet, the bonding phenomenon did not wholly satisfy her as an answer. But she was...the word *scared* skipped through her mind. Yes, she realized, she was scared to search too deeply for an alternate reason.

Abruptly the stranger's injured arm twitched, as though a tremor of pain coursed down its length. He moaned through twisted lips. Instinctively, Elizabeth laid her hand atop his, absorbing the quivering spasm into her very flesh.

"It's all right," she whispered, holding tight until the jerking slowed, then died to an exhausted stillness. And even then, for reasons she didn't explore, she didn't let go of his hand, but rather held its warmth in hers.

Who was this man? Where had he come from? How had he been shot? She wanted to believe he'd been shot while hunting or maybe while cleaning a gun. But what did one hunt in July, in a storm? And if he'd accidentally, innocently, shot himself while cleaning a gun, why hadn't he wanted her to call a doctor? Again, the answers frightened her, but come morning, she'd face whatever they were. She'd face whatever she must. Come morning, she was determined to find out just who this man was.

The tear-shaped flame in the kerosene lantern winked once, twice, thrice, before going out completely. The room was instantly invaded by a plush darkness. Elizabeth didn't notice. Still sitting in the rocker, she rested her head on the bed, her cheek within inches of a hard thigh, her hand still wrapped around the stranger's. Drugged with fatigue, she slept soundly, deeply.

The stranger, however, accustomed to noting the slightest sound, the slightest movement, the slightest change in setting or mood, registered the loss of light. He tried to open his eyes, tried to weave his way through the labyrinth fogging his mind, but couldn't. He methodically searched for the reasons he could not. Drink. He'd had too much to drink. He could feel the liquor—whiskey, wasn't it?—dulling his senses, weighting his eyelids, making his head pound to a hideous, hammering, why-the-hell-don't-you-stop? rhythm.

He twisted, winced and simultaneously realized that the pain was not confined to his head. His arm hurt, too. Badly. Excruciatingly. Why would his arm hurt? Why—

Images flashed quickly. A cotton mill. A gun. The cracking sound of bullets fired. A tearing pain. Blood spurting from his arm. The body of a black man, his eyes wide with death. The dark, yawning mouth of a well. The black man falling down, down, until there was a faint splash of water. More blood, his own, pouring, pouring, pouring. Or was that the rain? Or maybe a woman's dulcet voice? Yes, a woman. A woman with gray eyes. A woman with a gentle touch. A woman named Elizabeth.

Elizabeth, Elizabeth, Elizabeth—the name, as light as fairy dust, echoed through the fuzzy corridors of his mind. Friend or foe? Devil or angel?

Suddenly the memory of something hot searing his arm chased all else from his mind. God, it hurt! Why didn't it stop?

Five seconds. No matter what I say or do.

One ... two ... three ... the fairy voice chanted.

Stop it! God, stop it! I can't stand any more!

... four ... five.

He groaned and tried once more to rouse himself, but again the harsh pain in his arm was too much. He let himself slip back into oblivion. It was a peaceful land filled with a hint of her perfume, filled with the delicate whispers of her voice, filled with the softness of her breast as she anchored his hand against it.

But something about her troubled him. What was it? He tried to fish the answer from the murky mental waters, but it kept slipping back, disappearing beneath the jet-black surface. He knew only that it had something to do with not knowing her, yet knowing her. As if somewhere, sometime, they'd met before. Though that wasn't possible.

A new pain seized him, racing down his arm. His hand jerked, he moaned and her hand closed around his. He relinquished the troubling thought, content for now to take the comfort, the sweet succor, she offered. That in mind, he twisted his hand and laced his fingers with hers. Tightly. She answered in kind.

Though both were lost in a world of sleep.

Chapter Three

I kept a bedside vigil, all the while wondering, Who was he? *and,* Would I ever have the courage to ask? *After a day and a half, he rallied, but I feared an infection, for the wound grew red and angry. Eventually the infection came, and I fought again, this time for an endlessly long week, to save his life. On the eighth day, to my joy, he awoke clear-eyed and free of fever. Restless, he longed to stir about. I took him to the big oak in the front yard and made him comfortable on a spread quilt. We listened to the summer birds, whose chatter mingled with the peaceful rustle of the leaves, and felt a faint breeze skip across our warmed skin. The stranger's smile, at once both happy and sad, beguiled me, and I think it was there, under the sheltering limbs of the oak, that I first began to fall in love with him. And the more I grew to love him, the more my courage failed. To save my soul, to save my heart, I could not ask who, or what, he was.*

Elizabeth came instantly awake.

A shaft of warm yellow sunlight squeezed its way into the room through the door, which was still propped ajar, while the same mellow light, shoving through the barred window, striped the wooden floor. As if performing in the spotlight, dust motes merrily danced in morning play. Silence, complete and stunning, whispered from every corner.

Utter silence.

Utter stillness.

In that split second when wakefulness overtook sleep, Elizabeth realized that she had a severe crick in her neck. She also realized that the paper sack was now crumpled in her left fist, while her right hand, which had covered the stranger's—an image of entwined fingers flitted through her drowsy mind—now held... nothing. A cold, barren, absolute nothing.

She jerked her head up. The bed was empty. Furthermore, it appeared as though it hadn't been occupied. The bulge of the pillows was fluffed and precise; the feather mattress bore no indentation, except for the spot that had cradled her cheek. She quickly—frantically, even—ran her hand down the printed coverlet, searching for a revealing dampness. Nothing. No, maybe it was a little moist. She sighed, admitting that she couldn't really tell. Though she could tell that panic had begun to stalk her, bringing with it a faint rush of adrenaline.

Where was he?

She whipped her head around, absently wincing at the pain the action produced in her cramped neck. She fully expected to see the blond-haired, brown-eyed stranger standing behind her. After all, that would be logical, wouldn't it? He was wounded, weak. Surely he must be nearby. But he wasn't. Like the bed, the room held no trace of his ever having been there. His shoes were gone, his blood-drenched shirt was gone, and—the panic took a menacing step closer—so were the dish towels she'd used to soak up the blood.

Frowning, she stood, walked to the bedside table and poked through the knives, tweezers, tape, ointment and sterile pads. Everything was as she'd left it, with one significant difference. There was no longer any blood on the tweezers or the knives. They were clean, as clean as when she'd packed them in the picnic basket. What had happened to the blood?

An answer crossed her mind—maybe there never *was* any blood—but it was so ludicrous, so disturbing, that she refused to acknowledge it. Instead, she began a frenzied search for anything that would prove the stranger's presence. The candle? No. The lantern, now burned out? No. The whiskey bottle?

The whiskey bottle!

The whiskey bottle stood on the bedside table, exactly where he'd placed it. And it was nearly empty, proof positive that he'd drunk it. Elizabeth's frown deepened. Or was it only proof positive that *someone* had? Someone like . . . She suddenly remembered taking, at his urging, a swallow of the liquor, remembered, too, how it had burned traveling down her throat. Would an objective bystander simply say that she herself had consumed the bottle of whiskey? That the liquor was responsible for her outlandish memories of the night? No, she thought in defiance, she had not drunk it. *He* had.

And yet, with ever-increasing intensity, she sought something that would substantiate his presence and alleviate her fear. But nothing, absolutely nothing, appeared.

Dammit, even the spot of blood on her shirttail she'd meticulously washed out in the rain!

She suddenly remembered the blood that had dripped onto the floor by the front door seconds before he'd whispered a plea for help and slumped against her. Racing out of the stranger's quarters, she noted, as she had the night before, the loud creaking of the hinges. Considering the noise the door made, how could the stranger have left without waking her? Maybe she'd been too dead to the world to notice? Or maybe the stranger had simply walked through the wall? This latter possibility she pretended she hadn't thought at all, though it hastened her footsteps forward.

In the brilliant light of the sun that seemed dedicated to making up for the previous evening's storm, the square wooden columns and the latticed railing were blinding in their snow-whiteness. Elizabeth squinted against the glare, thinking that the bloodstains would vividly stand out against such a pristine background. And that she'd be able to see them any second now. But each step brought her nearer with no sight of crimson. Disbelieving, Elizabeth stooped and ran her hand over the planked floor.

Nothing!

Elizabeth glanced the width of the gallery. Maybe the rain had splattered off the eaves, or maybe the wind had driven the rain inward, obliterating what could only have been small spots at the most. Or maybe...

The panic that had been stalking her suddenly pounced. Dear God, she thought, rising from her kneeling position, what had happened last night? Had she been so steeped in her great-grandmother's journal, a woman whose life had always seemed mysteriously interwoven with her own, that the past had somehow, some way, come to life for her? Or was she simply walking in the unstable footsteps of the eccentric Jarrett women? Or maybe—her heart quickened at the prospect—she'd had her first encounter with Rose Haven's ghost.

Ghost.

My God, was she seriously entertaining the notion? Elizabeth leaned against the front door and raked unsteady fingers through her sleep-mussed hair. Beginning with her great-grandmother, history was dotted with people who claimed to have spotted the rough and rugged desperado. But Elizabeth had never seen him, though she remembered longing to in her youth. For hours she would sit beneath the giant oak tree in the front yard, where he reportedly often appeared. Day after day she had spread her schoolbooks around her and waited. But he'd never come. Until last night?

Elizabeth unthreaded her fingers from her hair and slowly began to lower her hand. She didn't know what to believe. She really didn't know what... Her gaze fell to her left wrist. There, three purplish-blue bruises marred her ivory skin. Three purplish-blue bruises that starkly revealed the imprint of two fingers and a thumb. *His* fingers and thumb.

Elizabeth's heart surged into a new rhythm at this indisputable evidence. Clasping her right hand around the bruise, she clutched both hands to her chest. She could feel the powerful pressure of his hand supplanting the gentle pressure of her own. She could hear his uneven, pain-racked breaths. She could hear his raspy voice commanding her to swear that she wouldn't call a doctor. How truly relative everything was, she thought. At the time, his grabbing her wrist had been physically painful. Hours later, it helped to ease the emotional pain of troubling, unanswered questions. Someone *had* been here. She wore the proof of that on her wrist. But who? Where had he come from? And how had he gotten shot?

In search of answers to these questions, she made a quick drive to the nearest convenience store, then returned and sat at the long wooden dining table, scanning the morning newspaper. Since the local paper came out only on Thursdays and Sundays, many residents looked to a larger city for daily news. As Elizabeth turned the pages of *The Shreveport Times*, she had to admit she was uncertain what she was looking for. Well, that wasn't exactly true, she thought, systematically perusing all articles for one that hinted at violence in the Natchitoches area. Which surely the paper would report, wouldn't it? Especially if the incident was serious enough for someone to have gotten shot? In the end, all she discovered was that the man who'd drowned the week before in the rain-swollen waters of Natchitoches's Cane River Lake had been buried in his hometown of Shreveport, some eighty miles away. But no one, accidentally or otherwise, had recently been shot in Natchitoches.

Again Elizabeth began to entertain unsettling questions. Could an apparition grab your wrist? Would he leave bruise marks if he did? And what kind of crazy loon was she for even considering such questions?

She was trying hard not to mull over the subject, and thereby mulling over it excessively, when the phone rang. The shrill summons made Elizabeth jump. She castigated herself for her edginess and reached for the phone on the kitchen counter.

"Hello?" she said, automatically looking up at the clock. It had stopped in the power outage but was now ticking away—with the wrong time. Sometime during the night the electricity had come back on. Until just this moment she'd been too caught up in her thoughts to give any consideration to the hour.

"Hi there," drawled the warm, familiar voice of her friend, Pamela Shaw. "Oh, hold on a minute, will you?" In an aside, the woman said, "No, you may not slime your brother in the house." There came the argumentative whining of a young child. "I don't care if he did slime you first. Now, take that stuff out into the yard. And keep it off the sidewalk! You hear me? Carol, do you hear me?" she added on a raised note. A mumbled reply followed before the woman's voice came back on the line. "If I ever get my hands on the man who invented that slime crud, he's dead meat."

Despite the night, the morning and the endless array of questions swirling in her head, Elizabeth smiled. "How come you're so sure it's a man?"

"You've got to be kidding. No woman would invent a toy whose instructions say 'May cause damage if applied to furniture, clothing, curtains, floors or walls.' My Gawd, what's left?"

"The yard?" Elizabeth ventured.

"Right. And hopefully someone else's. That stuff probably kills grass, too. What?" Pamela asked, obviously once more distracted. "She's in the front yard, Casey. Go get slimed." A deep sigh later, she said, "Thank the merciful heavens they were twins and not triplets."

Elizabeth's smile widened. In a small town like Natchitoches, where everyone knew everyone, lives were entwined practically from birth, but that didn't guarantee the solidity of friendship that had developed between her and brown-haired, twinkling-eyed Pamela Shaw. From the moment they'd entered first grade and Pamela's extroversion had so fittingly complemented her introversion, they'd become fast friends, a fact that the years had not altered. They had gone to Natchitoches High together, where they'd shared both giggles and growing pains, then later they'd been roommates at Northwestern State College, now Northwestern State University, where Elizabeth had majored in English and Pamela in history. Pamela had been the first person she'd told upon graduation that she was leaving Natchitoches to teach American literature at Bryn Mawr in Pennsylvania. Pamela had also been the only person not to ask why. In that moment, when Elizabeth had realized just how clearly Pamela understood her identity problems, the friendship had deepened into a rich maturity.

It was with the warmth of that friendship that she now asked, "Are you being ugly to my godchildren?"

"Trust me, I could make a far greater case for parent abuse." There was the scrambling sound of the phone being switched from one ear to the other. "Listen, can we make it twelve-thirty instead of twelve?"

A silence followed. Elizabeth searched through the chaos of her mind.

"Don't tell me you've forgotten our lunch date," Pamela complained mildly.

"No. No, of course I didn't forget," Elizabeth said, only partially lying. She did remember planning the lunch date for Tuesday, July eighteenth; she simply hadn't realized that Tuesday, July eighteenth, was today. This morning she was having trouble remembering anything not connected with a blond-haired, brown-eyed stranger who might or might not be a figment of her imagination, whose blood might or might not have stained her hands, her clothes and her veranda, whose— She suddenly realized that her friend had spoken. "What?"

"I said, Are you all right?"

"Sure. I'm fine. Why wouldn't I be?" Before Pamela could even venture an answer, she added, "I'll see you at twelve-thirty."

There was a slight hesitation, as if Pamela was trying to decide if everything really was fine. "Right," she said at last.

The phone was already leaving her ear when Elizabeth rushed it back and asked, "Hey, Pam, what time do you have?" She knew the clock in the drawing room would have the correct time, but she was reluctant to return to the scene where everything had begun. She knew she'd find her great-grandmother's journal on the sofa where she'd left it. Still open to the entry dated July seventeenth.

He came out of the night. Out of the dark, rainy night....

"Uh, I have five till ten. Your electricity was out, too, huh?"

"Yes," Elizabeth answered, her mind playing back images of faltering lights, a candle's glow and streaked lightning delineating rugged facial planes and blood trailing down a muscle-bound arm. Blood that dripped onto the white porch. Blood that, like the stranger, had been gone come morning.

"Boy, last night was something else, wasn't it?" Pamela said, referring to the storm.

"Yeah," Elizabeth agreed quietly before they hung up. "It was something else."

The town of Natchitoches, founded in 1714 by Louis Juchereau de St. Denis, was the oldest permanent settlement in the Louisiana Purchase. Originally a trading port on the Red River, its commerce flourished until the river changed its course, abandoning a thirty-two-mile stretch of water—which came to be known as Cane River Lake—to run through the heart of both city and parish. The demise of trade and thus of outside influence had allowed the city to preserve much of its history.

A riverfront drive, lined by cotton-candy pink and fuchsia crape myrtles and majestic live oaks, offered a scenic view of Cane River Lake's muddy green waters, which were often lazily spotted with colorful, graceful mallards. Above the riverfront ran Front Street, the town's main thoroughfare. In the early 1900's, red bricks were laid over what had previously been dirt streets, and the bricks had remained through the years, adding to the quaint, cobbled charm of the city.

Elizabeth, seated in the air-conditioned restaurant, absently stared out at these sun-dappled bricks, which seemed to shimmer in the sweltering summer heat. The restaurant, called Just Friends, was in Ducournau Square, a boutique-riddled restoration characterized by carriageways, courtyards and casks of ferns and flowers.

It was thoughts of red, however, that characterized Elizabeth's worry-riddled mind—the red of the hot bricks, the scarlet of her blouse—despite the heat, she'd chosen a long-sleeved shirt to hide the bruises at her wrist—and the crimson of the stranger's blood. Where had the blood gone? Where had the stranger gone? Where—

Elizabeth jerked her head around at a voice calling her name. Her gaze collided with the openly inquisitive soft blue eyes of her friend.

"Are you ready to order?" Pamela asked in a tone that suggested the question had been asked before, either by her or the woman standing beside the table.

Elizabeth glanced up into the warmly hospitable face of the waitress. Her pen was poised over a pad. Her look was expectant.

"Yeah. Yeah, sure," Elizabeth said, throwing open the menu she hadn't read and selecting the first thing she saw. "I'll have a turkey sandwich."

"Anything to drink?" the waitress asked.

"Uh . . . A glass of iced tea."

The woman nodded, scrawled, collected the menus and walked away.

Elizabeth lowered her gaze—right back into Pam's inquiring eyes. *What's wrong?* they clearly asked. Elizabeth ignored the silent question. Instead she said with a forced enthusiasm, "This is nice. Really nice." She made a gesture with her hand that encompassed the room—the gleaming wooden floors, the woven baskets attractively arranged on the wall, the hanging planters of green ivy, the patterned blue tablecloths, the small vase of fresh flowers on each table—none of which she truly saw. "It all looks—" Elizabeth's traveling gaze landed once more, this time in blue eyes still filled with questions "—nice."

Long, quiet moments passed, and Elizabeth feared a barrage of inquiries.

"Did Carol and Casey get slimed?" she hastened to ask, hoping the subject would distract her friend. If the six-year-old twins didn't do the trick, nothing would; though Pamela complained incessantly about the antics of her "cloned monsters," Elizabeth knew she adored them as only a mother who'd tried long and hard to have children could.

The subject worked its magic, and Pamela's expression passed from one of uncertainty to one of feigned annoyance. A blissful light, however, shone in her eyes. "Casey got Carol once, Carol got Casey twice, and both were talking in whispers when I left. My guess is that the baby-sitter got it before I backed out of the drive."

Elizabeth smiled. So did her friend. Elizabeth noted that Pamela, with her brown hair short and pixyishly wisped about her heart-shaped face, looked almost as youthful, certainly as innocently in love with life, as her six-year-old daughter, Carol. Mother-daughter. It was a relationship Elizabeth had never known from either viewpoint. She'd never known what it was like to have a mother, nor would she, in all likelihood, ever know what it was like to have a daughter. At least that was the road life seemed to be herding her down. Her heart grew heavy from both denials.

The tea, clear and golden, arrived, invitingly iced and served with a sprig of mint. Both women murmured their thanks.

"So how does it feel to be back at Rose Haven?" Pamela asked, selecting a packet of sugar.

Elizabeth considered before replying. "Strange." She, too, reached for a packet of sugar but realized that the blouse cuff had ridden beyond the bruises at her wrist and reeled her hand back in. She gave her dinner companion a quick look to see if she'd noticed the distinct purplish-blue marks. When she obviously hadn't, Elizabeth breathed a sigh of relief and reached for the sugar with her other hand. Yes, she thought, *strange* was definitely the word to describe what it was like to be back at Rose Haven.

Suddenly Pamela laughed. "Remember when we used to go to the attic and dress up in those clothes we found in the trunk? We couldn't have been more than eight or nine."

Elizabeth smiled in genuine amusement. "I loved those buttoned, high-topped shoes."

"And I loved that red felt hat with the black ostrich feather."

"Remember the ivory comb shaped like a flying bird? Remember how we used to twist up our short hair and try to pin it with that comb?"

Her friend nodded. "Remember that crocheted shawl?"

With each recollection, Elizabeth's smile had grown broader. Abruptly it disappeared, replaced by a sad, sober expression. "I used to pretend that I was dressing up because my mother was coming to visit me. The few times I remembered seeing her, she was so pretty, and I thought that if she could just see how pretty I was in those high-topped shoes, that shawl and ivory comb..." She trailed off, unwilling, unable, to finish the sentence.

Pamela gently finished it for her. "You thought that she wouldn't go away again."

Elizabeth glanced up from watching a bead of moisture pop on the iced tea glass. The exchange of feelings, warm and weighted with poignancy, was ostensibly woman to woman, yet, curiously, child to child.

"How naive, right?" Elizabeth said. Before Pamela could answer, before the moment could become intolerably maudlin, she added, "Did I tell you that they buried her in Italy?"

Pamela looked as if she wanted to say something more on the subject that was being left so quickly behind, but in the end chose to respect her friend's emotional privacy. "No, you didn't. Last time we spoke, you didn't know where she was being buried. Why Italy?"

Shrugging, Elizabeth said, "Beats me. Except husband number four—no, number five, I think—was Italian. Frankly, I suspect they just put seven names into a hat and Mr. Italy won."

"I would have thought her current husband—"

"They were already in the process of getting a divorce."

"Oh."

"Yes, oh." Again the atmosphere, like the storm of the night before, threatened to become oppressive. "Actually," Elizabeth said, dissipating the heaviness, "several of her husbands have been kind enough to send condolences. One, number six, a British lord or something—they were married all of three months—is going to send some of her things, which she obviously left behind in her haste to marry husband number seven."

"What about your father?"

"I called him. He hadn't heard." Elizabeth smiled wryly. "Which, of course, seems to be the story of his life."

Elizabeth had been nearly ten years old before her father, a French banker, had discovered her existence. Why Regan Jarrett had chosen not to tell him until then, why she'd chosen to tell him at all at that late date, remained a mystery. Elizabeth had always assumed it was part and parcel of her mother's erratic behavior. Her father's behavior, thankfully, had been less erratic. Though they didn't share a traditional father-daughter relationship, they had been able to maintain a long-distance friendship.

Pamela picked up her tea glass and offered a toast. "To Regan Jarrett, who certainly did it her way."

Careful to use her unbruised hand, Elizabeth reciprocated. "That she did," she said as the glasses clinked in agreement.

Their lunch came, and conversation was comfortably reduced to the mundane. The Hall Tree was having a summer sale on sundresses. The card shop had a new line of hysterically funny greeting cards, the A & P had some really good-looking fresh fruit. Elizabeth was grateful that last night had retreated to the back of her mind. Sitting here, with the sun streaming in so brightly, so ordinarily, with her friend talking so animatedly about sundresses and ripe peaches, she could almost believe that last night hadn't happened. She could almost believe it until she remembered what lay beneath the sleeve of her blouse.

Dessert and coffee had just been served when Elizabeth heard the familiar voice of Ben Adams. The tall, stout, khaki-uniformed sheriff had gone to school with Elizabeth and Pamela and had led the Northwestern Demons to more touchdowns than any other single player in the school's history. Following graduation, he'd played pro football for several years before a knee injury demanded that he stop.

He'd returned to Natchitoches to be elected to the post that his father was just vacating.

"I heard you were back," Ben thundered, grabbing Elizabeth up in a big bear hug, then pushing her to arm's length. "Lord, look at you. Pretty as ever."

"Still trying to score, huh, Adams?" Elizabeth teased.

A broad, white smile erupted across the sheriff's football-scarred, though handsome, face. "A man's gotta keep trying." The smile faded. "Sorry about your mamma."

"Thanks."

"How long you gonna be at Rose Haven?"

"Through the summer," she said, explaining about her arrangement with her aunt.

"If you're looking to sell, I'd like to talk to you about buying. I saved a little money before the knee bummed out, and I've always liked the plantation."

"I'll definitely keep you in mind," Elizabeth assured him.

"Sit down and join us," Pamela said.

"Sorry, I can't. Gotta get back to catching rowdies and rascals."

Elizabeth eased back into her chair and attempted to ease out her question. "Has anything really exciting happened lately? Like a burglary, a kidnapping, a shooting...?" She let the question suggestively taper to nothing.

"As a matter of fact, something did. Last night."

Elizabeth's heart picked up its rhythm.

"When the lights went out, old Miss Farber tripped over her cat and broke her leg. Miss Farber's leg, not the cat's."

Everyone laughed, even Elizabeth, who wasn't sure whether she'd wanted to hear that a shooting had or hadn't occurred. Her heart settled back into a slower beat.

Moments later the sheriff took his leave, and the two women slid back into casual conversation. Didn't Ben look wonderful? Why was it that men aged so much better than women? For that matter, everything seemed to age better than women. Why, look at Rose Haven....

Rose Haven, Elizabeth thought. With its picturesque live oak drive, with its elegant rose garden, with its resident ghost.

"Do you think a ghost would bleed if it got shot?" Elizabeth asked, surprising herself by vocalizing the question.

Pamela spooned up some of the spicy apple cobbler and responded. "Naw, he'd mess up his sheet." With the spoon midway to her mouth, she stopped, her attention suddenly hooked. "What's wrong, kid? That haunted plantation getting to you?"

Elizabeth squirmed at her transparency. "No. Of course not. I, uh . . . I was just contemplating the possible implications of having a ghost as a roommate."

Pamela said nothing, though the inquisitive look was back in her eyes.

Elizabeth began chatting nonstop, trying once more to nip any questions in the bud, and eagerly motioned for the bill, saying, "I really need to get back."

"What's the rush? No, this is on me," Pamela said, reaching for the bill at the same time Elizabeth did.

"I'll get—"

"No, I'll—" Pamela's argument abruptly ended as her gaze lowered to the dark marks visible on her friend's wrist.

Elizabeth sought the object of the other woman's sudden interest, and as her eyes fastened on her own wrist, she swallowed. And prayed that Pamela wouldn't question her. She had no earthly idea what she'd say; there would be no denying what the marks clearly were.

Slowly Elizabeth released the bill. "Thanks," she said, her voice spinning only a thin thread of sound.

It seemed forever before the bill was settled and they were stepping out onto the sidewalk. As if from the mouth of an open furnace, the summertime heat blasted against Elizabeth, instantly filming her skin in sweat. The red silk blouse, which had whispered her secret so indiscreetly, clung damply to her body.

Her car was parked directly in front of the restaurant, and Elizabeth began to rummage through her purse for the keys.

"Why don't you come over for a while," Pamela asked, visibly restraining herself from asking about the bruise and Elizabeth's rattled behavior. "I promise the kids won't slime you."

Elizabeth smiled weakly. "I'll be over later in the week. Right now I need to get back—"

The sentence came to a crisp halt as Elizabeth spotted the man step from one of the nearby stores. He was tall, lithely slender, and, though she saw only the back of his head as he moved away from her and toward the corner, his hair was the same honey-blond color as the stranger's. And the man held his left arm at an awkward angle.

Elizabeth's heart began a loud, thudding tattoo. She moved away from the car and instinctively started after the only person who had the answer to last night's confusion.

"Where are you going?" Pamela asked in astonishment.

Elizabeth didn't answer. Instead, she increased her steps to a clipped pace.

"Elizabeth?"

She hurried on.

"Elizabeth!"

She ignored the sound of Pamela's footsteps behind her.

The man, quickly outdistancing his pursuer, seemed oblivious to both women. At the Hughes Building on the corner of Front and Horn Streets, he turned, walked toward the rear of the building and had just placed his foot on the first rung of the iron spiral staircase when Elizabeth grabbed a handful of his shirt.

"Wait!" she cried, her breath heaving in and out.

The man turned. His eyes, surprise flashing in their depths, met Elizabeth's.

His green eyes, she acknowledged. Not the brown eyes she'd expected. Nor had she expected the blond mustache fringing his upper lip. Nor had she expected the injured arm to be nothing more than a package held closely to his chest, a chest far too narrow to belong to last night's stranger. Slowly she released the man's shirt, which she'd pulled from the waistband of his slacks.

Embarrassment flooded her, leaving rose tints in her cheeks. "I ... I'm sorry," she murmured. "I thought you were ... someone else."

"That's all right," the man said, sensing her distress. "No problem." He then tucked his shirttail into his pants and disappeared up the staircase and into the building, sparing only a brief backward glance at the strange woman.

Reluctantly Elizabeth turned to face her friend. Their eyes met. And in Pamela's she no longer saw vague concern. What she saw now was blatant, out and out worry.

She'd made a fool of herself. Lord, had she made a fool of herself! And her best friend was probably ready to lock her up. Furthermore, she couldn't truly say that wouldn't be best. Maybe she *had* reached the padded-cell point.

She recalled the worry in Pam's eyes. She remembered ineptly trying to excuse the scene with the man on the street. Even now she could hear her friend's silent questions. Thankfully Pam hadn't pushed, though Elizabeth knew her reticence had wounded their friendship. She vowed somehow to make it up to her.

But she couldn't talk about what had—or hadn't—happened last night. Not yet. Nor could she continue to think about it. The subject of the stranger had saturated her brain.

Elizabeth absently checked the casserole heating in the oven and began another restless trek through the plantation house, her attention scattered here and there, everywhere and nowhere. Was that another small plane going over? In the ten days she'd been at Rose Haven, she'd heard planes frequently, usually during the night. Her curiosity faded as the thrumming engine faded from earshot. Next she wondered why the caretaker hadn't shown up for work that morning. Big Joshua Boone came every Tuesday, Thursday and Friday. Employed by Aunt Siddie, he was responsible for keeping an eye on the abandoned plantation and for tending the numerous gardens, chiefly the rose garden, which Aunt Siddie refused to allow to suffer the slightest neglect. After Monday night's storm, however, roses still lay strewn about the estate—a mass of wilted petals, heaps of yellow, white, red, lavender, soft pink, hot pink...hot...hot...hot...

Lord, it was hot! Even with the air-conditioning, the large, high-ceilinged rooms were uncomfortably hot as the late-afternoon, typically muggy Louisiana heat poured ruthlessly through the windowpanes. The red silk blouse still insisted on clinging to her moist skin. She unfastened the pearl button at her throat and rolled up the cuffs, then slipped off the white sandals tied about her ankles, pressing her bare feet to the coolness of the wooden floor. That was infinitely better, she thought, scooping her black hair, which coiled in sweaty tendrils, off her shoulders. The traditional overhead fan, oscillating slowly, cooled the back of her neck.

At length, driven once more by restlessness, Elizabeth stepped to the drawing-room window and drew back the lacy curtain. Beyond, the world glimmered in a summery haze, and sunset streaked the sky in pink and salmon and lavender. Not a leaf stirred on the long line of live oaks guarding the drive; equally motionless were the scattered camellias, azaleas, and crape myrtle. Stillness, virginal and pristine, surrounded the huge magnolia with blossoms of purest white. From there, Elizabeth's gaze slowly, automatically, shifted to the mammoth oak, beneath which the ghost purportedly appeared to his romantic believers.

Emerald leaves, crusty brown-black bark, draping gray strings of Spanish moss, a man leaning against the massive trunk.

A man.

A tall, slender man. A blond-haired man. A man holding his arm to his chest. A man staring at her, intensely, as if the distance, as if the windowpane, in no way separated them.

Elizabeth's heart burst into a rapid-fire speed.

And even as she watched, the stranger from the night before slowly, lazily, pushed his shoulder from the tree and started for the house.

And her.

Chapter Four

He came often but always unexpectedly, and always I would see him beneath the oak tree, as the sun was setting, as if driven to me at day's end by all that he'd seen and heard and been. There was always something a little desperate about him, as if his hard life needed the balance of my softness. It was a softness I willingly gave, and, in return, I took his hard strength because my lonely soul so needed it.

Elizabeth had known he would come.

The realization came to her swiftly, clearly, the sheer depth and power of the intuitive thought leaving her breathless. It also left her head spinning to the wild cadence of her heart. Or maybe the whirling dizziness could be attributed solely to the sight of him slowly making his way forward.

Never questioning why, she stepped from the window to the door, which she opened. Standing there in the humid rush of the grasping heat, she waited . . . because this, too, somehow seemed ordained.

With each step he took, with each breath she drew, their eyes probed, silently, deeply into the other's.

He was exactly as she'd remembered him, yet not at all as she'd remembered him. She'd remembered generalities, not subtleties, and it was the subtleties that now loudly spoke to her. It was true that his hair was blond, but it was more than that. It was the color of honey and flax, a fair hue that had been streaked by long hours in the hot, bleaching glare of the sun. The same sun had bronzed his skin to a coppery glow.

His eyes, too, were surprising. Though indeed brown, she now saw that they were darker than she'd originally thought, the color of a mature autumn as it stoically awaits the arrival of harsh winter. And, like autumn, his eyes held a restless melancholy, maybe even desperation. They were also glazed with pain, a pain evinced by the inflexible way he held his arm and the careful but unsteady way he walked.

He was pale, a fact barely discernible with his tanned complexion, but the chalky shadows were there in the sharply chiseled planes of his weathered cheeks. A film of moisture sheened his creased forehead and dampened his upper lip. He had made no attempt to shave, which left a bristly growth of stubble on his face; Elizabeth thought it, combined with the dark ambience that naturally surrounded him, made him look a little wild. And a lot appealing.

A yellow oxford-cloth shirt, wrinkled as though it had been carelessly packed in a suitcase, molded his chest and was loosely tucked—obviously the arm had impeded dressing—into the waistband of his beltless jeans. The short left sleeve revealed the bandage she had wrapped around his arm. The bandage showed a dried bloodstain.

The jeans were not those he'd worn the night before. These were fresh and clean, though they similarly hugged the masculine contour of his legs. The image of denim-sheathed limbs, sprawled against a calico quilt, uninhibit-edly, disturbingly, sped through her mind. The image was immediately shattered by the reality of his feet thudding up the wooden front steps.

She angled her head to accommodate his height.

The stranger lowered his.

Her eyes were gray, he noted, gray like the steamy morning mist that sometimes rose from a jungle pond. And like that pond, they seemed immeasurably deep, timelessly inviting. They also seemed…hazily wistful…as if they were more accustomed to, more comfortable with, looking inside herself than outward at the rapidly changing, confusing world. Her face was square, dramatically so, relieved only by the slight curve of her chin. Her brows were heavy, her jet-black hair, peaked alluringly on her forehead, scattered about her silk-clad shoulders. Her mouth, lipstick free, appeared soft.

Soft.

The word, for reasons he couldn't explain, had coiled and curled and finally snuggled cozily into his consciousness. Something about her triggered memories of soft. Intuitively he knew that they were nice memories, memories he wanted to pursue, maybe even memories he needed to pursue.

Instead, he smiled by twitching a corner of his mouth. "Florence Nightingale, I presume."

In that second, with his low, rumbling voice falling around her, with the hint of his smile warming her in its mantle, Elizabeth was struck again by the possessiveness she'd felt the night before, only this time she realized that the possessiveness translated to feeling as though she'd known this man for a long while. *For a hundred years?* The question came out of nowhere, and she prudently refused to answer it. She could not, however, refuse to return his smile. She had no idea who this man was, not even *what* he was, but it really didn't matter. He had come, as she somehow knew he would, and for now that was enough.

Silently she stepped aside, allowing him entrance into Rose Haven, entrance into her life.

"I, uh . . . I was fixing supper," she said, her voice quavering. Even though—perhaps because—the moment seemed inexplicably ordained, she felt nervous. That nervousness drove her through the house and toward the kitchen, which was originally located outside but was now annexed onto the house. The stranger followed. "Are you hungry?"

"If it wouldn't be an imposition."

Elizabeth glanced over her shoulder, answering honestly and with a speck of teasing. "If last night wasn't an imposition, sharing a ham-and-noodle casserole certainly isn't."

The stranger smiled. This time the act involved his whole mouth, though it never quite cut through the pain in his eyes. Even so, the smile produced a kick in Elizabeth's stomach. "No, I guess you're right. After last night, very little's an imposition."

The subject was sobering. For both. And for long moments they simply stared.

"How do you feel?" she asked finally.

Without invitation, as though he'd used up what strength he had, the stranger eased onto a kitchen stool. He winced as he settled his arm. "As if I have a hole in my arm." He took a deep breath. "As if I have two holes in my arm."

She wanted to ask if he'd seen a doctor but knew that he hadn't; she knew, too, that nothing she could say would persuade him to. She asked instead, "Have you taken anything for the pain?"

He shook his head. "I don't need anything."

She recognized the lie for what it was and opened the drawer where she kept what limited medication she had. "All I have is aspirin or Tums or..." She hesitated as her eyes raked over the Midol container. When she glanced up, his eyes were taking in the same thing. They then rose to hers. She blushed in a way he thought made her look old-fashioned. Charmingly old-fashioned.

"I don't need anything," he repeated, taking mercy on her delicate sensibilities.

She shut the drawer and reached for any handy subject. "Do you like coleslaw?"

A teasing note danced in his voice, though, again, it never quite overrode the pain. "Lady, right now I could eat anything."

Why hadn't he eaten? Elizabeth thought. Because ghosts have selective palates? Because men on the run from the law rarely have the time and the opportunity for three square meals a day? She pushed the intrusive questions aside.

"That's an excellent state to be in when facing one of my meals," she said. "I spend my time teaching, not cooking."

"What do you teach?"

"American literature." She looked up from testing the casserole. Her eyes met his, and the question slipped out before she could monitor what she was saying. "What do you do?"

His eyes darkened. "Oh, a little of this, a lot of that."

She pursued. "And do you often get shot doing a little of this and a lot of that?"

"Actually, only rarely...and never with such a pretty rescuer." The pain-bleary eyes that stared out from the appealingly unkempt face bluntly perused her.

Elizabeth wasn't certain whether it was his evasion, his compliment or the look in his eyes that set her hands to trembling, but tremble they did. They continued to do so as she shoved the casserole back into the oven and set the timer for another five minutes, as she made the dressing for the slaw, as she placed the rolls on a cookie sheet and poured the glasses of milk.

All through her flurry of activity, the stranger watched. Quietly. Thoroughly. He watched as the ebony fall of her hair swayed about her shoulders, as the red silk blouse caressed the fullness of her feminine body, as her bare toes dug almost childishly, and endearingly, into the wooden floor. He watched as her hands trembled.

"Elizabeth?" His voice was low and whiskey-rough.

She almost dropped the milk carton.

When her eyes met his, he said, "You're trembling."

She glanced down at her hands, then back to him. "Yes."

"Are you afraid of me?"

She considered. She was confused by him, troubled by his appearance in her life and perhaps overwhelmed by a thousand other things she felt about him, but she wasn't afraid of him—any more than she'd been last night. "No," she answered firmly.

"Then why are you trembling?"

"I'm not sure."

He accepted her truthful answer. She turned back to the cabinet. When he called her name again, she again met his eyes. "Thanks...for last night."

"You've already thanked me," she said, remembering vividly how he'd passed out minutes after doing so. She remembered, too, how courageously he'd borne the pain until that second when his body had refused to consciously tolerate more. She wondered how it was humanly possible for him to be up and walking around after what he'd so recently been through. *Humanly.* Maybe that was the operative word.

"Considering the magnitude of your favor, two thank-yous don't seem excessive."

"Then you're welcome twice," she answered, adding with a slight smile, "although I don't remember your giving me a choice."

"You had a choice," he said, his voice suddenly notes lower, his eyes shades browner.

"No," she said, her eyes meeting his openly, honestly, "I didn't."

His look said that he expected her to explain, but she didn't. How could she tell him that she truly hadn't had a choice? That from the moment she'd opened the door to him, she'd been caught up in some mysterious something beyond her power to stop or to refuse? And that she was still incapable of stopping or refusing whatever else might lie in their future?

"Why did you leave without telling me?" she whispered, her question laced with that morning's confusion, panic and hurt—yes, she realized now that she had been hurt. "I . . . I didn't know what to think." *And if I told you the thoughts that had crossed my mind, you'd think me crazy.*

How could he explain, the stranger thought, to her or to himself, that why he'd left had been simple enough? It was why he was back that defied explanation. He had covered his trail, as years of experience had taught him to do, and left because he didn't want anyone to trace his having been there. There were too many things he didn't want to have to account for. Why, then, had he returned? He told himself that, because he was still weak, he needed her. He told himself that he wanted to determine if she knew what was going on on the far reaches of her property or if she was simply an innocent victim. The truth was, however, that he'd returned because he'd wanted to see her again. No, he felt compelled to see her again. From the moment she'd opened the door the night before, he'd been driven by a compulsion that was both inexplicable and painful in its demanding strength. *If he told her this, would she think him crazy? Was he crazy?*

"Why?" she whispered again, suddenly desperate for his answer.

"It seemed like the thing to do at the time," he said, suddenly equally desperate to say something that would ease her obvious hurt. "Right this moment, however, it seems like a foolish thing to have done."

She had no idea what his words meant, only that the way he was staring at her seemed to open up her vulnerable body and fill it with a warmth that was both savagely gentle and tenderly rough. She again strongly sensed déjà vu, as if this man had stared at her in just this way at another time, in another place, in another lifetime.

The man was lost in similar feelings. No, he was just lost, he thought. Lost in the fathomless gray of her eyes. Lost in the wistfully intriguing gray of her eyes. Lost in the soft gray of her eyes. Soft . . . soft . . . soft . . . Why did the word, the feeling, haunt him so?

Elizabeth swallowed.

The stranger lowered his eyes to her lips.

The oven timer pinged.

And both were washed ashore from the uncharted seas they'd been sailing.

They ate in the dining room, at the long cherry wood table, on Castleton china that was mint green and edged in richest gold. Overhead, a cut-glass chandelier spewed down a fine mist of light, while outside the sun had finally set, allowing the twilight to escape its daytime prison and slowly crawl across the land.

They said little, though both seemed comfortable with the silence. Occasionally their gazes met. When they did, something magnetic seemed to pass between them. More than occasionally Elizabeth studied him out of the corner of her eye. He ate well, though she could almost see the pain gnawing at him.

"Would you like some more?" she asked after he laid his fork down.

"No...no, thanks," he said, summoning a tiny grin. "I've eaten everything but the design off the plate. And you lied. You *can* cook."

She shrugged. "I'm only passably fair." She reached for his plate and stacked it in hers. "How about some coffee?" she asked, stretching for his empty milk glass. "My coffee's pretty decent, even if I say so myself." She smiled. "And so are the store-bought cookies I worked long and hard to pull out of the sack."

His grin grew until it almost, but not quite, looked at home on his stark face. "How can I refuse when you've gone to that kind of trouble."

As she carried the dishes away, the stranger noted that her hands had stopped trembling. The fact pleased him. What didn't please him was how tired he suddenly felt.

Ten minutes later, bearing a silver tray laden with steaming mugs of chicory-flavored coffee—if the stranger were a ghost, he was at least a Southern one—and a dish of coconut macaroons, Elizabeth entered the drawing room. The man, his tennis shoes removed, lay sprawled on the antique sofa. He was sound asleep.

A warm feeling washed over her, while a small smile played at her lips. He needed the rest. Eating had sapped what little energy he had arrived with. The smile drifted away. Where had he arrived from? Surely in his condition he couldn't have walked far. But then, maybe he hadn't walked at all. Maybe he had simply disappeared from some nether world and reappeared in the world of reality. Or maybe he existed only in the world of her mind? She left the logical interpretation of what was happening for another time. Seating herself in a nearby rocker, she willed her mind to blankness and sipped her coffee.

She also watched. The steady rise and fall of his diaphragm. The way that even in sleep his right hand protectively held his left arm still by crossing it over his chest. The way his blond hair fell onto his forehead with a shaggy, boyish charm. The way his beard seemed to be visibly darkening. The way his long legs were scrunched up to fit the short sofa. The way he occasionally grimaced.

At those times she longed to go to him and stroke the pain away, but she didn't. Simply because the urge to do so was so strong. Instead, she sat and wondered how old he was. Late thirties? Early forties? It was hard to tell from his harsh-looking face. However long he'd lived, it hadn't been an easy life. The fact was sculpted in the muscles, facial and body, that never seemed to fully relax. Not even in sleep.

A long while later, a short while later—she couldn't have said which—she discovered that his eyes were open and that he, too, was studying her. Quietly they stared, gray eyes to brown, brown eyes to gray. It was a strangely peaceful, wholly comfortable exchange.

"Hi," she said finally, her soft words mingling with the loud ticking of the clock. It was the same clock that had been her sole companion the evening before. Until one minute after ten.

"Hi," he returned, his voice husky with sleep. He swallowed, drew his tongue across his dry bottom lip, then said, "I'm sorry I nodded off."

"That's all right. You needed the rest." She was pleased to note that the circles under his eyes were fractionally lighter, though his eyes still held traces of pain.

He smiled slightly. "It's still a lousy way to repay your hostess's hospitality."

Elizabeth smiled back. "Your hostess didn't mind."

"I suppose that coffee's cold."

"Colder than cold." She stood. "I'll get you some more."

"I'd rather have that aspirin you offered earlier."

Elizabeth returned the tray to the oval mahogany table, carved in a rose motif, that Rosemary Jarrett, the illegitimate daughter of the desperado, had brought back from Paris. It had been the first of her many trips there to study art and, later, to exhibit her own. "Does your arm still hurt badly?"

"Actually, I could use the aspirin for my head." He produced a crooked smile that was like a velvet-clad fist sailing into her stomach. "There must have been twelve men with jackhammers in that bottle of whiskey."

"Oh," she said, her mouth wreathed in a knowing grin as she tried to ignore the one-two punch in her belly.

He both grimaced and grinned. "Could you say that softly?"

She smiled, then hurriedly slipped from the room, finding it easier to breathe out of his presence.

She returned minutes later, bearing the aspirin bottle, a glass of water and a handful of bandages, along with a tube of ointment.

Mutely he held out his hand, palm up, for her to tap the tablets into. Which she did. In the process, their hands brushed. Warm to warm. Their eyes met briefly, intently.

"Here," she said, giving him the glass and averting her gaze.

"Thanks," he said, awkwardly rising to a semi-sitting position and downing the pills with a gulp of water. "Put it on my tab."

The activity obviously brought renewed pain to his arm, for he suddenly bared his teeth, held his injured arm as immobile as possible and eased back down onto the sofa. He closed his eyes and let out a ragged breath of air. When Elizabeth lightly touched his arm, his eyelids opened.

She was kneeling on the floor beside him, her face closer to his than it had been all evening. In fact, she was so close that she could see the darker, chocolate-brown chips in his deep brown eyes. And she could hear, as well as see, the rhythm of his breathing.

"The bandage needs changing," she said in explanation. She was aware once more that her own breathing had deviated from normal.

"It's all right," he said, his eyes relentlessly gazing into hers.

She glanced away. "No, it isn't. The bandage is soiled." She loosened the tape and, with an insistent gesture, forced him to raise his arm so she could unwind the wrapping. Keeping her eyes on her task, she said, "I have some clean pads to place over the wound."

She worked quickly and as gently as possible. Even so, she could tell the jarring motion took its toll. More than once she heard his single breath break into two distinct sounds. When she at last tried to pull the square pad away, she found that it was stuck, dried into place. The stranger hissed between his teeth.

"Sorry," she said, knowing that she had to remove the pad despite the pain involved.

Gazing down at the wound, it was all she could do not to gasp. The smaller entry hole was healing nicely, but the larger hole looked less than pretty. Though the cauterization had sealed the opening, it had also burned the adjacent skin, leaving two blisters behind. The burn, however, was the least of his worries. Streaks of red, like uneven spokes of a wheel, suggested an infection on the rise. It was a suggestion further confirmed by a heated swelling.

Her gaze rose to his. She saw in his eyes that he, too, knew an infection was brewing—maybe even that he'd suspected what she would find before she'd removed the bandage. He saw in hers the silent plea she'd made repeatedly.

"No doctor," he said quietly. The soft, unemotional, unyielding tone contained more power than had he shouted the refusal from the rooftop.

"But it's getting infected," she insisted, looking as if she were ready to plead her case from here to eternity.

He stopped her short. "Just give it your best shot, Florence."

In the end she did what she could, knowing it wasn't nearly enough. She applied the ointment liberally, but she suspected that the whole tube, and twenty besides it, didn't possess the medicinal power needed. After all, it was only over-the-counter medication meant for superficial scrapes and cuts, and nothing about the stranger's wound was superficial.

She rebandaged the arm, discovering as she had the night before that it was easier said than done. Only this time the patient was at least conscious and could offer some assistance. Which ultimately proved to be more disastrous than had he been unconscious. She was careful not to prop his hand against her chest as she'd done the night before, but it was seemingly impossible to keep his hand from brushing her breast. The first time his knuckles grazed her, she ignored it. The second time, her fingers increased their wrapping speed. The third time, as his knuckles passed beneath the silken-covered fullness, her fingers stopped. Along with her breath. Their eyes met slowly.

Something in his said that, though he'd been unconscious the night before, he remembered touching her. Softly remembered. Something in hers said that she remembered, too. Warmly remembered.

She looked away, hastily finished bandaging his arm and breathlessly proclaimed, "Finished."

"Thanks," he murmured, his voice low, thick.

She could have risen from her knees, but she didn't, just as he could have said a thousand things except the one thing he did.

"Who is she?" he asked, nodding toward the portrait over the mantel.

The question surprised, yet didn't surprise. Elizabeth didn't even look behind her. "My great-grandmother."

"You look like her."

"Yes," she said. "I'm named after her."

"Her name was Elizabeth?"

The name, her name, sounded sweet on his lips. So sweet that Elizabeth had to concentrate on the question.

"Yes," she managed to say. A silence followed. She heard the ticking of the clock, then heard herself saying, "I don't know my great-grandfather's name. Not even my great-grandmother knew it."

The statement was guaranteed to be intriguing. The stranger expressed his interest with the slight narrowing of his eyes.

"He was an outlaw. Blond-haired. Brown-eyed. He showed up at Rose Haven one summer evening during a storm. Exactly a hundred years ago last night. He'd been shot."

A flicker of something—astonishment? disbelief?—flashed through the stranger's eyes.

"My great-grandmother removed the bullet, cauterized the wound and took care of him. They became lovers."

The word *lovers* drifted through the still room like a satin caress.

"She had his child. A daughter. When the baby was three weeks old, he was hanged for robbery." Another silence ensued. "My great-grandmother thought that his ghost came back to visit her and the baby. In fact, many people say they've seen him . . . beneath the oak tree in the front yard."

The stranger said nothing. Nor did anything in his face give away what he was thinking. In that moment Elizabeth knew that whoever he was, whatever he was, he was accustomed to, superbly talented at, not showing his emotions.

"Do you think I'm the ghost?" he asked at last, his voice cutting through the thick silence.

It was strangely comforting to have the question out in the open. It was also comforting to realize in that surreal moment, with his brown eyes burning into hers, that it didn't matter whether or not he was, for, real or unreal, she was swept away on a tide of feelings she couldn't explain.

"It doesn't matter," she whispered.

Again there was no indication of what he thought. Suddenly, though, his eyes seemed to scorch her with their relentless intensity.

"I...I'll go get you some coffee," she said, starting to rise to her feet.

"Wait," he said, grabbing her wrist. Her left wrist. Though his grip was gentle, a marked contrast to the pressure he'd exerted the night before, Elizabeth nonetheless winced. His eyes lowered immediately to the source of her pain.

He swore, softly but vehemently.

Her eyes rose to his.

His were contrite. "I'm sorry."

"It doesn't hurt," she lied.

"No, I can see it doesn't." His sarcasm was self-aimed, and as he spoke, he began to massage the bruises with the pad of his thumb. "I didn't realize," he said. "I swear I didn't mean to hurt you. I swear . . ." The words trailed off, but his touch remained.

His gentle touch. His insistent touch. His masculine touch.

She watched his hand, mesmerized by its warmth.

He, too, watched his hand, mesmerized by the feel of hers tucked into it.

Small into large.

Soft into hard.

Hard.

Soft.

Slowly images floated through two minds—images of their hands entwined throughout the long night as pain ran its dark race, he seeking comfort, she granting it.

Seeking, granting. Giving, taking. Man to woman, woman to man.

So natural were they that Elizabeth was unsure of the exact moment when the warm, drizzly, sexual feelings began. She *was* aware that the spot at which his hand touched hers glowed with a tingling sensation not unlike sprinkled stardust. And that the tingling spread, slowly, inexorably, throughout her body, leaving in its wake a need, a physical need, that flooded each cell of her being. In places uniquely feminine, the need became an exquisite heaviness, bearing down with savage force. Her body begged for the completion of his.

It was a completion that she'd somehow known before. Intuitively she knew what it was like to be this man's lover. Not what it *would* be like, but what it *was* like. She knew the gentleness and the fury of his passion. She knew what it was like to lose herself in the sweetness of his touch. She knew what it was like to share his soul, and have him share hers.

The realization was stunning, perplexing, frightening.

She raised her eyes to his. And saw there everything that she was feeling. The same bewilderment—he, too, knew what it was like to have her as his lover—the same blatant need.

They stared. Neither coyly pretending that what was happening wasn't. There were no maidenly denials, no camouflage of the desire hardening his masculine body. He wanted her, and she wanted to be wanted by him, to be possessed by him, to be consumed by him.

The air around them crackled with a brittle sensuality.

She sighed.

He swallowed.

Sanity reigned.

Slowly she pulled her hand from his. Slowly he released her.

"Elizabeth...?"

"I...I'll go get that coffee," she answered without turning around.

Minutes later, when she returned, he was gone. She wasn't surprised. She, too, felt the need to flee. From the aching desire still burning her body. From the stranger who seemed more familiar than even herself. From the dozens of questions that seemed to have not a single answer.

Chapter Five

He called me Lizzie. I called him naught, for I knew not his name. I never asked it; he never volunteered it. It was as if he felt my not knowing would shield me from his life. And perhaps it did, though it did not shield me from worry. Each time he went away, I worried whether he'd come back, though I always knew he would if he could. And each time he did, he would bring me a single rose, which he'd plucked from the garden—red for the depth of his love, he had proclaimed, or white for my purity, or yellow for the sunshine I'd brought to his life, or pink for the softness of my lips . . . or the blush that stole into my cheeks when he'd say such foolish things. And always when I'd blush, he'd smile and whisper my name. "Lizzie, my sweet Lizzie . . ." he'd say.

Elizabeth made the call first thing the next morning.

"Good morning. Dr. Haywood's office," came the receptionist's professionally polite voice.

Elizabeth swallowed down the knot that had suddenly jumped into her throat. "This is Elizabeth Jarrett. I'd like to speak with Dr. Haywood, please."

"I'm sorry, but Dr. Haywood's with a patient. Could I take your number and have him call you?"

"Yes, please," Elizabeth said, leaving her name and number and hanging up. For long, fortifying seconds she clutched the receiver, as if holding on to anything was preferable to holding on to nothing.

Damn! she thought. She had psyched herself up to make the call, but making it had proven totally anticlimactic. Now she was going to have to psyche herself up again. If she could. *Please, God,* she prayed, knowing it was an unorthodox prayer at best, *let me be an effective liar.*

Images of beet-red, puffy skin, fire-hot from a soon-to-be raging infection, crowded her mind, and she heard a voice deep inside her chime that she had no choice but to be effective. He had no choice but for her to be.

She eased her hand from the receiver to the coffeepot and was refilling her mug when the phone gave a loud, sharp ring. She jerked, puddling coffee on the kitchen counter. Throwing a dish towel over the brown pool, she snatched up the receiver.

"Hello?"

"Elizabeth? Dr. Haywood."

Elizabeth's heart revved into gear. Dammit, she hadn't had time to psych herself up again! "Yes, Dr. Haywood, I . . . I wasn't expecting you to return my call so soon. Your receptionist said you were with a patient."

"I was, but I'd just finished. My nurse handed me your message as I was headed back to my office. By the way, I was going to get in touch with you. I was sorry to hear about Regan.''

Grover Haywood had been the Jarrett family doctor for over twenty years. Though Elizabeth had never stopped to consider his age, she assumed he was somewhere in his mid- to late-fifties. It was hard to tell, however, because he had begun balding early and had always worn a salt-and-pepper beard that had further hidden the years. Even though he was younger than her mother, rumor whispered that the two had once considered marriage. Which didn't surprise Elizabeth a bit. Her mother had evidently considered marriage with every man she met.

"Thank you," Elizabeth said in response to his condolence.

"What can I do for you?" he asked.

Elizabeth took a deep breath, put her hand at the lie's back and pushed it forward. "I, uh... I'm having trouble with tonsillitis again."

"You still haven't had those things out?"

It was a running commentary between the two, going back to Elizabeth's teenage years. Dr. Haywood always recommended a tonsillectomy; Elizabeth always pleaded cowardice.

She now manufactured a laugh. "Only when they can be taken out some way besides surgically."

"Unfortunately, that's still the only way. Come on in and let me see how badly they're infected. Hold on and I'll give you my receptionist, who'll make an appoint—"

"No! There's no point in my coming in. I mean, I don't want to mess up your schedule."

"You're not messing—"

"Couldn't you just call in some antibiotics, like you used to, and I could pick them up at the pharmacy?"

"Sure, but if it's a bad infection—"

"It's not bad. I mean, it is, but it isn't any worse than it usually is, and antibiotics have always done the trick before."

Dr. Haywood hesitated.

Elizabeth prayed.

Reluctantly he said, "All right, but if the infection isn't better in forty-eight hours, get back to me."

Elizabeth felt as if the gun aimed at her head had just misfired. "Right. I will."

"How long are you planning on being down?" Dr. Haywood asked after the pharmacy she preferred had been determined.

"For the rest of the summer."

"That long?" he asked, clearly surprised.

"Aunt Siddie and I are trying to decide what to do with Rose Haven."

"I assumed you'd sell it."

"Yeah, well, I imagine we will."

"Frankly, I thought you'd sell when Siddie went into the nursing home."

Frankly, Elizabeth had, too, but her aunt had remained steadfast. It was only after Regan's death, when Elizabeth had broached the subject again, that Siddie Jarrett had relented, promising to do what Elizabeth wanted if she'd just live there for the summer. Elizabeth assumed her aunt's change of heart had been part of the natural process of coming to terms with the fact that she was truly ensconced in the nursing home and would never be returning to Rose Haven.

"When you decide to sell—" Dr. Haywood broke through her reverie, and Elizabeth noted he'd said *when*, not *if* "—I'd like to talk to you about it. Sylvia—" Elizabeth recognized his wife's name "—has always had a fondness for Rose Haven."

"Fine. I'll be happy to talk to you about it."

Seconds later, she hung up the phone with hands that were still unsteady. She made two quick resolutions. One, to stop worrying about selling Rose Haven—she'd already had two nibbles. And two, never to take up lying on a consistent basis. She wasn't constitutionally constructed for it.

The full implication of what she was doing struck her as she stood at the pharmacy counter writing a check for the antibiotics. She expected the stranger to return. It was the kind of all-pervasive feeling that left no room for even the smallest doubt, the kind of feeling that spread through her body with the sudden warmth of pleasurable anticipation.

Unknowingly she smiled.

The cashier, assuming the smile was for her, smiled back. "Will this be all, Ms. Jarrett?"

"Yes. No! I need some bandages. Some gauze, some pads, some tape."

"What size?"

The size of a gunshot wound.

Elizabeth explained what she needed; the clerk selected several boxes and packages from the shelves around her.

"Oh, and some peroxide."

The clerk reached for a bottle. "Anything else?"

"No, that's all."

As Elizabeth was exiting the store, "Have a nice day" floated after her.

"Yes, I think I might," she returned.

She was several blocks away and halfway to her destination before it finally sank in that she wasn't headed home. The parking lot of the A & P was, in typical Wednesday fashion, sparsely occupied. As Elizabeth cut the car engine, grabbed her purse and started into the grocery store, she asked herself exactly what she thought she was doing.

She immediately answered herself: planning supper... for two. Again, a feeling of certainty sluiced through her—certainty that the stranger would return—and again, the realization produced a warm, comfortable glow.

Where was he?

What was he doing?

Did he like shrimp creole?

It took her no time to round up the ingredients she needed, ending with lush, plump, Gulf shrimp. She also added a bag of rice, over which she'd serve the spicy, tomato-based dish. As she was headed for the checkout stand, she made one last sweep down the fresh vegetables aisle and selected lettuce, tomatoes and crinkly-skinned avocados for a salad. It was while she was standing in the short line, waiting her turn to pay, that the chocolate Hershey kisses first tempted her. The bags of foil-wrapped candies were piled hill-high in an alluring display nearby.

No, she thought, staunchly positioning herself against the sugary temptation. She didn't need the cavities. She didn't need the calories. She didn't need the cellulite on her thighs.

The foil winked in the morning sun.

Elizabeth groaned, grabbed a bag and greedily embraced the three C's.

Minutes later, the groceries stored beside her, she started the car, turned the air-conditioning to high and let the cool air wash away the muggy humidity that had already dampened her clothing. She reached for a candy, shucked its foil and popped it into her mouth. The sweet taste spread across her taste buds.

Something in the sultry heat, something in the wild abandon of eating chocolate in midmorning, caused her mind to zero in on something Pamela had mentioned the day before. The Hall Tree was having a sale on sundresses. That tidbit, like the chocolate, was suddenly very appealing—so appealing that Elizabeth backed the car from the parking space and headed for the dress shop. She conveniently denied that a new sundress had anything to do with her anticipatory mood or, more directly, that it had anything to do with the stranger.

She hastily bought a chambray sundress that buttoned all the way down the front and was trimmed in a flounce of white eyelet lace. She didn't even try it on because she'd left the car running so that the air-conditioning would preserve both shrimp and candy. She also bought a white cotton lawn camisole and tap pants that caught her eye as she was leaving the store. Their demure sensuality seemed more appropriate to yesteryear than the present, but she'd had an odd feeling when she'd seen them—as if she had little choice in purchasing them. Because the feeling had been so odd, yet so overwhelming, she'd deliberately refused to think about it. Just the way she'd deliberately refused to think about what had happened the night before.

The day passed quickly, the day passed slowly, but mostly the day passed restlessly. Though she checked the clock as often as a young girl awaiting the appointed hour of her first date, Elizabeth refused to admit that she was eager for the pastel sunset to paint the sky, marking the time when the stranger would return.

Was he in pain?

Was the infection worsening?

Was she going to go crazy if she didn't find something to occupy her time? Assuming, of course, that she wasn't crazy already?

That thought in mind—prevention rather than acceptance of what already might be—she slipped out to the rose garden just as the clock was striking four. The garden, which was always maintained at a hundred healthy bushes, lay to the side of the plantation on a sunny strip of land.

Storm-ravaged petals, their colors suggesting an earthen sunset, still lay scattered about the ground, and Elizabeth began to scoop them up by the handfuls. She heaped them into a pile that she would later put in a plastic lawn bag.

As she worked, she wondered again why the caretaker hadn't come the day before. And why hadn't he called to explain his absence? If he missed tomorrow, *she'd* call *him*. Aunt Siddie would have her hide if she let the rose garden suffer. She had promised her aunt that periodically she'd check out the rest of the property as well. Way at the back of Rose Haven's boundaries were some shacks, pre-Civil War slave quarters. Her aunt had used the nearer ones for storage. Elizabeth vowed to take a long walk sometime during the next few days to make certain everything was all right.

While the storm had shattered the mature roses, those just budding had remained undamaged. A few had unfurled their velvet petals, and it was from these that Elizabeth gathered a simple, fragrant bouquet, which she carried into the house. She arranged the flowers in a cut-crystal vase and placed them on the dining-room table…near the two place settings of fine china that she'd earlier laid beside the silver candleholders, each bearing a white taper that she would later light.

In the end, after all her clock-watching, she was late. The shrimp creole and salad took longer than she'd planned, so that sunset was already threatening when she stole up the outside stairway to her bedroom. The sweltering late-afternoon heat moistened her skin like a fiery rain, leaving her sticky and uncomfortable.

Though she'd long fought her association with the other Jarrett women, there were times, like this, when she was suddenly awed by the fact that what she was feeling had been felt by each of them. They, too, had stood, each in her turn, on this stairway, with the summer swaddling them in heat. But, with the exception of Aunt Siddie, they hadn't known what it was like to anticipate the air-conditioned coolness of the bedroom, didn't know to lament the design of the home that allowed no indoor stairways, or closets, since both, at one time in Louisiana's history, had led to heavy taxation.

At the top of the stairs, Elizabeth paused and looked back at the oak tree. No one stood beneath it. Stepping inside the bedroom, she was instantly, and gratefully, wrapped in coolness.

The bedroom was simple but elegant. The focal point was a four-poster bed with a canopy of ivory peau de soie; an armoire, substituting for a closet, and a chaise longue, also in ivory silk and lace and trimmed in blue, stood nearby. Delicate lacy curtains decorated the bay window. The bathroom, modernized to include a shower, still contained an old-fashioned porcelain hip bath. Beside it sat a white pitcher in a white bowl.

Elizabeth stripped immediately, showered, and afterward piled her hair atop her head, with little sprigs, moist from the shower, curling about her ears and the nape of her neck. As always she applied a minimum of makeup. She slipped into the new sundress, which she quickly learned she couldn't wear a bra with. Tying the sandals about her bare ankles, she took one last look at herself in the mirrored panel of the armoire. She felt the eyelet lace swish against the back of her knees, felt the soft chambray fabric caress the fullness of her breasts, felt the lowered waist hug her hips. She felt a sudden nervousness seep through her body.

Will he like the sundress?

I didn't buy it for him.

Didn't you?

No!

Aren't you lying to yourself now, just the way you've lied to yourself all day?

What have I lied to myself about all day?

You've lied to yourself by trying to deny what happened last night, by pretending that the two of you didn't feel what you did.

No, Elizabeth thought, though even as she did, desire welled deep within her, soft and sweet, primal and harsh.

"No," she whispered, knowing full well that for the second time that day she'd spoken far less than God's truth.

She saw him the moment she stepped from the bedroom.

And he saw her. Or perhaps he heard her... or felt her. Pushing from the oak tree, he headed slowly for the gallery steps as she started slowly down the stairway. They met at the front door.

He had shaved, giving him the superficial appearance of feeling better. On closer inspection, however, his eyes still seemed clouded, and he still held his left arm motionless. In his right hand he carried a pink rose.

"Hi," she said, her heart suddenly as heavy as the humid air that fell about them like a damp whisper.

"Hi," he said, his voice as low and throaty as the lonesome whippoorwill that called in the distance.

He handed her the rose.

She took it, raised her eyes to his and, not in the slightest surprised with his gift, murmured a simple, "Thank you."

A grin slow-danced across his mature, masculine lips. "I, uh... I stole it... from your garden."

The infectious grin jumped to her mouth. "An honest thief."

Considering their unconventional relationship, considering that Rose Haven's ghost had been hanged for robbery, her choice of words proved awkward. For both of them.

She quickly changed the subject. "How do you feel?"

He let the subject be quickly changed. "Like hell."

Her gaze lowered to his arm. The bandage was clean—the wound had stopped weeping—but Elizabeth almost wished it wasn't. She feared his injury was now inwardly festering. The striations of red peeping from beneath the gauze confirmed her fear.

She was suddenly irritated. It was the kind of irritation that comes from caring and having your hands tied behind your back. At least, she noted, trying to console herself, they weren't tied as securely as the day before.

"Come on," she ordered, marching into the house and the kitchen.

The stranger followed and stood watching as she filled a glass with tap water and placed it, and a brown plastic medicine bottle, on the cabinet.

"Here," she said, "take this before your arm falls off and you expect me to put it back on." She realized vaguely that part of her irritation came from impatience. She'd been impatient all day for the man to begin the medication.

"What is it?"

"Antibiotics."

His eyebrows arched in surprise. "Where did you get them?"

"At the pharmacy, of course."

"Let me rephrase my question. *How* did you get them?"

"I called my family doctor and told him I had tonsillitis."

"And he wrote a prescription from just—"

She cut him off. "I have a history of tonsillitis."

He said nothing; he simply studied her. Her generosity was obvious, as was the fact that her act had been performed on the solid ground of belief—she had believed he would come back. How could she have known what he himself did not? Or had he, too, known and had simply refused to accept it so easily, so honestly?

"They're not doing you any good on the cabinet," she pointed out, her tone still crisp with concern.

He reached for the bottle and with the thumb of the same hand pried up the lid. He tumbled two capsules into the palm of his left hand.

"Only one—"

"I'll take two to get the ball rolling."

She nodded in agreement and watched as he downed both pills together. His throat moved convulsively—his tanned, thick throat. She suddenly wondered what it would be like to press her lips to the deep hollow. *Sweetly salty* came her answer. Again, it was a certainty recorded somewhere in the memory bank of her being.

"Thanks," he said, dragging her from somewhere in the past to the confusing present.

"What?"

"Thanks. For going to the trouble."

"You're welcome," she said, deliberately withdrawing her gaze from his throat. "Here," she said as she shoved the pill bottle forward, "take them with you."

She busied herself with wiping up a clean cabinet, though out of the corner of her eye she saw him shove the small container into the pocket of his jeans—tight jeans that bulged with everything from muscles to masculinity.

"Supper's going to be a little late," she said, her voice riddled with breathlessness.

"Mind if I rest?"

"No. Of course not," she answered, grateful for anything that would put a little distance between them.

He was at the kitchen door, headed toward the drawing room, when he stopped. "Elizabeth?"

She turned.

A grin sauntered across his lips. "Anybody ever tell you you're pretty when you're angry?"

Before she could react, he walked from the room. Which was just as well, because she didn't know what reaction to give. She didn't know whether to laugh or to cry. She knew only to wonder why this man had come into her life. She knew only to wonder who he was.

"Supper's ready."

The stranger glanced up from what he was reading.

Elizabeth's gaze dropped to her great-grandmother's journal. Her eyes instantly rose to his. In his autumn-dark irises she saw every emotion, every bewildering emotion, that she felt. She sensed that for the first time he truly realized the magnitude of what was unfolding around them. She longed for him to say something that would explain everything, but he didn't. Silently he laid the diary aside. Silently he rose. Silently he followed her into the dining room.

The meal was just as silent, partly because neither felt the need to fill the void with idle talk, partly because neither knew what to say. Elizabeth knew he was still reeling from what he'd read. And that he still wasn't feeling well.

She'd brought the single pink rose from the kitchen cabinet to the table, where it had lain beside her plate for the entire meal. Its fragrance, combined with the sweet scent of the bouquet's, wafted about the room like a delicate secret hinted at but not disclosed. Careful of the thorns, she picked up the flower and prolonged its survival by arranging it in water with the others.

"Is the plantation named after the rose garden?" he asked, the question echoing loudly in the looming silence. His eyes lingered on her lips, lips as pink, as soft-looking, as the wakening petals of the rose he'd given her.

Soft.

The word still haunted him. And he now hungered, with a need he could hardly control, to touch her to see if she was as soft as some memory told him she was.

Candlelight, rippling across the cherry wood table, played across his face, screening half in golden incandescence, half in mysterious shadow. Elizabeth felt drawn, particularly to the shadowed facet of him.

"Yes," she answered, her voice sounding as loud as his. "The garden was my great-grandmother's pride and joy. Over the years, whoever lived here tried to preserve it." Elizabeth swallowed the last of her mint tea. "My aunt, who lived here until a year ago, kept the caretaker on. He tends the rose garden." She frowned. "At least when he comes."

The stranger's hand hesitated only slightly as he lowered the fork from his mouth. The memory of a mammoth black man flashed through his mind. Skin as black as the night. Teeth gritted in a murderous growl. A dead weight that he could hardly carry, especially with the injury to his own arm. The hollow sound of an abandoned well. The delayed splash of water.

"What are you doing?" Elizabeth asked suddenly.

"The dishes," he said, his voice oddly strained as he pushed back his chair and stood.

"I'll get them."

"You got them last night."

"No," she said firmly as she, too, came to her feet. "You can get them when you're feeling better."

The implication was there. Heady and strong. He would return...and they both knew it. It was acknowledged in the intense way they stood looking at each other.

A few minutes later she left the coffee perking and walked into the drawing room. She found the stranger, his shoes kicked off, perched in the corner of the sofa. At first he didn't see her, and she watched as he continued to read the journal. As he read he chewed a candy kiss, which he'd taken from the bowl on the table. Without losing his place, he wadded the foil into a ball and, favoring his injured arm, stretched and placed it atop the table. Leaning back, he readjusted his hips.

The action pushed his pelvis forward. His legs, spread in typically male fashion, formed a cradle, the apex of which was a considerable bulge, made all the more pronounced by the tightness of his jeans—a tightness that threatened to split the seams.

Elizabeth swallowed hard and prayed that the Levi seamstress had taken her job seriously.

The stranger, still not noticing her, turned the page of the diary.

His arm, bunched with muscles, corded with veins, settled back across his stomach. The hard, lean stomach that Elizabeth remembered vividly from the night he'd shed his shirt. She remembered his navel, nestled in golden-tipped hair. The same hair was densely spread across his chest and even now peeked, in beckoning swirls, from the V of his shirt.

Elizabeth swallowed again.

The stranger again turned the page...but stopped short when his eyes found her. A volt of sizzling electricity suddenly seemed to have been unleashed in the room.

Wordlessly she stepped forward, walked toward the gaming table with the massive, lion-footed legs and gathered up the bandages and peroxide she'd placed there earlier. She started toward her patient.

He lay the journal aside, saying, "I don't suppose it would do any good to tell you the bandage doesn't need changing?"

"None whatsoever."

"Then I'll save my breath."

"Prudent choice," she commented, trying to be prudent herself by banishing images of his powerful torso from her mind.

She was only partially successful. She might have been more successful had he not slid his hips in to make room for her by his side. The invitation was natural, and to refuse it would have been conspicuous. She sat down—and felt her thigh meet his. He felt warm, hard and...and *there*—a substantial something in the lonely nothingness of her life. Funny, she hadn't realized how lonely she'd been, what poor company a textbook could be, what poorer company the long nights were. Nor how warm and hard and downright good a man could feel. She glanced up to find him openly studying her. She quickly looked away.

"It should be changed every day," she said, clumsily grasping at the subject of the bandage. Her movements, however, were not awkward; she'd dealt with the dressing too many times now for that. Efficiently, confidently, she cut the gauze from his arm and pulled the sterile pads away. His flesh was hot with a budding, headstrong infection, and only the knowledge that he'd started the antibiotics gave her any peace of mind. Still, she couldn't help but investigate the red-streaked area with gently probing fingers.

"Is it sore?"

He shrugged, a gesture intended to minimize what she was certain wasn't minimal.

Uncapping the peroxide, she soaked a cotton ball. "I don't know whether this burns or not."

And she still didn't know after she'd dabbed the wound. The stranger didn't make a sound, didn't flinch a single muscle. After drawing the cotton ball one last time across the injury and watching the liquid fizz its cleansing white, Elizabeth smeared on some ointment, using her finger to distribute it evenly. The task shouldn't have been sensual—she was treating a wound, after all—yet the smooth, slippery gliding of her flesh across his had her fighting to keep the moment purely platonic. When she glanced up, she saw that he was engaged in the same battle. They both worked hard, as she rewrapped the bandage, to keep his hand from contacting her breast. Unfortunately their efforts called more attention to the moment than had he deliberately reached and done what was on both their minds.

"You're a widow, aren't you?" he asked suddenly.

Her hands paused; her eyes found his.

"Yes," she said, recommencing to wrap. "My husband's been dead a long time. So long that it seems strange to refer to him as my husband. And we were married such a short time. Not even two full years."

"Was he a teacher, too?"

"Yes. He taught physics at Bryn Mawr. That's where I teach," she added.

"How did he die?"

She raised her eyes to his, and she could see that he knew what her answer would be.

"A heart attack."

"Totally unexpected," he added, recalling what he'd read in the journal about the death of the first Elizabeth's husband.

"Yes."

Though she'd finished bandaging his arm, she still held it. Neither spoke. Ultimately she lowered his arm, and as she did, his knuckles accidentally grazed her breast. Her bra-less breast. The sensation that blazed through Elizabeth was startlingly painful. A similar sensation seared the stranger. The air seemed to have been sucked from the room . . . and from two pairs of lungs.

Elizabeth started to rise.

"Wait," he said huskily, throwing a detaining arm about her waist.

His arm felt heavy, hard.

Her waist felt trim and soft.

Hard.

Soft.

His eyes drifted slowly, heatedly, over her, taking in her slightly flushed face, her bare arms and practically bare shoulders, the gentle thrust of her breasts.

"I like your dress," he said, surprising them both: she because he didn't seem the kind of man to concern himself with compliments, he because he knew he wasn't that kind.

"It's new," she said, the words scarcely audible, her skin aflame everywhere his eyes had touched. The breast he'd skimmed felt unbearably full, overwhelmingly achy. So much so that she wanted to cry out.

"It's pretty." The lace-edged hem fanned out enticingly, and he slowly, sensually, crushed the eyelet frills in an enormous fist. "I like lace."

"I know," she said, though she didn't know she knew until just that second. Had it been the reason she'd been attracted to this dress?

"How do you know?" he asked, visions of a dainty-laced, old-fashioned, handmade camisole suddenly coming to his mind through the swirl of years. The camisole had tiny buttons that his large fingers fumbled with, tatted trim that brushed softly against his rough hands; it was hauntingly scented of lavender. Behind it lay an even more exquisite softness.

"I don't know," she answered, she, too, thinking of a lace-trimmed, white lawn camisole. The image reminded her of the garment she'd just bought, only the one now dancing through her mind smelled of lavender and had delicate white-on-white embroidery, embroidery that she could feel her own hands painstakingly working into the fabric. She could also feel the sheer material caressing her breasts. Just as she could feel a man's hands—*this* man's hands—gently worrying the old-fashioned seed buttons open.

Her breath fled.

His followed.

Moments passed, belonging only to lace and longing.

"I—I'm sorry I cut out last night," he said finally, hoarsely. "It's just that what you told me was pretty heavy."

"I know."

"And what I was feeling... it was pretty heavy, too."

"What were you feeling?" She had to hear him say it. God, she had to hear that the madness engulfing her was not of her own making, that she hadn't simply imagined that he, too, felt what she did!

They stared. The stranger lowered his eyes to her lips and swallowed. Would she think him crazy? Would she turn from him in fear? Would she deny feeling the same thing?

"I felt... I feel... as if we've been lovers," he said, waiting for her reaction. She didn't condemn him, obviously wasn't afraid of him, and in no way denied what he saw in her eyes. "I don't know how it's possible," he said, his body bombarded with the sweetest memories, "but I know what it's like to touch you. I know what your mouth tastes like, I know how you feel in my arms, I know there's a tiny brown mole..." His eyes lowered to her breast as his words trailed off.

Elizabeth's breath scattered, both from what he was saying and the accuracy of his last remark. Until that moment she hadn't known that her great-grandmother had had a similar mole on her breast. It wasn't the kind of thing one normally recorded in a diary.

"And I know what it's like to feel you beneath me," he said, mesmerized by the heaven-hell feelings washing through him, feelings leaving him hard with a desperate need. "I know how you move, shift, how you whimper softly. I know how wet your body gets, how hot and wet, how—" he paused, sharply breathing in and out, and when he spoke again, his words were nothing more than a fractured whisper "—how it feels sliding deep inside you."

Emotion thickened the air until neither could breathe or think. They could only feel. And marvel at the beauty of the mysterious feelings. At their beauty and at their primitive and pagan power.

Elizabeth felt a tingling, a tightening in her breasts, felt the nipples stab the thin fabric covering them, felt a weighted heaviness pressing on the hurting, hollow core hidden between her thighs.

Touch me! she screamed silently.

The stranger felt his uneven breath burning his chest, felt his turgid body burning with the heat of desire.

If he didn't touch her soon, he'd die!

He reached up, cupping her cheek in his rough, callused palm.

Hard.

Soft.

The pressure of his thumb angled her head; tendrils of her hair wisped against the back of his hand.

Hard.

Soft.

With impatient insistence, he drew her forward; with willing compliance, she followed.

Hard.

Soft.

"Ah, Lizzie," he whispered, not even realizing he'd abridged her name, "what in hell's happening to us?"

She didn't know, but even if she had she couldn't have answered. The crush of his mouth prevented all except the sweet fall of heaven around them.

Chapter Six

... and when he kissed me, my lungs forgot to breathe, my heart to beat, my soul to be lonely. I forgot who he was, what he was, and remembered only the feel of his lips on mine, the feel of his heart throbbing beneath my palm, the feel of his hot breath desperately whispering sweet words against my burning skin.

Hunger had never been so raw.

The stranger's mouth took hers in fierce possession, angling, slanting, urgently seeking a way to join their bodies as intimately as a kiss would allow. His lips pressed recklessly hard, painfully hard, giving hers no choice but to part, to unfurl her vulnerable softness like the petals of a pink satin rose. When her mouth opened, he groaned. And thrust his tongue deep into the moist waiting warmth.

Unknowingly, Elizabeth clutched at his shirt, anchoring herself in the onslaught of the sensual storm. His tongue was rough and nimble and sought out every part of her mouth. It flicked the corners, slid across her teeth, moved against her tongue in a sinuous, inviting way that suggested a mating dance. Her tongue responded, climbing onto, then under, his, curling and coiling in erotic play.

She whimpered.

He moaned, splaying his hand across her almost bare back and urging her forward until she lay sprawled across his chest. Beneath her hand, his heart beat rapidly. Her own heart echoed the chaotic rhythm.

He's kissed me this way before! she thought.

God, it's been so long since I've kissed her! he thought, accepting the feeling as fact. And then, because he was still so starved, as if too many lonely years had left him thus, he deepened the kiss to an urgency that neither could long tolerate. Though her face was cradled by his hand, the pressure of his kiss forced her head backward. His lips drove into hers. Bitingly. Furiously. Just a little madly.

She gasped from pleasure and from pain.

Rather than hurt her—for controlling the kiss was beyond him—the stranger broke away. They stared, their breath hissing raggedly through lips that were shiny wet, through lips that were already beginning to swell.

Ultimately, when breath was a surer thing, he lowered his hand from her cheek and traced her tender, bruised mouth with the pad of his thumb. His touch, careful and unhurried, carried a silent apology for his prior roughness. Their eyes never wavered, gray swimming in brown, brown drowning in gray, until he, once more willing to trust himself, shuttered his eyes, leaned forward and, slipping his thumb aside, replaced it with his mouth.

This time the kiss was as slow, as gentle, as the first had been wild and uncontrolled. It was no less sensual, however. In fact, it was more devastatingly so. As sweetly as the night had fallen around them, he worshiped her mouth, pecking, nibbling, sliding his lips against hers in a wet, circular pattern. He tasted of chocolate and man. His tongue, once the savage invader, now swept her mouth in slow, long, broad strokes that conquered even more surely, even more sublimely.

Elizabeth melted. Within her chest a golden sun burst, spilling its heated rays into every secret part of her body; its molten rivers sensuously flowed, like hot silken ribbons, through her breasts, her middle, her thighs, leaving her weak, yet at the same time deliriously exhilarated. She sighed, vaguely astonished at the strength of what she was feeling. Rather than contemplate this power, however, she simply succumbed to the sweetly wicked heat.

"Soft . . . God, you're so soft," the stranger murmured against her lips, he, too, slow-burning with blatant desire. He angled his head, nudged hers aside and dropped tiny kisses to her neck, then to her ear, where he again whispered "Soft" before trailing his mouth, in slow, breath-stealing increments, back to hers. This time, when his tongue entered her mouth, it was to the in-and-out rhythm of making love. It was not something he'd planned—he was beyond such conscious choices. It had just happened. And he couldn't have stopped it even if he'd tried.

God, she was soft, sweet! And she was making him so hard. . . .

Elizabeth felt his tortured sex pressing against her belly, felt the carnal cadence of his tongue, felt new fires—bolder, hotter fires—licking at her senses. She became the personification of need—a profane need, a holy need, a familiar need.

Familiar.

Everything about this man was familiar. Hauntingly familiar. The way he breathed, the way he whispered her name, the way his tongue moved gently, provocatively, into, out of, into her mouth.

Slowly the memory came, transporting her back to a nebulous, gray-misted past—to a night that stood shimmeringly still in time, to a night that wandered through her mind like a diaphanously clad dream. Cadence. Rhythm. Feeling. Into, out of, into, out of. But it was no longer his tongue plying the gentle magic. It was his body, moving heavily, lovingly over hers. She could feel his scattered breath rasping against her neck, could feel the warmth of the long summer evening, could feel the salty sweat slickening their love-heated bodies. She could feel him driving deeper, deeper, deeper inside her. She could feel herself receiving each thrust, glorying in it, giving it back. Over. And over. And over. Until... Suddenly she could feel herself responding to his drugging movements in a way that was consummately feminine, naturally ordained. She could feel her body spiraling toward relief.

When Elizabeth realized what was about to happen, not in the fantasized past, but in the very real present, her first thought was disbelief—no, this couldn't be happening! Her second thought was nothing, for her mind was already emptying for celebration of the supremely physical act. She wrenched her mouth from his, gasped and closed her eyes as the tiny, rippling shudders started. She cried softly as each convulsion claimed her, swathing her in a tender ecstasy. Clenching his shirt in her fists, she buried her face in his stomach, her breath splattering short and wild against him.

She was having an orgasm.

The fact registered in the stranger's mind with the impact of a diesel truck at top speed. With one exception. He wouldn't have been quite as stunned if a diesel truck had struck him. One part of him said that he must be mistaken, while another said that there was no way he could be. The act was perfectly recognizable for what it was. What wasn't recognizable was the emotion that erupted deep within him. It was like nothing he'd ever felt. It was a burning need to shelter her during these moments when she was helpless to shelter herself. Something in her softness, her emotional softness, tugged at his strength, making him feel more needed, more powerful, more a man than he'd ever felt before.

His right hand spread wide across the back of her head, his fingers entangling themselves in her hair until tendrils waywardly fell from the topknot. Gently he pressed her face more tightly to him; her breath was scalding as it penetrated the fabric of his shirt and bathed his skin. He raised his injured arm to the small of her back, then lower onto her hips, which she was unknowingly, gently moving against his leg in a seeking, corresponding rhythm to the contractions. Though it hurt his arm to do so—he grimaced back the pain—he urged her hips in their motion. And he spoke to her, softly, sweetly, in words she couldn't fully cling to but in a tone she couldn't mistake. For himself, it was a tone he didn't recognize, for no one had ever drawn it from him before.

"Easy...easy...yes...ah, Lizzie, my sweet Lizzie..."

Slowly, after a seemingly endless rapture, her body quieted. She turned her head, nuzzling her cheek to his stomach. Her hands released their frantic hold on his shirt, splaying now in relaxation, exhaustion. She lay quietly, her eyes closed, the weight of his hands a strangely comforting burden on her head and back. She was content to simply be.

Contentment, however, was short-lived. Embarrassment came stealing through the stillness. Embarrassment more accurately defined as mortification. What had happened? What would he think? Lord, how could she face him again?

Tears stung her eyes.

The stranger felt the sudden dampness through his shirt, heard her slight sniffle. She was crying. Whether as a release or as a reaction to embarrassment, he didn't know. From a little of both would be his guess.

"Elizabeth?" he called softly.

Nothing. Except another sniffle.

He tried to nudge her head up.

She resisted.

"Elizabeth," he said again, applying more force.

He raised her head, though she carefully kept her eyes averted. She swiped at the tears. "I...I'll go get the coffee," she said, rising before he could stop her.

"Forget the coffee. I want to talk."

Ignoring him, she started toward the kitchen. He grabbed the hem of her sundress. She turned but kept her eyes on the hand holding a fistful of fabric.

"We need to talk," he said huskily.

Still keeping her eyes from his face, she swallowed. "N-o," she said, the words cracking wide open, "not now. Please, not now."

There was such a desperate plea in her voice, such a lost look on her face, that when she pulled her dress from him, he let her go without an argument.

The last thing she saw out of the corner of her eye as she exited the room was the stranger standing and adjusting the front of his jeans.

Just how long she stood with her hands spread against the cool kitchen counter, her forehead leaning against the overhead cabinets, Elizabeth couldn't have said. All she knew for certain was that her mind was steeped in turmoil. The intimacy that had just happened she found embarrassing. What had inspired her intimate reaction—the memory of the stranger's lovemaking—she found downright frightening. It was one thing to feel they had been lovers, another to recall the actual act—so clearly, so vividly that she'd responded as if that moment their bodies had been entwined. And the power his body had had over hers . . . Sighing, Elizabeth shoved this equally disturbing feeling to the back of her mind and reached for two mugs.

She was all the way through excuses for postponing her return and midway through the dining room when she saw the headlights of a car as it turned into and slowly made its way up the tree-lined drive. The lights, looking like giant fireflies, cut through the dark night. They also cut through the troubling muddle in Elizabeth's mind. Who could it be? It had to be Pamela, she decided, feeling her pulse rate soar. Visions of an awkward confrontation between a curious Pam and a reticent stranger hurried her forward.

"There's someone—"

The drawing room was empty, the words falling impotently into a loud silence. Where was he? Why did he always vanish like a . . . Like a ghost? Ignoring the thought, Elizabeth placed the mugs on the table. Even as the knock sounded on the door, she realized that the bandages, the bottle of peroxide and the ointment had been stashed into a basket containing magazines. As she looked around for other telltale evidence, she noticed that the foil wrapper from the candy was missing. He'd obviously taken it. Just the way he'd destroyed all evidence of his presence that first night. Just the way someone on the run might—

The knock came again.

Elizabeth stepped forward and opened the door. As she'd expected, Pamela Shaw stood there, concern in her eyes.

"Hi," the woman said, adding in explanation for her unannounced appearance, "I called this morning, then again this afternoon, but I got no answer."

"I went shopping this morning, and I worked in the rose garden this afternoon."

"Oh. Well, I must have called then."

Neither spoke, but Pamela's eyes roved from the tumbled mass of Elizabeth's hair to her kiss-bruised lips. Self-consciously Elizabeth lifted her hand to her hair but lowered it when she saw her friend's eyes fasten on her wrist and the bruises that were turning from purple to yellowish-green.

"Are you alone?" her friend asked.

Elizabeth's heart thumped at the question. "Of course."

When no invitation was forthcoming, Pamela asked, "May I come in?"

Elizabeth stepped back. "Sure. I'm sorry."

The woman entered the house. Elizabeth closed the door behind her.

"Where's Carol and Casey?"

"With their father," Pamela answered, sitting down on the sofa.

Was the sofa still warm from their lovemaking? Elizabeth thought, taking the chair and folding her feet beneath her.

Pamela's gaze drifted about the room and finally rested on the table before the sofa. Elizabeth glanced down to see the object of her attention. The *objects* of her attention. *Two* mugs filled with coffee.

Elizabeth looked up. Guiltily. "Uh...I, uh...I saw your car pull in...and I was just pouring coffee."

"How did you know it was me?"

Elizabeth gave a small, unconvincing laugh. "C'mon, who else would be stupid enough to drive this far out just to check on a friend?"

Pamela said nothing. Elizabeth ran her tongue over her swollen lips.

"Are you all right?" Pamela asked, ending their charade of casualness.

What would her friend say if she were to answer honestly? Well, funny you should ask, Elizabeth longed to say. My body is still flushed and drowsy from making love. Well, actually I was only kissing in this century, but making love in another, and, you know how it is, sometimes your centuries get mixed and mingled, and well, right there on the very sofa you're sitting on, I embarrassed myself totally. With a stranger who seems anything but a stranger. With a stranger who may or may not be a ghost. With a stranger who may or may not be wanted by the law. With a stranger who may be all of the above or none of the above because I may simply be losing my mind.

"I'm fine," Elizabeth said finally, the lie tripping from lips that quivered with emotion. "But thank you for caring."

By the dark of the moon, the land lay in peaceful slumber. Night creatures called among themselves in a lonely, hushed communion, while stars, dazzling in their bright gowns of silver, twinkled in a black, low-hung Southern sky. Not a breeze stirred, not a whisper of air rustled the death-still leaves, which only intensified the grass-muffled sound of footsteps.

Dammit, it was hot! the stranger thought, worrying the candy foil between restless fingers. His clothes had immediately stuck to him as he'd hurried out into the hot, humid night after sighting the car pulling into the drive. Who had it been? Whoever it was, their timing was impeccably lousy. Lousy. The one word summed up his sour mood. He hadn't wanted to leave so abruptly. He hadn't wanted to leave without talking with her. He hadn't wanted to leave without satisfying himself that she was all right.

Satisfy himself?

The stranger laughed harshly, the sound strafing the breathless, ebony night. If he'd satisfied himself, he would have buried his aching body so deep in hers that neither one of them would have been able to walk straight for a week. Maybe two. In reaction to the thought, he drew his hand along the buttoned closure of his jeans, hoping that rearranging the fabric would ease the problem. It didn't. If the ache didn't abate soon, he snarled silently, he'd be a shoo-in for *The Guinness Book of World Records* under the dubiously desired heading of: Man With the Longest-Held Erection. Maybe even the hardest. God, how he envied her release!

Release.

Even now he could hear the catch in her breathing, her whimper, the way she'd folded into him when the climax had started, as if she'd suddenly melted like wax brought too close to a fire. He'd never seen anything like it, or, more precisely, he'd never reacted as he had with her. He'd seen women have orgasms before, but nobody, nobody, had moved him the way Elizabeth had. Aside from it being so unexpected, apparently to her as much as to him—God, he'd only kissed her!—it was so . . . so honest. Just the way his reaction had been. He'd quite simply wanted to pull her somewhere deep inside him.

He frowned. He wasn't comfortable with emotion . . . for more reasons than he cared to acknowledge. When your home was a Detroit ghetto, when your father could have been half-a-dozen men, none of whom gave a hoot in hell what happened to you, when your mother gave only half a hoot, and then only when she was sober and out of jail, when the only game in life was survival, you didn't cultivate emotion. And you sure didn't when you were in the business he was in.

And yet . . .

Even before he'd met Elizabeth Jarrett—hell, what kind of spooky historical reenactment had he stumbled into? And why did he feel as if he'd known her forever?—he'd felt his emotions getting the better of him. They'd started tumbling downhill when he'd heard that Jake Jennings had been fished from the Cane River Lake in Natchitoches, the victim of an apparent accidental drowning. Accident? No way! Jake Jennings had gills and more swimming medals than he'd had common sense. Why else would the jerk have risked his butt pulling yours truly from the Mekong River when .50-caliber machine gun slugs were raking the water faster than a man could pray?

His first mistake had been sneaking out of the jungles of Guatemala to go to Jennings's funeral in Shreveport, his second going on down to Natchitoches for a look-see. His third mistake had been not being able to turn his back on the suspicion that Rose Haven's caretaker, Joshua Boone, had killed Jennings. In his old, emotionless days, he could have controlled his feelings—postponed them at any rate—and bid for a better time to even the score, a time when he wouldn't be placing a long-planned operation into jeopardy. But these hadn't been his emotionless days, and thus he'd committed mistake number four: he'd followed the caretaker, risking discovery, which had ultimately come, and when Boone had shot at him, he'd shot back. And killed.

Not wanting the body to be found, he'd carried it to an abandoned well and tossed it in. Though he'd felt no remorse in killing the man, the insensitivity of the well had stuck in his craw. But, like always, he'd done what he had to. Besides, he himself had been bleeding, and lugging around a man who weighed two hundred plus pounds wasn't doing anything for the injury—except making it bleed more.

And then he'd made mistake number five, the biggest of them all, though he'd had little choice. He'd walked center stage into Elizabeth Jarrett's life. Elizabeth Jarrett, who was doing things to him that no breathing man could ignore. Elizabeth Jarrett, the lady with the mysterious gray eyes. Elizabeth Jarrett, who he would swear on a stack of Bibles had a brown mole on her right breast, though heaven alone knew how he knew that.

God, was he going crazy?

Or did all this emotion simply mean that he was finally burning out? Had he seen and done one too many violent things? Had he not cared one time too many? Had he not felt for so long that it had become a case of feel or die?

He cursed his lack of answers, flinging the candy foil onto the ground and prying open the door of the sweltering shack he'd called home for almost a week. He cursed again, this time for the long, sleepless night he knew lay ahead. How could any man sleep in this damnable heat... and with a record hard-on?

Elizabeth slept poorly.

And awoke the next morning with a dull headache, which she treated with a Bayer cocktail—two aspirins taken with orange juice. From there the day got progressively worse, with one vexing irritation layered upon another until by mid-afternoon she was forced to surrender to a nap or jump entirely out of her skin. But once again sleep eluded her, and she was left wide-eyed with a filmstrip of the night before playing over and over again in her troubled mind. She relived the stranger's kiss, her embarrassing, frightening reaction to it, Pam unexpectedly showing up on her doorstep. In retrospect, she was glad her friend had intruded. It had spared her from facing the stranger—at least for the time being.

Following the sleeping debacle, Elizabeth dragged herself from bed, took two more aspirins and prowled the house like a restless beast. Suddenly realizing that the caretaker hadn't shown up again—today was Thursday, wasn't it?—she called his home but got no answer.

When the phone rang a couple of hours later, she half expected it to be Joshua Boone. It wasn't.

"Elizabeth? This is Ruth Dixon."

Ruth Dixon? Elizabeth tried to place the name. Finally bits and pieces of recognition came. Red hair. Fortyish. A Daughter of the American Revolution and snobbishly proud of it. The few times Elizabeth had seen her after they'd become adults, she'd had the odd feeling that Ruth Dixon viewed them as competitors. From an old family herself, Ruth took great pride in her pedigreed name, her *legitimate* heritage, though she was never crass enough to do more than subtly hint that Elizabeth's lineage was founded on illegitimacy. Elizabeth reflected on how galling it must be to Ruth that the notorious Jarrett family always got more attention than the proper, never-a-skeleton-in-their-closet Dixons.

"Yes, Ruth. How are you?"

The conversation pursued a predictable social path before Ruth got down to business.

"Actually, what I'm calling about is Rose Haven. I hear it may be on the market soon."

The small-town grapevine was still healthy, Elizabeth noted. "Yes, we're thinking about selling, but we haven't reached a decision yet."

"I understand, but I wanted you to know that the Association for the Preservation of Historic Natchitoches—I'm president this year; well, actually I've been president for three years—"

Elizabeth glanced at the clock, wishing the woman would hurry up and get to the point. The hour for the sun to set was fast approaching.

"... anyway, the Association is interested in acquiring Rose Haven..."

Would he show up? Yes. Yes, of course he would. She had no doubt of that. And, curiously, she both wanted to see him and didn't want to see him.

"... and opening it to tours. Maybe even establishing it as a bed-and-breakfast..."

What would she say to him?

"... I've even considered moving in, managing everything..."

How could she possibly look him in the eye after last—

"Would you?"

Elizabeth clasped the phone more tightly. "Would I what?"

"Would you call us if you decide to sell?" The voice that was obviously repeating the question betrayed its carefully tended, socially acceptable tone by registering faint irritation.

"Yes. I'll be glad to. And thank you for calling."

Elizabeth hung up, grateful for another avenue to pursue should she and her aunt choose to sell, but increasingly fidgety with the approaching hour. Her mood hadn't changed forty-five minutes later when, showered and dressed in jeans—she denied choosing the jeans because they covered so much of her body—she moved barefoot around the kitchen. If anything, her mood had worsened, a fact substantiated by her nervous mumbling.

"Tomatoes... lettuce... pastrami... turkey... mustard. No, mayonnaise. No, mustard. No..." She raked her fingers through her hair. "What difference does it make, Elizabeth? Put both mustard and mayonnaise on the darned

sandwiches. Or don't put either. Who cares?'' In exasper-
ation she reached for the tomato and sliced through it with
all the frustration she was feeling. She had just positioned
the knife for a second sweep through the flesh of the tomato when she heard the noise.

A scuffling.

Behind her.

She whirled and, clutching the knife to her chest, gasped.

The stranger stood in the kitchen doorway. Silently. Fa-
miliarly. As though there was no other place in the world
where he should be standing. Elizabeth's first thought was
that she could have sworn she'd locked the front door, the
second that maybe it didn't matter in this man's case.
Though she hadn't thought it possible, in her surprise her
eyes met his. They looked more free of pain than she'd ever
seen them. However, they were veiled with fatigue, under-
scored by dark circles. She could almost believe that he
hadn't slept any better than she had. And that he was just
as emotionally hung over as she, which she deduced by the
grim squaring of his jaw and the intense way he was staring
at her.

"I didn't mean to startle you," he said, his eyes brooding, his voice low and scratchy.

He looked and sounded exactly like what she suspected
him to be—a modern-day desperado...or the ghost of one
from yesteryear. The rapid beating of her heart, however,
was not caused by fear. It was caused by the sublime re-
membrance of what had happened in his arms.

She turned and, her fingers trembling, started whacking
at the tomato with great imprecision. She heard him cross
the room, felt him move to stand beside her without crowd-
ing her, saw him lazily prop his hip against the cabinet. His
jeans were as tight as they always were, and they did the
same reedy things to her breath.

"How are you?" he asked.

She absently thought the question created a curious role reversal. "Fine," she said, keeping her eyes on the task before her, which was turning out to be the slaughter of an innocent vegetable. "How are you?"

"Better. The antibiotics are helping."

"Good," she said, focusing her attention on the head of lettuce she was now ruthlessly butchering.

"The arm's moving better, too," he said, and she could see him flexing it out of the corner of her eye. It was one of the arms that had held her so tenderly the night before as her body had shuddered against his.

She didn't look up. Whack! Whack! Whack! The lettuce fell into shambles.

"We're having sandwiches."

"That's fine."

"I hope you like pastrami."

"I do."

"And turkey."

"Yes."

"Do you want mustard or mayonnaise?"

"Whichever."

"I'll put both on the table or..."

"Elizabeth?"

"...I think there's some sandwich spread..."

"Elizabeth?"

"...or if you'd prefer..."

"Dammit, will you look at me!" he shouted, stilling her hands with his.

Her heart ran wild, clamoring loudly in her ears, yet still she didn't look at him. She couldn't.

His thumb and forefinger gripped her chin, none too gently, and forced her head up. "Look...at...me!" he growled.

She had no choice but do as he bade. Reluctantly her eyes slid into his.

"Why wouldn't you look at me?" he asked after what Elizabeth would have sworn was an eternity.

She said nothing, though she could feel her cheeks growing warm.

His eyes lowered to the pretty pink. "Ah, Lizzie," he whispered, tracing her blush with the crook of his finger, "don't you know what happened last night was okay, was normal?"

She shook her head, spraying her hair against the inside of his arm. "Not for me."

"So there's a first time for everything."

"You don't understand," she said, pulling away from him.

What he understood was that her sudden absence felt more powerful than any other woman's presence ever had. He wanted to reach out for her. But didn't. Instead, he said, "Then help me to."

She had turned back to the cabinet but now stood staring at her hands, which were idly folded atop it. "We . . ."

"We what?"

"We were making—" She swallowed and collected what courage she could. "We were making love."

The words gave birth to a momentary silence before he said softly, gruffly, "I know."

"No, you don't know!" she cried, whirling, her fear and frustration bubbling to the surface. She was aware that she was unfairly taking her negative emotions out on him, but she couldn't stop herself. "No, you don't know," she repeated, raking her fingers through her hair.

When nothing followed, he asked, "Well, are you going to tell me, or are we going to play twenty questions?" He knew his response had been curt, but his emotions were on a short fuse. He hadn't slept, he was tired and he was hungry. At the word *hungry* he lowered his eyes to her jean-covered hips. He fought to concentrate on what she was saying.

"S-something happened last night. I mean, beyond the obvious." She hesitated but forced herself to go on. "I, uh...this memory...it came from out of nowhere. It was sometime in the past...a long time ago...we were..."

She had his attention. "We were what?"

Her voice was barely audible when she said, "We were making love." She swallowed again. "I could feel...I mean, it was as if...you were moving inside..." She stopped.

The stranger stared. "You mean...?"

Elizabeth replied with a breathless, "Yes."

The silence that followed was complete. And lengthy.

At last Elizabeth asked imploringly, "What's happening?"

It was a question he had once asked himself. He shook his head, splaying his hand through his hair. "I...I don't know." His level of confusion seemed equal to hers. Finally, simply because it felt the right thing to do, he took a step toward her.

She took an immediate step backward and held up her hand, as if warding him off. "No! Don't come near me." He stopped. Though his eyes were accustomed to showing little emotion, she thought she saw hurt flash deep in his brown irises. "I...I can't think clearly when you're near me."

Nor could he, he acknowledged silently.

And so both stood, each looking at the other, neither thinking clearly anyway.

"Who are you? What are you?" The questions drifted tremblingly from her lips, from her heart.

The stranger thought of all the nowhere days and the empty, nothing nights of his life. He thought of dark alleyways, steaming jungles, two-bit hotel rooms crawling with loneliness and cockroaches—all of which had one thing in common: they were the backdrop of his carelessly lived life. He thought of endless lies, tiresome charades and his constant courting of death. He thought of the shell he'd built around his heart, a shell so hard that he could kill a man and not feel an ounce of regret.

"Believe me, Lizzie," he said quietly, "it's better if you don't know."

"Better for whom? You? Or me?"

"Better for both of us," he said, knowing that she could never grow accustomed to his hardness but that he could grow dangerously accustomed to her softness.

Silence reigned. Both stared. In the far distance there came the faint sound of a small, light aircraft.

"Leave me alone," she whispered with sudden desperation. "Just go back to wherever you came from."

Hell. He had come from hell. He'd been born there and would die there, and he in the meantime was going through hell standing here listening to her, watching her, wanting her in a way that defied all reason.

His eyes lowered from hers to the cheeks that blushed so becomingly, so endearingly.

Hers lowered to the dramatic set of his jaw.

His gaze slid to her lips.

Hers sought his out as well.

Memories of the night before flooded them both.

Suddenly both reached the end of their emotional tethers.

Tears glazed her eyes.

He took a step backward, then another, then whirled and started for the door.

The plane sailed overhead.

"Wait!" she cried out because she couldn't stop herself, but when his eyes—his hopeful eyes—found hers, there seemed nothing more to say.

Finally, with not a flicker of emotion, he turned and disappeared through the doorway.

Elizabeth felt him take a part of her, the heart of her, with him.

Chapter Seven

Am I a fool to love him, knowing what he is? Yes, un-questionably. Though the heart does make fools of us all. I know only that I'd rather be foolish with him than the wisest of all women without him.

The stranger lay facedown upon the Louisiana earth, his chest nuzzling soft sprigs of green grass, his nose buried in bitter-smelling weeds. Undergrowth, heavy and lush, hid him from all except a hungry mosquito, whose incessant buzzing he ignored, along with the slithery sounds that came from somewhere nearby. His attention was fully focused on the scene before him.

At the edge of the woods, at the very back of the planta-tion, was a clearing just long enough to allow a skillful pi-lot to land a small aircraft. A skillful and daring pilot, the stranger amended as he watched the Cessna bump to a shaky halt. The motor died, the propellers whirled to a stop and two men, pilot and passenger, crawled out of the aircraft. They were the same two men he'd seen land twice before, both times after nightfall and with the help of flashlights aimed at the sky, flashlights worked by Rose Haven's caretaker. Rose Haven's recently deceased caretaker.

A plane had also flown over Tuesday evening, at sunset, but the gunshot had been too fresh, too painful, for the stranger to do more than register its arrival. And to wonder. Was the caretaker's unavailability the reason the landings had been rescheduled from night to late-afternoon? Had someone already missed the man? Was that someone already growing suspicious? Was that damned emotional indiscretion going to cost him even more?

And did Elizabeth Jarrett know what was going on at the back of her property? Was she actively involved? Or passively involved, which demanded that she did nothing more than turn a blind eye, for a handsome cut of the profits, of course? Or was she simply a vulnerable victim?

Vulnerable.

Soft.

We were making love. I could feel . . . I mean, it was as if . . . you were moving inside . . .

Stop it!

Don't come near me. I . . . I can't think clearly when you're near me.

Dammit, stop it! the stranger seethed, carelessly shifting positions and hurting his arm in the process. He grimaced. Will you just give the subject of Elizabeth Jarrett a rest? You almost didn't hear the plane going over at all because you were too preoccupied with that little scene in her kitchen.

Dangerous.

Emotions are dangerous.

Don't ever forget that.

He forced himself to concentrate on what was unfolding before him. The two men were unloading a long, obviously heavy wooden crate. One of the men stumbled, jarring his share of the load, and a curse stung the air. With frowns on their faces, and muscles bulged to the limit, they started off through the woods. The stranger didn't follow. He knew where they were headed, just as he knew what the crate contained. Their destination was the dilapidated mill where the Jarrett cotton had once been ginned. There, the men would pile the crate alongside the dozen or so others, each filled with firearms—M16 rifles, grenades, Uzis, anything dedicated to maiming or killing, anything that would appeal to restless, ruthless revolutionaries or any number of unscrupulous people who made their living through violence.

It was at the mill that the stranger had encountered the caretaker, at the mill that he'd killed him, in the nearby well that he'd dumped him. It was the guns that he wanted. It was the guns he would have. In time. With patience. If he didn't screw up everything by getting too involved with Elizabeth Jarrett.

Leave me alone. Just go back to wherever you came from.

Good idea, the stranger thought. No, it was better than a good idea. It was a damned good idea. But even as he thought it, memories crowded his mind, memories of haunted gray eyes, memories of an old-fashioned blush, memories of a feminine body, warm and unforgettably soft.

And the memories persisted, even after the plane had taken to the air, even after the stranger had returned to the sweltering shack, where he'd spread peanut butter onto stale crackers and called it supper, even after the night sang with lonely darkness. When it was obvious that another sleepless night was upon him, the stranger cursed. Why was it that the path of a good idea, even a damned good idea, was so hard to follow?

Impossible.

Sleep had been impossible for the second night in a row, Elizabeth thought the next afternoon, a hot Friday, as she pulled her car into the parking lot of the nursing home. Clouds patchworked a sea blue sky, suggesting that maybe rain was in the day's forecast. While she wasn't opposed to a cooling rain, what she needed most was rest, sleep, blessed surcease from thoughts of a stranger.

Shutting off the motor, she drew her compact from her purse and checked to see if she looked as bad as she felt. She did. Maybe worse. Which Aunt Siddie was certain to point out first thing.

"You look awful," Aunt Siddie said, laying the Big Chief writing tablet and pen onto the TV tray she was using as a side table. The table was already piled high with an assortment of magazines, newspapers and books.

"And aren't you a dear to point it out?" Elizabeth said good-naturedly as she bent to kiss the older woman's cheek. Siddie Jarrett smelled of something sweet and familiar, and Elizabeth fought the urge to fall at her feet, bury her head in her lap and simply absorb the comfort this woman had always given so unselfishly. Instead, she did what an adult does best: she pretended to be an adult. Taking the chair by her aunt, she said with a nod toward the tablet, "Who's catching hell now?"

Seldom did a week go by when Siddie Jarrett didn't write a scathing editorial to the Natchitoches or Shreveport newspapers. And always on a Big Chief writing tablet. When teased about her stationery, she'd reply that you could buy more expensive but you couldn't buy better. And she ought to know, she'd invariably say, because she'd used the tablets to teach second graders for thirty-odd years.

"The town council is trying to rezone an area that's perfectly zoned as it is. Why everyone always thinks that change is better is beyond me. The scourge of our society is this endless preoccupation with improving things. I say if something is right, leave it alone. If it isn't broken, don't fix it. Just look at that toothpaste ad...." Siddie Jarrett frowned. "No, that's an example of false advertising, but you get my point."

Which, of course, Elizabeth didn't; but then, she didn't expect to.

"Enough of me and the council's rezoning shenanigans," the older woman said. "What's wrong with you?"

Elizabeth shrugged. "I'm fine."

"Uh-huh. And I can see that 'fine' puddled beneath your eyes."

"Truly, I—"

"Aren't you sleeping well?"

Elizabeth started to lie but settled on the truth. "Actually, no." When her aunt said nothing, but rather raked her with soft blue eyes, she felt compelled to add, "I, uh...I guess it's just everything catching up with me." She conveniently left the impression that "everything" meant her mother's recent death.

Siddie said nothing, yet her eyes probed more deeply.

Under her intense gaze, Elizabeth rose and restlessly walked to the window. The sky seemed increasingly cloudy. Would it rain?

He came out of the night. Out of the dark, rainy night.

"We, uh...we've gotten several nibbles on Rose Haven," she said, trying to divert her own thoughts. She went on to report the doctor's, the sheriff's and Ruth Dixon's expressions of interest. "Plus, we had a letter today from Leland

Webster. He asked if we were considering selling the plantation.''

Webster, Webster, Dennison, and Devereaux had served the Jarrett family in a legal capacity ever since there'd been a Webster and Webster and long before there'd been a Dennison and Devereaux. The elder Webster had died years before, and Leland, his son, had risen to seniority. Elizabeth had always suspected that Leland Webster was not a happy man; he'd always had aspirations to practice law in a larger city, where he could have become a Melvin Belli or an F. Lee Bailey.

"Leland?" Siddie asked. "What in the world would Leland want with Rose Haven? For that matter, what would anyone want with a house that's too hot in the summer, too cold in the winter and impossibly drafty all year round?"

"Oh, I don't know," Elizabeth said. "It has a certain charm, an undeniable graciousness, a certain—" She stopped, studied her aunt and smiled at the sparkle she saw in her eyes. "Have I just been outsmarted?"

"Oh, my, no, I wouldn't presume to match minds with a Jarrett. It would be too much like jousting at thin air."

The two women grinned. Siddie's smile faded first. "So, have you decided to sell?"

Elizabeth turned, walked toward the double bed Siddie had been allowed to bring from Rose Haven to personalize her room and stroked the ecru crocheted spread. She'd stroked it a thousand times before as she'd stood in her aunt's bedroom, pouring out her soul about everything from braces to boys to mothers who made promises but never made good on them. "We have a deal. I'll make no decision until the summer's over."

Siddie nodded, as if pleased. "And I'll stand by my part of the bargain. If you want to sell at the end of the summer, I'll agree."

"Why?" It was a question Elizabeth had wanted to ask before. "Why agree now and not last year when I asked you to sell?"

The woman, youthful despite her seventy-seven years, considered and reached a decision. "I don't want to sell Rose Haven. You know that. But neither do I want you to hang on to it if doing so makes you unhappy. I don't want that now; I didn't want that a year ago."

Elizabeth looked puzzled. "Then why—"

"It was your mother who didn't want to sell."

Few things had ever so startled Elizabeth. "Regan?" she asked disbelievingly.

Her aunt nodded. "Last year when the subject of selling came up, I called her in Rome, explained that I'd broken a hip and was going into a nursing home, probably for good, and told her that you wanted to sell Rose Haven." At Elizabeth's silence, she went on. "She begged me to talk you out of it."

Elizabeth could feel some emotion building. It felt like anger, but she told herself that she no longer felt anger for her mother's scattered behavior. It was another little game adults learned to play: they told themselves that they were over things when the truth was that maybe they weren't.

"Why?" she now whispered. "Why would Regan want me to hold on to Rose Haven? She didn't care a fig about the plantation." The emotion was building, building, building, until it finally erupted. And its name was anger. "She didn't care a fig about us...me! If she had, she would have come home occasionally! She would have remembered occasionally that she had a daughter!"

Silence reigned like a supreme despot in the wake of the outburst.

Siddie Jarrett patted the seat next to her. "Come here." Thrusting her fingers through her hair, Elizabeth went and eased onto the seat's edge. Her aunt took her hand. "Your mother loved you—" At the protest Elizabeth started to make, Siddie interrupted, "In her way, she loved you. And in the end, all any of us has is our own way. As for why she wanted to keep Rose Haven in the family..." She shrugged. "Human nature is complex, Elizabeth. Sometimes what we run from is what we most want to run to."

Like a blond-haired, brown-eyed man? Elizabeth thought.

"You're very much like your mother," Aunt Siddie continued. "Neither of you was, is, comfortable being a Jarrett."

"It's not a question of being comfortable," Elizabeth said. "It's a matter of feeling ... I don't know ... lost ... in the family's history. No one ever sees *me*. I always come bearing the trappings of the family."

"The trappings of a colorful family?"

"Yes."

"The trappings of a slightly crazy family?" The sparkle was back in Siddie Jarrett's eyes. "Do you think we're crazy, Elizabeth?"

Despite the emotions weighting her, a smile tweaked Elizabeth's lips. "I don't know. Are we?"

"Lord, I hope so. Sanity is such a bourgeois state of being. It's for those people with no creative imaginations. Reality, my dear Elizabeth, is too cumbersome a thing to be stuck with for too long."

Elizabeth smiled. Her aunt smiled, too, then brushed a strand of hair from her niece's cheek. It was a gesture warmly remembered from childhood.

"Can you stay awhile and help me with my puzzle?" Aunt Siddie asked.

"Are you still forcing pieces into place?"

"Only when I have to."

The statement sounded so like her aunt, and in its way was profound. Everyone tried to make the pieces of his life fit. Only sometimes they just didn't. And this was one of those times. Elizabeth couldn't even begin to force together the pieces of the puzzle that was unfolding around her.

They sat at a card table, searching, selecting, trying out, rejecting and searching again. The puzzle, when completed, would depict a fat, contented cat. Because the animal was golden, pieces of the puzzle ranged from maize to sunshine-yellow to a pale ash blond. Elizabeth found herself gravitating to the jagged pieces whose color most closely matched that of the stranger's hair.

She had told him to leave her alone, to go back to wherever he'd come from. And he had left. Leaving her desolate even before he'd disappeared. It was a desolation she couldn't shake, a desolation . . .

She jerked her head up. "What?"

"I said, it's going to rain."

She glanced out the window. "Probably."

"Did Monday night's storm damage the roses?"

"A little."

Aunt Siddie discarded one piece of the puzzle for another that looked more promising. "Has Joshua gotten the mess cleaned up?"

Elizabeth's hand hesitated. "It's cleaned up," she answered, failing to mention that she herself had done the work. She didn't want her aunt to worry about the gardener's continued absence. She had called his house again today with the same negative results.

Both women inserted pieces of the puzzle at the same time. A triumphant silence rained down.

Finally Siddie said, "Grover Haywood stopped by yesterday."

Elizabeth's heart faltered.

The older woman never looked up, but rather kept searching and selecting. "Sometimes he tools that little Maserati of his out to the nursing home and rewards us with a visit. Imagine *vrooming* about at his age. Of course, maybe at his age he still needs to prove he can *vroom*."

Ignoring Grover Haywood's penchant for flashy sports cars and deciding it would look better if she took the initiative, Elizabeth asked, "Did, uh...did he mention my tonsillitis?"

Siddie glanced up. "Do you have tonsillitis?"

"Just a little," she answered, hating the lie. "He prescribed some antibiotics."

The other woman went back to the puzzle. "You ought to have them taken out."

"Yeah. Someday," she said and felt her heart returning to normal. She still hated the lie.

A few minutes and several mismatches of the puzzle later, Elizabeth said, as casually as one could say such a thing, "Do you think Rose Haven's haunted?"

"Of course it is," her aunt replied, as if the subject matter fell under the heading of normal conversation. "No self-respecting plantation isn't."

"Have you, uh...have you ever seen him? The ghost, I mean?"

"Certainly."

"What does he look like?"

"Blond hair...longish and a bit unruly...dark, brooding eyes—not very handsome really, but...I don't know, there's something magnetic about him...intense. He has a troubled, haunted look, if you'll pardon the pun."

Elizabeth instantly pardoned it to pursue the thought that jumped into her mind. Reaching for the Big Chief tablet, she asked, "Can you sketch him?"

Siddie Jarrett keenly studied her niece before accepting the tablet. Quietly, quickly, she drew pen across paper with the natural talent she had inherited from her artist mother. When Siddie passed the tablet back, Elizabeth took it, almost fearfully. She lowered her eyes.

And felt her heart begin a dull thud. Though the sketch was simplistic, the figure was recognizable. Familiar. So familiar that her face paled, her throat dried to the consistency of cotton, her eyes stung.

"Is that what this is all about?" Siddie asked softly. "Have you seen the ghost?"

Elizabeth glanced up but said nothing. Deep within her, logic warred with the drawing she held in her hands.

Her aunt saw the battle. "Ah, child, don't limit yourself to only those things you understand." She smiled with the wisdom of all her years. "Don't you know that then you'd miss half the beauty of life?"

The words taunted and teased Elizabeth as she drove home, until by the time she pulled into Rose Haven's tree-lined drive, she was certain of nothing. Except that she'd never been more confused in her life.

Or more lonely.

The promise of rain became the threat of a storm.

By late afternoon not a leaf stirred, not a blade of grass swayed, not a shrub or bush danced to the melody of a windsong. The cloud-streaked sky had melted from blue to lavender to purple, as if bruised by the pressure of harsh, unseen hands.

Standing on the gallery porch, her clothes sticking to her body in the muggy heat, Elizabeth fought to breathe in the still, stagnant air. She glanced down at her wrist. The bruise was little more than a smudge now, a faint telltale reminder of something she couldn't forget anyway. No more than she could forget what had transpired the evening before. She had told the stranger to go away, banished him to wherever he had come from.

Where had he come from? Elizabeth mused, putting her hands behind her and leaning back against a square column. Some world between then and now, yesterday and today, insanity and reason?

Don't limit yourself to only those things you understand. Don't you know that then you'd miss half the beauty of life?

Elizabeth sighed, her emotions as roiling, as unsettled, as the storm brewing about her. Did she regret sending him away? Did she regret his being so willing to comply? Did the hollowness inside her hurt more than anything had ever hurt her? And why should she feel anything at all for this man?

When the phone rang, she was relieved. Any distraction was worth its weight in gold. The caller turned out to be the sheriff, Ben Adams, who, after inquiring about her health—he had heard she was feeling poorly from a bout of tonsillitis—asked her for a date the following week. Elizabeth had been so surprised that she'd stammered through what she hoped was a tactful rejection. What had surprised her even more was the reason she'd rejected him. There was no way she could say yes, no way she wanted to say yes, with the blond-haired, brown-eyed visions running through her mind.

Where was the stranger?

What was he doing?

What wouldn't she give to see him one more time?

No, she didn't want to see him.

Yes, she did.

No! Just leave me alone! Please!

But her troubled thoughts stayed with her for the rest of the afternoon. Ultimately, she carried them to the attic, which she seemed intractably drawn to. There, amid shadows and memories and the aged smell of sandalwood, she sat rummaging through the trunk. She found the high-topped shoes, their leather cracked and rivered with age. The red felt hat with the black ostrich feather—both hat and feather had seen better days, better years—brought a smile to Elizabeth's lips. Just as the crocheted shawl brought a warmth that had nothing to do with the fact that it was spread about her shoulders. Who had worn the shawl? The first Elizabeth? Or perhaps her daughter, Rosemary?

The shawl was suddenly forgotten as Elizabeth's eyes lowered to a new treasure peeking from the corner of the trunk. Slowly, she reached for the . . .

. . . ivory comb in the shape of a bird's spread wings.

The thought flashed through the stranger's mind with searing clarity. He had no idea what it meant, yet he strangely felt some affinity for the comb, as if at some time in his life he'd seen a woman wearing it. Maybe one of the Central American women? Probably. They were always piling their dark hair on their heads to get it off their hot, sweaty necks.

Hot, sweaty.

God, it was hot and he was sweaty!

Shrugging his shoulders out of the shirt he'd long ago unbuttoned, he wadded it up and threw it onto the torn, dirty mattress lumped on the floor. His chest glistening with moisture, he checked the bandage wrapped about his arm to see if the perspiration was loosening the tape. It was, and he tried to adhere it back onto his skin, noting in the process that the bandage was soiled. It should have been changed last night—probably would have been, if the evening hadn't taken the turn it had.

Leave me alone. Just go back to wherever it is you came from.

"Fine, lady," he said, his voice rumbling darkly. "That's exactly what I intend to do. *Maybe tomorrow, if the arm continues to improve. To tell you the truth, I've already hung around too long.*

One kiss too long?

He ignored the question and moved to the doorway of the shack. One hand propped on the rotting door frame, one hand wedged at his waist, he stared out at the storm-shadowed sky. It was going to rain. Until the bottom fell out. Which was all right with him. He didn't have anywhere to go tonight.

Not even to her?

No way. The smart lady doesn't want me anywhere near her.

What do you want?

Same thing. Something strange is happening here. Besides, all that sweetness is poison to a man like me.

Then why can't you get that sweet kiss out of your mind?

It's out.

Anyone ever tell you you're a liar?

Anyone ever tell you you're a pain in the ass?

The sunset hour came and went.

Lightning scrawled its electric message across the ebony sky, while thunder bayed like a pack of wild dogs. The rain, however, held off, as if the world were poised for some cataclysmic occasion its commencement would herald.

Elizabeth, her nerves reverberating with the same anxious sentiment, felt the restlessness deep within her as she forced down a tasteless ham and cheese sandwich. A similar restiveness slinked through the stranger as he dug his meal out of a tin can, warm potted meat and pork 'n' beans, which he chased down with warmer slugs of beer.

Beer and antibiotics. He wasn't sure of the medicinal appropriateness, but life wasn't so accommodating as to always present appropriate scenarios.

Antibiotics.

Elizabeth.

What was she doing? Eating? Waiting for the storm to strike? Would she be all right when it did? Of course she would! And yet that strong sense of protectiveness he'd felt before flooded him, and he was left with the need to feel her in his arms, the need to crush her to him, the need to shelter her. This need inexorably gave way to another need. The need of a man's hard body for the softness of a woman. At the heat that infused him, at the ache that traitorously thrust against his jeans, the stranger growled a curse.

Elizabeth cursed, threw the sandwich into the trash and roamed the house. Just as the stranger roamed the shack. Finally she decided to go to bed, even though it was only a little after nine. As she passed through the drawing room, the lights flickered, and she stopped long enough to light a precautionary candle. She then turned out the downstairs lights, stepped out onto the gallery and made her way up the stairs to the bedroom. The air was still. Hot. Thick. Or was hot and thick the way her blood ran whenever she thought of the stranger? Minutes later, her body flushed from thoughts of him, she stepped into the shower.

The stranger moistened the tail of one of his shirts in the can he'd filled with water from a nearby pond. He drew the cloth across his face, his neck and, raising his arm, down his furred chest. The water felt cool, like a refreshing reprieve from hell. In seconds he'd bathed his belly and legs and had slipped back into his jeans. Grabbing a shirt, he slipped it on, leaving both it and his jeans unbuttoned. He stepped to the door, flung the water into the yard and paused. The air was still, sticky, hot. And he was restless.

Why not go to her?
Mind your own business.
It is my business. Go to her.
When hell freezes over!

The frosted waves of the air-conditioning rippled over Elizabeth's skin as she stepped from the shower, producing a rash of goose bumps. She had just reached for the towel when the lights flickered again, then faded entirely. The cool air died in midwave, and a silence descended into which Elizabeth's groan fell heavily. Drying as she walked, she felt her way out of the bath and into the candlelit bedroom.

Thank goodness she'd had the forethought to plan for this contingency. She now had to plan for a very hot evening, for there was no telling how long the electricity would be off. With the towel draped about her, she opened the windows; only a whisper of air flowed through. That done, she rummaged through the dresser drawer for something cool to wear.

Her eyes fell to the tap pants and the matching camisole she'd purchased several days before because she'd been unable to resist them. She now knew that the fine cotton lawn, with the tiny buttons and the lacy tucked front, had eerily reminded her of another camisole, the memory of which had been delicately hidden in her mind until only recently. Pulling them from the drawer, her heart pounding erratically, she slipped into them, then drew her hair off her neck, twisted it into a knot and pinned it in place with the ivory comb she'd brought down from the attic that afternoon.

As she lowered her arms, the filmy fabric of the camisole skimmed across her breasts. Though as soft as a spring breeze, the contact hurt. She gritted her teeth at the exquisite ache and thought of what it would take to ease it.

His hands. They could ease it, had eased it in the past. Of this she was certain.

At the same moment Elizabeth was thinking this, the stranger's hands caressed a warm can of beer. Restlessly caressed it. As if remembering something far softer, far warmer.

Had she been a fool to send him away? she thought. It had been like sending herself away.

The stranger lolled his head back, took a deep breath and tried to swallow down the feeling that some siren something in the velvet night air was teasing his senses.

What would she do if he were there now, Elizabeth wondered. Turn him away again? Or plead with him not to leave her? Now or ever.

He wouldn't go to her, he thought. It would be a stupid thing to do. For him, for her. Wouldn't it?

Lightning tore through the sky.

Thunder crashed.

The world stood still.

Suddenly the stranger cursed, pulled to his feet and, crossing the narrow width of the shack, threw open the door. He moved quickly, as if skimming over ice. But then, the motion was appropriate. It appeared that hell had just frozen over.

Chapter Eight

He awakened within me things that I did not know could be felt. He made me feel like a woman; he made me feel special; he made me feel wonderfully wicked. So wicked that I feared it must be a sin. Would God punish me for the stolen hours of bliss I found in this man's arms? No. I cannot believe God would be so cruel. No god could proclaim something wrong that felt so perfectly right.

Elizabeth whirled at the sound of the bedroom doorknob turning.

The figure of a man, tall and uniquely familiar, stood silhouetted in the shadowed night. Flickers of lamplight swam to meet him, lapping greedily at the rugged, harsh planes of his face, washing up on the shores of his broad shoulders, bathing that part of his chest and belly exposed in the open slit of his shirt. Elizabeth couldn't see the stranger's eyes, yet she could feel them—hot, intense, filled with a hunger that was almost angry because it was so great and so urgent.

All in one seemingly choreographed move, he started toward her, her heart burst into a breathless rhythm, and rain, so long the tease, fell from the sky. She watched him as he crossed the room, watched the sure saunter of his hips beneath the partially unfastened jeans, watched the sway of his shirttail, watched the hard, set expression on his face. As always, he looked tough, rough, even dangerous. As always, Elizabeth felt an emotion far removed from fear.

He stopped directly in front of her. And let his thirsty eyes drink of her, as if it had been eons, not hours, since he'd last seen her.

"I tried to stay away," he said, the words low, dark, again tinged with anger because he hadn't had the self-control to keep his distance.

"I'm sorry I said what I did. I was upset," she whispered, her voice as fragile as the heartbeats fluttering in her chest.

"You were right. I shouldn't be here. It would be better—"

"No! Please stay."

His eyes lowered to the mouth that had once told him to go but was now begging him not to. The sweet, soft mouth that he was going crazy to feel against his own. He bit back the sharp taste of desire. And let his gaze again wander over her, from the lace-edged camisole to the ivory comb thrust into her hair. The comb. It was the one that had flashed through his mind earlier in the evening, the one that was now bringing a whole new series of sensual images to his mind, images from another time and place, images that devastated the close check he was holding on himself.

"You look exactly as I remember you," he whispered in awe. "How is it possible that I can remember what I've never seen before?'' He obviously didn't expect an answer. ''The comb...I remember it...I remember how it feels to pull it from your hair...how your hair feels wrapped around my fingers...how it feels against my skin.'' His eyes lowered, inch by sensual inch, to the camisole, through which he could see the misty buds of her breasts. ''And I remember this...I remember what it feels like to unbutton it...what it feels like to draw it from your shoulders...what it feels like to touch your breasts.'' His voice had grown so thick that he was forced to stop simply in order to breathe.

In the silence, she asked, ''Are you real?''

He studied her. Was he real? Hell if he knew! All he knew was that he had a very real ache straining against his jeans. And a very real need to lose himself, physically, emotionally, within her.

''I'm as real as you want me to be,'' he answered huskily.

As real as she wanted him to be. Right now he only needed to be real enough to end the sublime ache that was gently gnawing at her body, the ache that had eaten away at her from practically the first moment she'd seen him. Though she didn't understand anything about the mystery she was caught up in, she was determined to heed her aunt's advice. She would not let this beauty slip from her hands. As if to keep it from doing so, she reached up and trailed her fingertips across his sternly chiseled face.

Her touch pierced his very soul. No one had ever touched him so lovingly. No touch had ever burned so deeply, so searingly, and he quite literally couldn't stand the intensity of it, the sheer, utter and complete beauty of it. In emotional self-defense, he manacled her wrist and gently pulled her hand away. He was breathing hard. Much too hard for such a simple thing as the touch of a woman's hand to his cheek.

"Ah, lady," he whispered, his voice like heated whiskey, "we're dealing with something here that I don't understand."

"I don't, either," she said, "but does it matter?"

What mattered, he realized with startling clarity, was the feel of her in his arms. With the hand still at her wrist, he tugged. She leaned. Their bodies collided and meshed. Fire to fire. Need to need. Emotions too long contained burst their bonds. An instant frenzy jumped from one body to the other.

"Don't go!" she pleaded, angling her head for the kiss he was nuzzling to her ear.

"No!" he said, his lips frantically leaving the side of her neck for the slender column of her throat. As they did so, his hands searched for the comb in her hair. Finding it, he wrenched it out. It fell to the rug. Her hair tumbled to freedom. At that same moment, his mouth found the vulnerable hollow of her throat. She whimpered, arched her neck and felt the loosened hair shimmying about her shoulders and down her back. He buried his hands in the thickness of the ebony satin.

"Don't go!" she whispered again, almost deliriously. A thousand feelings were flooding her from all the places he was touching—his hands in her hair, his lips at her throat, his jeans chafing the suddenly super-sensitive skin of her thighs.

"I won't!" he promised, dragging his mouth down, down, down, to the peaked softness of her breast. "I couldn't even if I wanted to!" he breathed, kissing her through the sheer fabric of the camisole.

Elizabeth cried softly, unknowingly arching her back to give him more of what they both wanted. He took what she offered, tugging her deeply into his hot mouth, then sucking once, twice, before releasing her breast. Urgently, he sought her mouth.

"I can't leave!" he growled, crushing her mouth with his and trapping the words between their hungry lips.

The kiss was hard, harsh, as volatile as kerosene meeting fire. Instinctively, Elizabeth knew the kiss was like the man. She welcomed his dark energy, his light fury. Sliding her hands through the opening of his shirt, she wound her arms about his lean waist. He felt solid and full of strength; he filled her hollowness, eased her loneliness.

She felt soft. So damned soft he could die! Which he was going to do if he didn't touch all of her. Deepening the kiss—don't hurt her!—he drew his hands all along her body. He investigated her warm, perfume-scented shoulders, examined the slender curve of her back, spanned her trim waist. He then pushed his hands lower, seeking the rounded fullness of her derriere. The filmy fabric glided and slid beneath his roaming hands, and his fingers grazed her bare skin. Her silken bare skin. Skin he couldn't resist knowing more intimately. Working his hands beneath the wide-legged tap pants, he cupped the cheeks of her hips, his palms pulling her up against him.

Elizabeth felt a patch of her exposed tummy mating with his. His stomach was warm, and coils of his chest hair tickled her. The denim of his jeans was shoved tightly, erotically against her feminine mound, her aching, craving mound. She could feel that the top button of his jeans was unfastened, suggestively so. The masculine power that lay beneath the denim was more than suggestive. It was pure sensuality. Pure sexuality. Pure man.

He pulled her higher, and his hands rhythmically urged her to ride him with a sweet desperation. The motion, combined with the tongue that masterfully slid into her mouth, was her glorious undoing. She whimpered, wanting more, straining for more, but knowing that too much more would plunder her senses beyond her shaky control.

The stranger heard the strangled little cry in her throat and felt her body crumbling around him. He stilled his hands and jerked his mouth from hers.

"No!" he whispered. "This time it's going to be with me deep inside you."

She blushed at his directness, but her pink cheeks were instantly shielded by his chest as he scooped her into his arms.

"Your arm," she managed to say.

"To hell with it!" he growled.

He lay her in the middle of the four-poster canopied bed and followed her down until he was sprawled gently across her thighs. He had intended to love her slow and long, but that was before he saw her, felt her, stretched out beneath him. Her black hair fanned wildly about her face, a face flushed with passion, while her eyes were all misty gray from the same emotion. Her lips still bore the wetness of his. She was breathing in tiny, sweet gasps. And shifting her hips. God, she was shifting her hips! Unknowingly, instinctively trying to make room for him between her legs.

"Ah, Lizzie," he gasped, suddenly on a very ragged edge as he slipped into the cradle she provided, slid the length of her and buried his mouth in hers.

She was lost.

He was lost.

With only heaven waiting to be found.

Their bodies, listening to the pagan music of their tattered breathing, found ancient, provocative rhythms.

"Oh, God," he whispered into her mouth, the sound wild and guttural, as he wedged his hand between their straining bodies. He ripped open the waist of her tap pants and somehow managed to shove them from her legs. Even more miraculously, he relieved himself of his jeans. When bare, heated flesh met bare, heated flesh, he tumbled over the precarious edge. "Oh, sweet God," he growled, adjusting, readjusting, sheathing himself wholly, deeply within her warm moistness. He had enough presence of mind to recognize that this was part of the softness he'd been remembering, a softness that first destroyed him, then healed him to the core of his being.

Elizabeth cried out at their joining.

He glanced up. "Did I hurt you?"

She shook her head. "No... no... good." She wriggled her hips, bringing him more fully into her.

"Yes, oh, yes... ah, Lizzie, move... just like that..."

"... deeper..."

"... wider..."

"... oh, please..."

"... soft... soft... so soft..."

Her head thrashed on the pillow. "... please, please, please..." she chanted, clutching at the sheet. "Yes, yes... oohhhh!!"

"... that's it... oh, yeah... yes, yes... ah, Liz-zie!"

It was an ending; it was a beginning.

Slowly, finally, with his body still buried deep inside her, the stranger raised himself on an elbow and stared down at the woman beneath him. Her hair was totally dishevelled, her eyes hazy, her lips swollen and bruised.

With exquisite care, and not questioning too closely how atypical such a display of gentleness was in his life, he brushed the hair back from Elizabeth's sweat-dampened face and eased his mouth to hers. Softly, tenderly, as if to heal the bruises that he, and passion, had inflicted. They kissed, exchanged tremulous breaths, then kissed again before lazily dueling with their tongues. They were sated, relaxed, drifting in another world, a world far removed from mysteries, a world of feeling that had neither to be explained nor interpreted.

Elizabeth sighed, the warm, gossamer sound falling on the stranger's mouth. It stirred him to speech.

"You're so wet...and so hot...and so soft...God, Lizzie, how can you be so soft?" His lips played in her hair, found her ear, whispered kisses while his tongue traced and tasted. "And you cry these soft little sounds...and make these soft little movements around me when you come...and blush this soft shade of pink when I talk like this."

As if on cue, her cheeks pinkened.

He grinned, started to lower his mouth back to hers, but grimaced instead.

Elizabeth's hand went to his arm.

Gritting his teeth, he said, "I think I'd better be kind to it." As he spoke, he started to roll to his side. Elizabeth started to pull away. "Don't move," he said, drawing her toward him to keep their bodies joined, "I'm not finished with you yet."

The remark deepened her blush.

"Every time you blush is just one more time I'm going to make love to you."

She blushed yet again.

He grinned, then growled, "At this rate, it's going to be a long night, Lizzie."

She'd seen him grin so seldom. She had the feeling that grins came very rarely to him. Because of that, she cherished the one he was now bestowing on her. She also cherished the sensual promise he was making.

As he lay down on his side, he managed to peel his shirt from his shoulders, so that he was now boldly, divinely naked. In the golden glow of the candlelight, she could see that his body was slick with sweat. Just as she could feel it. Just as she could smell it, wafting and mingling with the scent of lovemaking.

Lovemaking.

Who was this man she'd just made love to? Who'd just made love to her? He was real. She had no doubt of that now. She could feel his realness deep inside her. She'd sensed his very real need and had heard that same real need released as he'd grunted her name at that mindless moment when passion had ruled supreme. But if he was real and not some shadowy figure from a bygone world, then how had he been shot? She let the question be washed away by the rain pounding against the house.

The lightning had stopped; the thunder had diminished to an occasional rumble. The rain, falling in punishing pulsations, seemed to be cooling nothing off, but rather seemed only to be turning a hot day into a steamy night. The air was breathless, still, begging for relief. And so humid that inhaling was painful.

The stranger's sweat-sheened body drew Elizabeth's attention to the glistening, tanned expanse of his chest. Tanned. She'd noted the tan before, but never how even it was. Wherever he lived, he often went without a shirt. Which seemed appropriate, since he had such a magnificent chest. So magnificent that she desperately wanted, needed, to touch it. Reaching out, she grazed her fingertips across the width of his shoulder and slowly down his arm. The muscles were bunched and toned. Trailing her fingers over their bulge, she gingerly skimmed across the area that was bandaged, then skipped to follow a full vein on the inside of his elbow.

The stranger didn't move; he simply watched her and soaked in every delicate nuance of her tentative yet curious touch.

Elizabeth spread her eager fingers in the hair matting his chest, testing the texture of skin, the contour of muscle. Teary drops of moisture clung to the curly sprigs of hair like lush morning dew. She raked her thumb across the tawny-brown nipple peeking from the golden forest. It knotted, hard and tight, but still the stranger didn't flex a muscle, didn't make a sound. When she glanced up, however, she saw the infinitesimal darkening of his eyes.

His response challenged her, and she ran her fingertips down over the ripple of his ribs, then to his waist. There, she hesitated.

"Don't stop," he said, molding his hand over hers and drawing it toward the damp length of his thigh. Here, his skin was much paler, as if exposed to the sun far less frequently. Her reach took her only to mid-thigh, and he urged her fingers to the inside of his leg. Removing his hand, he abandoned her to her own resources.

Slowly she trailed upward, feeling his muscles tighten beneath her caress. When it came time, however, to spear the crisp curls nesting where their bodies were joined, she glanced up shyly and removed her hand. Instead, she flattened her palm across his belly. His stomach grew taut.

A bead of moisture wended its way from his throat, down the middle of his chest, through hair and over sinew to splash onto her finger. She drew the finger to her lips, sucked the drop into her mouth and tasted the warm saltiness of his sweat.

The act was so consummately sensual that he moaned, brought his mouth to hers and sipped his own taste from her. That part of him buried inside her swelled.

She felt him expand and whimpered softly, needily.

The camisole was damp with her own perspiration and clung to her breasts in revealing patches. The stranger's fingers made their way to the first button, which he worried from its mooring. The second he tried to do the same thing with but had to make three attempts before completing the task. He was trembling. God, he was trembling! He, whose aim on the trigger was always cool, always smooth, never riddled with emotion. He willed his hand to be steady; his hand didn't pay the least attention. Finally, however, he unbuttoned the last button and edged his hand into the opening to draw the fabric from her breast. Slowly he lowered his eyes. His breath ceased to be.

In that moment he told himself that he'd seen everything there was to see in life. He'd certainly seen enough women's breasts to make this occasion just one of many. As he took in the sight before him, however, he had reason to confirm the conclusion he'd arrived at once before. He'd seen too much of the harsh side of life. And maybe, just maybe, he'd seen too many of the wrong women's breasts.

The sweet mound of flesh was rounded into perfection, standing high and firm. So firm. And the skin was silk and ivory—the color of a cameo he remembered seeing once—while the nipple was almost as dark as chocolate. Would it taste as sweet? Would it—

He saw the tiny brown mole peeping from the underside of her breast. His eyes found hers. But since neither knew the answer to the unspoken question of how he'd known about the mark, neither spoke. Slowly he lowered his head, nudged her breast gently with his nose and kissed the brownish-black dot.

Elizabeth sighed, then caught her breath as his lips shifted and closed around the nipple. He cupped her other breast in his hand, kneading gently, as he tugged and sucked surely, competently, with the experience he'd learned from all the wrong women. It was experience he treasured if it allowed him to please this woman for only a moment.

Elizabeth's nipple beaded painfully, and her gasp turned into another soft cry.

The stranger's body hardened even more, and his voice was ragged when he said, "You're so..."

"...beautiful," she finished, her thoughts fragmented in the face of the feelings claiming her. "You're so...beautiful."

At the unexpected words, he laughed. Elizabeth felt the laughter dancing through her womb. "Lady, no one's ever accused me of being that."

"But you are," she said sincerely, her eyes burning into his. "Your touch is beautiful, your body is beautiful, you make me feel beautiful, you taste—" she leaned, drawing her breast from the heaven of his hand and placing her lips against his chest "—so beautiful." Kittenlike, she nuzzled her damp cheek against his damper chest. "You—"

He tore the dangling camisole from her arms and, spearing his fingers into her hair, rushed her lips to his. He pushed her back into the mattress, his body following and covering hers. His hips instinctively began the movement that would bring relief to his tortured body. And to hers.

This time, however, hungry, impatient thrusts gave way to more patient undulation. His body rolled against hers in ripples, flowed in a ceaseless pattern, one sensation beginning before the former had even ended. His lips ate at hers, while his hands slicked over her sweat-moist body. Her breasts, swollen with desire, slid wetly against his chest. Their bellies rubbed in dewy unison.

"We're going to come slowly and easily and all over each other," he growled in her ear.

She wound her arms about his wet back and let the fire-hot, candy-sweet sensations flow from head to toe, from breast to loin. "You...make me feel...so alive," she breathed.

"You make we want to live." It was a curious response that neither had the time to ponder, for all beginnings have an end.

This one came as he'd promised—slowly, easily, but no less intensely. At that moment when their bodies could stand no more pleasure, Elizabeth cried out, a sound raw and loud, a sound that would have made her blush had she realized what she was doing.

The stranger followed seconds, strokes behind her. At the pinnacle, when his life jetted into her, he called her name. "Lizzie, ah, Lizzie..." he groaned.

"You've never asked my name."

Elizabeth's hands halted in the task of cutting away the soiled bandage. She glanced up. The stranger's eyes looked incredibly dark, mysteriously unfathomable, in the gleaming candlelight. Outside, the rain had dwindled to a peppery drizzle. Inside, it was still stifling.

Forcing her attention back to his arm, she snipped the scissors through the gauze. "I assumed you'd tell me if you wanted me to know."

Both were aware that her great-grandmother had never known the name of her lover. Neither spoke of that fact now. Just as neither had said anything when Elizabeth had returned from the bathroom minutes before wearing a towel. The stranger's displeasure had been obvious, and he'd made no attempt to accommodate her modesty by covering himself with the sheet. Instead, he'd unabashedly made room for her beside him so that she could change the wrapping. Elizabeth had worked to keep her mind above his waist.

"Cougar," he said. "Cougar Collins."

She halted again. This time the bandage fell away in her hand, quite forgotten.

"Cougar?" she asked, as if the name were some bright gift she'd been given, a gift she had to touch again and again before she could fully realize it was hers.

"Well, actually, Charles Lawrence. My Marine buddies tacked on the Cougar part."

"You're a Marine?" she asked, eagerly seizing what he'd just offered. A Marine? If he was a soldier, it might explain how he'd gotten shot. Soldiers handled firearms. His comment, at least, opened up a whole new world of possibilities.

"I was."

The two words shattered Elizabeth's new world, and she waited with keen impatience for him to do the logical thing and tell her what he did now. When silent minute stretched into silent minute, her disappointment grew.

To end the embarrassing silence, Elizabeth finally asked, "Why did they call you that?"

It wasn't what she'd wanted to ask. Cougar Collins knew that. She'd wanted to ask if he was a thief, a murderer or something just as vile. But then, he hadn't asked what he'd wanted to, either. If he had, he'd have asked her if she, for all her sweet, old-fashioned blushes, was involved in gun-running.

He shrugged again. "My hair, I guess. Plus they said I moved as quietly, as quickly, as a cat." And that I was just as ruthless, that I instinctively went for the jugular, he thought, wondering what she would say if he dropped that little tidbit of information. Or, more important, what would she do? Recoil from him? The thought hurt. Much more than he thought it should have.

In that second, Elizabeth was doing her own share of hurting. Why didn't he ease her mind by telling her that there was a perfectly logical excuse for the bullet that had ripped through his arm? In an attempt to ignore her own pain, she spoke. "That makes sense. I mean, your buddies giving you the name. Somehow I can't see a mother calling her baby Cougar."

"Actually, my mother didn't call me much of anything. She was never sober long enough. And when she was sober, she was usually in jail." The moment it was out, Cougar wished he hadn't said it. He'd always had one standing rule in life: never expose yourself. Not in any real way that mattered. Why, then, had he opened up to this woman? "I, uh . . ." he said, trying to cover his discomfort, "My grand mother did what raising I got."

Elizabeth sensed his reticence to go on, maybe even his regret at having said so much. She offered what comfort she could. "My aunt raised me."

A slight arching of his brow asked the question.

"My mother was one of life's great flitters. She flitted here, there, everywhere." She smiled, an expression filled with sadness, not mirth. "Mostly everywhere I wasn't."

Cougar fought the urge to pull her into his arms. "What about your father?"

"He's French. Very nice, but I don't really know him. His biggest contribution to my life was my middle name. Regan—my mother—named me Elizabeth Noel."

"Elizabeth Noel." He repeated the name, somehow making it sound like a love song he was playing only for her ears. And the look in his eyes could have melted Arctic ice. It was certainly melting Elizabeth's insides to a warm, funny-feeling liquid.

Swallowing, she glanced back at the wound. "Your arm's better."

"It would have to be to do what I did tonight."

A rose color seeped into her cheeks.

"Four."

"Four?"

"Four more times to make love tonight. Unless, of course, you want to blush again and make it five."

Predictably she blushed more deeply.

He grinned, a crooked smile that sat contentedly in the corner of his mouth. "Five it is."

"Will you be still?" she said, devoting her flustered attention to changing the bandage.

The wound did look a great deal better. After cleaning, salving and placing sterile pads over the sensitive areas, she rewrapped the gauze around his arm. As always, the task was a cumbersome one. This time it was made even more difficult by the towel she tried to keep fastened around her and by the liberties her patient was taking with his knuckles. At last she made one movement too many and the towel popped open. Instinctively she reached to catch it.

"No." The word drifted about her like a silken caress.

Her eyes found his.

Slowly he stretched his arm out and gently pried her clenched fingers from the terry cloth.

"Let me look at you," he whispered, drawing the towel away. His eyes lowered. And feasted. "I like seeing you naked," he said. "I like looking at your breasts. They're so round, so soft. They taste so sweet, so full, in my mouth." At this, the nipples tightened into pebbled knots. Elizabeth fought back a moan. "Ah, Lizzie, I don't even have to touch you to make you respond. Do you have any idea what your responsiveness does to me?"

Actually she did. She could clearly see his reaction. It jutted powerfully below the waist she was trying not to look beyond.

"I'll bet I could *talk* you to a climax."

She wouldn't have bet against him, not with the hot, syrupy feelings drizzling through her.

"Let me finish... with your arm," she said. "It'll only take a minute. I've just got to cut a piece of tape. No, that's too small," she said, impatiently wadding up a strip of tape and stretching out another with fingers that trembled. She was very aware that her breasts swayed with her every movement and that the man before her watched her every sway. "There, that's better. The arm looks good. It—"

"You're mumbling, Lizzie," Cougar said.

"I always mumble when I'm nervous or excited."

"Do I make you nervous?"

"You know you do," she said breathlessly as she adhered the tape to his arm. She didn't look up.

"Do I excite you?" He could hear the new, faster cadence of her breathing in the silence. "Do I, Lizzie?" he repeated, his thumb raking across her tautened nipple.

Elizabeth made a sound that was half-sigh, half-moan.

"I've got just the thing for nervous, excited mumbling," he whispered, suddenly placing his hands at her waist and drawing her forward.

In seconds, Elizabeth felt her back sinking into the soft mattress and felt a hard body sprawling across hers. She looked up into very dark eyes, eyes that promised very masculine things.

"But I—"

His lips brushed hers.

"But you—"

His lips brushed hers again.

"But we—"

The mumbling stopped as his lips, his body, meshed purposefully with hers.

Despite the heat, they lay snuggled together in sleep.

The dream began to crawl through Cougar's mind like the slow, slithery movements of a sun-warmed snake. It brought the same adrenaline-chased reaction the serpent itself would have had had he come upon it unexpectedly in the jungle.

Cougar shifted and moaned a protest. The woman in his arms stirred.

Suddenly, as can happen only in a dream, the snake coiled around his arm and became the gauzy-white, benign bandage. The feeling of fear persisted, however. Out of nowhere, a woman with beautiful, moody gray eyes appeared and began to unwrap the bandage.

Elizabeth Noel . . . Elizabeth Noel . . . Elizabeth Noel . . .

Unwrap . . . unwrap . . . untie . . . undone . . .

His life was coming undone just like the gauze falling away in her soft hands. As she unwound it, the gauze coiled at his feet, reverting back into a red-striped snake.

The snake spoke. "When no one cares about you, you don't care about yourself." Slowly, as if melting like candle wax, the red dripped from the snake and puddled in a pool.

Blood.

His arm was bleeding. A giant of a man stood before him. A black man, laughing viciously. He was pointing a smoking gun at Cougar.

Cougar taunted him. "It doesn't hurt. I can't feel . . . can't feel . . ."

"Nothing?" the man asked in disappointment.

"No, I feel nothing. Not pain, not happiness. Nothing . . . nothing . . . nothing."

Suddenly, however, pain tore through his injured arm. Hot and scalding and stealing his breath. He could feel. He did feel. The realization pleased him but frightened him.

Fear crawled like the serpent beginning to wind its way around his leg.

"No," Cougar mumbled, trying to wake himself.

Elizabeth shifted.

"No," Cougar called again.

The snake, now hissing a repeated "Feel or die, feel or die," slid higher and higher, its sleek, thin head climbing along Cougar's thigh. Cougar tried to shake the reptile off.

Elizabeth moaned, shifted, came awake enough to realize that the man beside her was moving.

Mysteriously, an aura of sexual desire coiled its way through Cougar's body. He suddenly hurt with need, yet all sensations were overridden by fear.

Fear. Terror. At feeling, at not feeling.

"No!" he cried out, catapulting himself to a sitting position.

"Cougar?" Elizabeth called softly.

His breath rasped against the room's silence; his chest heaved rapidly. "Go back to sleep," he growled, shoving his fingers through his sleep-mussed hair. "It was...just a dream."

She sat up beside him, unerringly finding his cheek with the palm of her hand. She turned his face toward hers, and, even though it was dark, each could feel the other's eyes.

"It's all right," she whispered, feeling perspiration that she suspected had little to do with the hot summer evening. "It's all right."

Her touch pierced him just as it had once before, but this time he didn't push her hand away. Instead, he placed his atop it and smothered it to him. Her hand was soft, something he desperately needed.

Needed.

Entwining his fingers with the hand at his cheek, he lowered her back to the bed, and, keeping their hands joined, he slid between her legs. His lips sought hers.

"Make me feel," he pleaded as his warm mouth found hers.

This time when he tunneled inside her, the action was more than sexual. Far more than sensual. This time he was a man in search of emotional sanctuary.

Chapter Nine

He made love the way he did everything—with tender roughness, with thinly veiled desperation. As if each smile, each kiss, each whisper of my name might be the last. And because of that, each small thing became painfully precious, while the love in my heart, not a small thing at all, grew each day to be preciously painful.

When Elizabeth awoke, she was alone. Disappointment raged through her, a disappointment that not even the yellow rose on the adjacent pillow could temper.

Shifting, she ignored the intimate tingle of love-stretched muscles and picked up the flower. She brought it to her nose and breathed in the sweet fragrance. As pleasing as the scent was, she would have preferred the musky smell of the man who'd lain beside her all night. And though the petals were as soft as a lover's promise, she, without a single reservation, would have exchanged them for the hard, sensual planes of Cougar's body.

Cougar.

Charles Lawrence Collins.

She said the name out loud, trying to fill the emptiness surrounding her, but all it seemed to do was intensify it. Why hadn't he stayed? Where did he go when he left her? And why was she so disappointed—no, hurt—that he hadn't lingered after what they'd shared?

Neither a cooling shower nor a hot, strong cup of coffee yielded answers to the questions, and she was left as restless as the morning sunshine that leaped from one rain-washed leaf to another, once more possessively gilding the world in heat.

Drawn outdoors, she walked through the rose garden, then picked up a few small limbs the storm had driven out of the oak tree. Wandering farther, she was halfway to the shacks located toward the far reaches of the plantation when she realized where she was headed. Maybe the outing would quell her restlessness. And she did need to check out the property. Hadn't she promised Aunt Siddie that she would?

The dozen simple, single-room structures stood in a row roughly a quarter mile from the house. Elizabeth imagined that long ago, in the days when the plantation utilized slave labor—she shuddered at the so-called "civilized" barbar-ism—a path had been worn between the stark quarters and the house proper. Now all that existed was a field of ne-glected, knee-high grass and weeds. Was the cotton mill still standing? She remembered slipping off to play dolls in the cool, shaded buildings. Just as she remembered echo-singing, against Aunt Siddie's implicit instructions, in the nearby abandoned well. She also remembered wading, again against Aunt Siddie's wishes, in the cattail-fringed pond near the shacks. And once, on a dare from Pamela, the two of them had walked what was probably a mile and a half back from the shacks. All Elizabeth could remember about the incident was that thick woods crept along both sides of a natural clearing and that, from a child's perspective, the woods had seemed menacing and filled with shadowy things, snaky things, she'd rather not know about.

Things she'd rather not know about. Like the stranger's—Cougar's—past? Maybe even his present? Was it easier to run from it than face it? Was that typically how she coped with life's uncertainties, life's unpleasantness? Was that the real reason behind wanting to sell Rose Haven? Elizabeth eagerly shelved the troubling questions at the first sight of the shacks.

The weathered gray cabins stood more or less intact. At each dwelling, two steps led to a small eaved porch, which led into the single square room. Each shack had a red chimney, though most were missing bricks and had tumbled into some degree of disgrace. Some of the structures were practically swallowed up by grass and weeds, while the closer ones were surrounded by only a smattering of ground cover. Elizabeth headed toward the first cabin, partly because its openness beckoned, partly because she thought she remembered that her aunt had used the nearest ones for storage.

Her hand had already curled around the loose railing, her foot had already anchored itself on the first step when the sun bounced off a metallic-looking object on the ground, attracting her attention. She frowned, eased her foot from the step and, stooping, picked up the glittery item. Her frown deepened. What was it? She rolled the small gleaming ball into the palm of her hand. It looked like . . . foil. A piece of foil. The kind that was wrapped around . . . candy kisses.

Elizabeth's heart jolted into a heavier, quicker rhythm. And she glanced up at the closed door of the cabin.

As if drawn by a force stronger than she, she climbed the first step, the second—it tilted at an awkward angle—then stood on the porch under the sloping eaves. She stretched out her hand, turned the knob and, not daring to move, pushed open the door. Slowly, on screeching hinges, the door slid back until it gently bumped against the wall. Elizabeth peered into the dusky interior.

No one was there.

Swallowing her heart back from her throat, she stepped into the room. The floor creaked with her weight. The room was small, so small that again Elizabeth shuddered at the thought that it might have once accommodated an entire family. Several dusty boxes, their contents marked with Aunt Siddie's precise, elementary-teacher printing, lined one wall. That made sense. What didn't make sense was the mattress, cotton bubbling from seams and tears, that sprawled on the floor. Some fabric, white and yellow, had been wadded up as a makeshift pillow. On closer inspection, Elizabeth saw that the pillow was two shirts rolled together. They were shirts she recognized as those worn by the strang—Cougar.

Her heartbeat thundered in her ears.

She glanced about quickly, searching for other signs of his presence. They were easy to find. A pair of jeans lay across a straight chair that had a slat missing from the seat; keys and some change were piled on the worm-eaten mantel above the fireplace; at the other end of the mantel was a flashlight, along with a brown plastic pill bottle. Elizabeth picked up the bottle and read her own name on the prescription label. She set it back with a hand that had begun to tremble.

Below the mantel, in the fireplace, lay discarded food tins and several crushed beer cans. Miller Lite beer. He drank Miller Lite. Was he watching his weight? she wondered, realizing how totally absurd the whole line of thinking was. She should try to hang on to at least a thread of sanity.

That in mind, she looked about her again. The bloody rags—her dishcloths—which she'd searched for that first morning, lay heaped in a corner. Beside them slouched a lightweight canvas travel bag. Kneeling, she pulled back the unzipped sides and probed through the bag's contents. A fresh shirt carelessly folded. A can of spray deodorant. A pair of knit briefs... just like the pair he'd worn the night before...just like the pair that had stolen her breath as he'd slipped them from his lithe frame... just like...

Her eyes latched on to the long, cylindrical object protruding from beneath the knit briefs. She knew from the shape of the gray steel barrel what the object was, yet she had an overwhelming need to deny it, to prove that her eyes were lying to her. But they weren't. She saw that when she dragged the briefs aside.

Curiously, carefully, somehow divorcing herself from the reality of the moment, she picked up the gun and stood. She'd never held a gun before. It was heavy. Cool. And a sinister shade of gray. It sickened her.

Who was this man? What dark secrets did he keep? What—

At the creaking of the floor, Elizabeth whirled. Her eyes collided with those of the man lazily leaning against the door frame.

Her brain registered that he'd apparently been using the nearby pond for bathing, for his bare chest glistened with moisture and his blond hair was wet and slicked back from his forehead. His jeans, splotched with water, were obviously slipped on over damp legs and hips. The top button was unfastened. That, plus the fact that he wasn't wearing any underwear, produced, even under the circumstances, a warm, heavy response in her suddenly very feminine-feeling body. In one hand he carried his tennis shoes, in the other a leather shaving kit. But what Elizabeth primarily noted was his expressionless face, his hooded eyes. They were the face and eyes of a stranger, not those of the man who'd loved her all night. This man was...dangerous...unpredictable...as sinister-looking as the gun she held. The gun she had instinctively pointed at him.

At the moment when she'd curved both hands around the gun and awkwardly aimed it at him, something had died in Cougar's heart, though his expressionless face, his hooded eyes, would never reveal the loss.

"Who are you?" she whispered.

"Don't you mean *what* am I?" he asked. Calmly he added, "If you're going to shoot me, you'd better release the safety."

Elizabeth glanced down at the gun. She couldn't have released the safety if her life had depended on it—which it might, she realized—because she had no idea what or where the safety was.

Cougar shrugged away from the door frame, dropped the shaving case and shoes and padded, barefoot, toward her. Standing directly in front of her, the gun only inches from his stomach, he accommodatingly released the safety. His eyes met hers, recklessly daring her.

A thousand images flashed in her mind—his lips devouring hers, his arms enfolding her, his body moving over, and into, hers, his voice whispering sweet, sensual secrets. Suddenly, slowly a new and very different emotion burned in her heart. So powerful was the emotion, so painful was its intensity, that she shied away from its dazzling brilliance. In its wake, her already trembling hands began to tremble even more.

Cougar felt the nose of the gun wobble against his bare belly. His eyes deep in hers, he reached and eased the gun from her hands. She surrendered it without a struggle. Resetting the safety and laying it on the mantel, he bent and brushed his lips against hers.

"Good morning," he said, as if nothing out of the ordinary had happened.

It was the soft, vulnerable trembling of her lips that tumbled his strength. That and the trembling of his heart as it accepted the priceless knowledge that she hadn't wanted to shoot him, hadn't tried to "turn him in" to anybody. With a rough groan, he hauled her into his arms. She buried her cheek in his hair-matted chest and banded her arms tightly about his waist. His warm breath fell unevenly against the top of her head. Neither spoke; each simply clung, soaking in the other's trembling.

"Ah, babe," he said at long last, "I haven't given you many choices, have I? I'm either a ghost or a desperado." He pulled back until his eyes found hers. "What if I could give you a third choice?"

"Can you?" she asked, the words bordering on desperation.

Cougar released her and walked to the window. It was only partially covered by a piece of battered screen, and flying insects flitted back and forth across the unprotected threshold. Sliding a hand into the back pocket of his jeans, he turned and asked bluntly, "Are you involved in gunrunning, Lizzie?"

The look that crossed her face was so comical that it was all Cougar could do not to laugh aloud. Hell, not only wasn't she involved in gunrunning, she wasn't even real sure what it was! He should have felt relieved, but the truth was, he realized, that he'd never really believed her guilty. Maybe not from the moment she'd opened the front door and stared up at him with those soulful gray eyes. Certainly not from the moment those gray eyes had looked at him through a haze of passion.

"Never mind," he said huskily, his body acutely reminding him how pleasurable it was to satisfy her body's needs.

"No," she said heatedly, "you don't just ask that kind of question, then say 'Never mind.' What do you mean by gunrunning?"

"Look, just forget—"

"What do you mean?"

"Smuggling guns and ammunition into a foreign country."

She stared blankly at him until, finally, a look of disbelief spread across her face. She raked back the long black hair from her forehead, making the widow's peak more pronounced. "You think I'm smuggling guns?"

"No."

"But you just said . . ."

"I know what I said."

" . . . that I was gunrunning."

"I *asked* if you were."

"Same difference."

"Forget what I said. Forget what I asked."

"But—"

"Come here, Lizzie," he said, taking her hand and pulling her down to sit across from him on the mattress.

"I don't understand—"

"Shhh."

"I don't—"

"Shut up, Lizzie," he said tenderly, his finger slanting across her lips. Her warm lips. Lips that his eyes couldn't help but search out. She felt his eyes like a caress and was very aware that he wanted to kiss her. But he didn't. Instead, he dragged his eyes back to hers, while her body adjusted to the disappointment of not receiving his kiss. "Just listen to me, will you?" he said roughly as he fought to rein in his desire. Taking a deep breath, he added, "Someone is using Rose Haven as a point from which to smuggle guns into Central America."

It took some time for the comment to register. "But that's . . . that's absurd."

Cougar shook his head. "The small planes you've heard going over—you have heard them, haven't you?"

"Yes, but—"

"They're bringing in crates of guns, which are being stockpiled in the old cotton mill."

"No—"

"I've seen them, Lizzie. Both the planes landing and the guns in the mill."

The sincerity of his voice, coupled with the intensity of his eyes, persuaded her in his favor. Belief, however, clarified nothing. "I . . . I don't understand."

"It's really quite simple. They—revolutionaries and drug dealers primarily—want guns in Central and South America and are willing to pay for them. Handsomely. Unscrupulous people on this side of the border are willing to provide what they need, which usually translates to stealing weaponry from government installations. They provide the goods for a profit, of course. There are even gun-trading cartels that act as brokers for buyer and seller. Again, of course, for a commission of the profit. It's all very organized, all very efficient, all very illegal."

She was afraid to ask the question, but more afraid not to. "How do you know all of this?"

"I'm a federal agent," he said simply. "I work for the Bureau of Alcohol, Tobacco and Firearms."

Another silence ensued. She'd heard what he'd said but couldn't make it make sense. Agents, to her, were figures totally out of the realm of fiction. "You mean...like James Bond?"

Cougar's mouth worked into a grin. "Not exactly. He's got a helluva lot more glamorous job."

The realization that she'd been wrong about his identity was flowing over her like molten honey. Elizabeth smiled. "You're a federal agent?"

"Yeah."

"But I thought—"

"I know what you thought."

Elizabeth's smile vanished, swallowed up by the enormity of what he had just said. For days she had believed that he was possibly a criminal. To discover now that he wasn't— the relief was almost more than she could bear. To keep from drowning in her feelings, she tried to channel her thoughts in a different direction. "But why Rose Haven?"

"It's perfect. It wasn't being lived in. Plus it has a natural clearing where planes can land."

"But who...?"

"That I don't know." He paused, adding, "All I know is that a big buy is going down in a couple of weeks."

"And you're here looking around?"

"Actually, I'm not supposed to be here." At her silent inquiry, he explained, "A friend of mine, Jake Jennings, was fished out of the Cane River Lake—"

"The man who drowned?"

"He was killed."

"Killed? But the newspaper said—"

"I know what the paper said, but he was killed. He was working on this case, and I figure he got too close to someone. Anyway, I went to the funeral, then stopped by here to..." He trailed off, thinking again that he'd stopped by to peg the sonofabitch who'd killed Jennings. Again, he acknowledged that it had been a dangerously emotional act. About as dangerous as staring into gray eyes more sultry than a Southern summer night. "I shouldn't have come," he said, and they both knew that he was referring as much to the evening before as to traveling to Natchitoches. "I guess my getting shot just proves that."

Elizabeth tried to imagine what it would have been like never to have known this man. But she really couldn't because she could never get a step away from the fact that she'd known him forever. Reaching out, she brushed her fingertips against the bandage, which he'd obviously worked at keeping dry while bathing. Her touch went through him like a bolt of tender electricity. The feel of his skin sensuously shimmied through her senses. "How? Who?"

"The man I think killed Jake." He paused. "Your caretaker."

Her fingers stopped tracing his injury. "Joshua? But surely you must be—"

"It's my guess that he was hired to baby-sit the guns and to assist the planes in landing. Monday night I followed him to the mill. I got careless, and he spotted me. He shot me. I shot him back." Cougar's eyes fastened to hers. "I killed him, Lizzie. And dumped him in the well because I couldn't risk his being found yet." He deliberately added, making it sound as shocking as possible, "He isn't the first man I've killed, and he won't be the last." Cougar braced himself. "I'm good at what I do."

He watched the play of emotions across her face, watched his harsh words settle in, and thought that if she was now afraid of him, he'd die. Which was curious, because he'd never before looked so fearfully on death. It had always been something that he'd known would catch up with him sooner or later—probably sooner.

When Elizabeth said nothing, did nothing, he forced the issue. Reaching out, he stroked his thumb across the hand limply lying in her lap. Still she did nothing except stare at his hand, a hand capable of such violence, of such gentleness. His desperation growing, he covered her hand with his. He felt no return squeeze of her fingers, no commitment to his touch. A blankness, a void, a renunciation. His soul had already started to die when her fingers had at last laced themselves with his. He tightened his grip until it was painful for both of them.

Her eyes found his. "Why? Why did you come to me Monday night?"

"I reasoned that I needed to know if you were guilty or innocent. I also reasoned that I was going to bleed to death without some help."

"And what about last night?"

"What about it?" he asked huskily.

"Was it some kind of test to see if I was guilty or innocent?"

"No," he answered firmly.

"Is it what you federal agents always do? Seduce the lady of the house into spilling everything she knows?"

"No."

"Was I just your entertainment while you waited for your arm to heal?"

"Dammit, no!" He willfully lowered his voice. "No," he said, his hand leaving hers to find the smoothness of her cheek. He brushed back a wisp of ebony hair. "I came to you last night for the simple reason that I couldn't stay away. I came to you because I was going crazy from wanting you. Just the way I want you now," he whispered, coming to his knees and looming over her. His face was chiseled into the severe planes of sensuality; his eyes were dark with passion. "I don't understand what I walked into the middle of, I don't understand why I feel I've known you before, I don't understand anything except that I—" his head lowered "—want—" his breath stirred against her lips "—you."

Suddenly, urgently, he encircled her waist with his arm, jerked her full against him and crushed her mouth with his.

With his lips smothering hers, with his heart wildly strumming beneath her palm, with his need hot and hard against her stomach, she realized that she'd believe anything he told her. That black was white. That night was day. That he was a federal agent, Mikhail Baryshnikov, a starman from a far galaxy. Anything. Just as long as he made love to her.

A breeze, like the chatter of fairies, faintly blew through the leaves of the oak tree. Elizabeth arched her head back against the gnarled trunk and let the whiff of air tiptoe down her throat and onto the shoulders exposed by the blue chambray sundress. The sun, greedily grabbing at the shade surrounding the spread quilt, warmed her bare feet. She closed her eyes, inhaled the sweet summer afternoon and supposed that she'd been happier than at this moment, though she truly couldn't remember when.

Opening her eyes, she let her gaze lazily wander over the man stretched out before her. He was asleep, and had been for the better part of fifteen minutes. She knew he was asleep because she could see the rhythmic rise and fall of his wide chest and the crescent spray of golden eyelashes across his cheeks. His bare feet were crossed at the ankles, his arms across his stomach at a point just above the navel peeping through the slit of his unbuttoned shirt.

How often did he sleep so peacefully, this man whose life demanded that he measure everything and everyone? Rarely, she knew, and she felt the warmth of satisfaction that he could do so with her.

After their confrontation in the cabin, after their desire had been both stoked and slaked by soul-deep kisses, they had returned to the house, where by mutual, silent consent the subject of his job, and what was going on at Rose Haven, was not broached again. Both knew they would have to tackle the subjects at some time, but it was as if both understood that he'd said all he could, that she'd heard all she could, for the moment. So they'd done what any couple with time to kill would do on a lazy Saturday afternoon: they'd packed a picnic lunch and sought a cool, caressing shade.

Their talk had been personal. He'd wanted to know all about her, all about her family, particularly her great-grandmother. Once again, neither knew what to say about the strange parallel of their relationship with the couple of a hundred years before. Consequently neither said anything, though both were consummately aware that the relationship had ended traumatically. This realization was the only shadow that drifted across the afternoon's tranquillity. That and the fact that Cougar was not eager to share his past. That alternately hurt and troubled Elizabeth...at least until he kissed her, and then she thought of nothing beyond the seductiveness of his mouth.

Elizabeth's own mouth wreathed into a sudden smile. There was something about wanting a sleeping man to wake up that could turn even the most righteous woman into a devilish imp. Sitting up, she folded her legs beneath her and reached for the pink rose Cougar had earlier pilfered from the garden and presented to her. She now took the rose and ever so lightly drew the satin-soft petals across his hair-swirled navel. The muscles in his belly contracted, and he moaned. Elizabeth grinned. And brushed the rose across the back of his hand. He absently swatted at the nuisance, while she bit back a laugh.

Slowly, carefully, she leaned forward and traced that sensitive spot between nose and upper lip. He twitched his nose, gave a tiny groan of protest and brushed at thin air. Soundlessly giggling, she swayed out of his way. She allowed a full fifteen seconds to pass before once more bringing the rose to his nose. This time the petals had barely connected with skin when two hands swooped out of nowhere, conquered her wrists and tumbled her backward.

Startled, Elizabeth cried out, laughed, then stared up into Cougar's stern face.

"You're in a lot of trouble now, lady," he drawled, adjusting his long legs until they heavily sprawled across hers.

"Yeah? What kind of trouble?" she asked, breathless from being tossed onto her back and from the implication of his remark.

"The worst kind," he said, leaning into her. "I mean to have my way with you."

She tried to look shocked, fearful. "Oh, no!" she proclaimed. "Anything but that!"

Cougar's stern features crumbled into a grin as he gazed down at her unrepentant smile, the sassy, provocative angle of her chin. A thin layer of moisture beaded her upper lip, while her chest heaved, bringing her breasts against his arms with every breath. Her hair fluttered, beckoning his attention. Suddenly Cougar's grin disappeared. Something deep inside him burst wide open and spilled forth an emotion he intuitively knew it was best not to label.

"God, you're beautiful," he said, slowly releasing her wrists. His fingers made their way to her hair, where he threaded strands back from her sweat-damp face. "So beautiful." The callused pad of his thumb traced her lower lip. "So very...very...beautiful." This last was all but lost in the sealing of their mouths.

The kiss was sweet; the kiss was scorchingly sexy; the kiss reduced everything in life to simply man and woman. Elizabeth moaned and made her lips malleable to the mastery of his. At the subtle pressure he exerted, she parted them.

"That's it, Lizzie. Open up for me," he whispered, flicking his tongue into the moist hollow, then withdrawing before either could be satisfied. "Give me all you have," he demanded, his thumbs at her cheeks anchoring her head. He urged her mouth even wider, and his tongue again slid inside, this time filling her, this time swirling with hers in lazy erotic play. When they were both breathless, he pulled his mouth away and laid his forehead against hers. "Sweet...so sweet...too sweet," he whispered.

Elizabeth breathed in his warm, moist breath.

"Close your eyes," he demanded when the rhythm of their hearts was a shade slower.

"They're closed."

"Then keep them closed," he said, pulling his forehead from hers. She immediately opened her eyes. Just the way he knew she would. He frowned in mock anger. "Keep them closed."

She obeyed, saying, "Why?"

"You'll see."

"Why?"

"A little matter of retribution."

"A little matter of what?" She gasped, then giggled as the rose, dripping its fragrant scent, tickled her nose. She giggled again as the petals flowed across her kiss-damp lips, then trailed down her throat, across the curve of her shoulder, and down—slowly, maddeningly—her arm. As the rose caressed the inside of her wrist and started up the sensitive underside of her arm and elbow, her giggles turned to moans and sighs.

When he began to unbutton her sundress, she opened her eyes.

"Keep them closed," he said, unfastening another button and folding back the fabric. Elizabeth felt the warm, humid air breathe against her bare skin. She also felt his eyes devouring her. The nipple peaked under his delicious scrutiny, and he groaned softly, proving to her that he was, indeed, looking at her. She opened her eyes. His were hot.

"Somebody could see," she whispered.

"There's no one here but you and me."

"But someone could drive up."

"We could see them a quarter-mile away." He grinned. "I've just now figured out why Southern homes have such long drives. A lot of hot things besides the weather were going on outside."

As he spoke, he drew the satiny pink petals across her richly brown nipple. If possible, it tightened more. It was a curious feeling—her being so hard it hurt, yet being swathed in something as soft as a rose's caress, in something as soft as the gentle look in Cougar's eyes. She knew that those eyes were unaccustomed to such gentle looks. Cautious looks, wary looks, hard looks, but not gentle looks.

She sighed. And Cougar lowered his mouth to the aching summit of her breast. His tongue washed across the tender, pebbled flesh, then curled around the bud, drawing it deep into his mouth. He sucked gently, then roughly, then gently again, abandoning the rose in the process and using his hand to mold her breast.

Elizabeth threaded her fingers through his hair and let the warm, gooey feelings melt over her. She moaned, a low, whimpering sound—the kind of sound a woman makes when she needs a man. Cougar raised his head and melded his eyes with hers. Hers were slumberous.

Easing down beside her, his body a shield between her and the drive, he kissed her mouth. Slowly. Thoroughly. As his fingers inched beneath the hem of her dress. She started to protest.

"No one can see," he whispered, once more kissing her before easing back to find her eyes with his. "Remember the first time I kissed you?"

She nodded.

"Remember what happened?" he asked, his hand trailing up and over the jut of her hip, then onto the silky softness of her panties.

She blushed.

"Do it again," he said, not understanding why he needed her vulnerability. He knew only that it had awakened some protective something in him that he wanted to feel again. "It was so sweet...so sweet...and it made me feel...so good...so strong...so alive."

"Cougar—"

"You want it...you need it...let me give it to you."

"But—" She gasped as his hand eased into the elastic waistband of her panties and his palm smoothed over her heated skin.

"Take it, Lizzie," he whispered, inching his hand lower until it feathered the downy raven curls nesting her femininity. "And give me your softness." Softness. That was what it was all about, wasn't it? He craved, had to have, her softness—the softness of her body, the softness of her life, the softness of her at that vulnerable moment when she was most clearly a woman.

She moaned as his hand eased between her legs, sliding through petals far sweeter, far softer, than those of the forgotten rose. Petals damp with a musky, dewy moisture. She arched, cried out, as he touched in one ecstatic stroke her every nerve ending.

Protectively folding himself over her, he whispered darkly exciting things in her ear as his fingers stroked, rubbed, breached the interior of her love-heated body.

"So wet...so hot...," he whispered feverishly.

She had never felt as she did at that moment, as if she were exploding from the inside out. She'd never felt so needy. So greedy. So feminine. So totally oriented toward feeling. A single feeling. It was that warm, bright, brilliant, burning feeling she'd felt in the shack. Yet, still she had no name for it. She knew only that she'd never felt it with anyone but this man. This man who was doing things to her body that no one had ever done before.

At the beauty of the feeling, she gasped, clutching his open shirt in her fists. And then it was happening. The tremors began. And though one part of her tried to be embarrassed, the other wallowed in the rightness of his lovemaking. Lovemaking. Love. The word somehow seemed important, appropriate.

At that moment when he felt her completion, his mouth sought hers, swallowing in her every pant, her every moan, her every breath. When he was certain he couldn't give her another stroke of pleasure, he pulled his hand from her and, rolling to his side, took her with him. He cupped the back of her head, nestling her face into the hollow between his throat and shoulder. He just held her.

"I need you, Lizzie," he whispered. "I need you."

Even as he said it, he was quite certain that the need he spoke of went far beyond the hard, physical need straining against his jeans. It was a need of the soul, of the heart. He needed her softness as an absolution to his hardness. He needed it to cancel out the things he'd done, the things he'd seen, the things he knew he'd do and see again because lying with her this afternoon, in the sweetness of the summer, with her body singing to his touch, did not change his life.

He was who he was, what he was. Leopards didn't change their spots. Just as cougars didn't shed their ruthless dispositions.

And yet, for the first time in his life, he longed that things could have been different.

Chapter Ten

Hell was saying goodbye. Hell was watching him ride away into the misty arms of dawn. Hell was not knowing where he was. Or if I'd ever see him ride back into my life again. Hell was hoping and wishing and praying, but never truly knowing.

There was a limit to how often the male body could sexually perform, Cougar thought as he stood before the steamy bathroom mirror, a towel draped around his damp hips, his eyes keeping Elizabeth's image constantly in view. And more was the pity, he added as he drew the sharp razor across his stubbly cheek, because she was so damned sexy—sweetly sexy, innocently sexy—that she almost took his breath away.

Which is what they'd spent the afternoon doing—stealing each other's breaths and leaving behind doubled heartbeats and exquisite pleasure. They'd been forced, for

propriety's sake, to move from the oak tree to the house—
what he'd wanted to do to her, what he ultimately had done
to her, simply couldn't be done in a front yard. No matter
how long the driveway.

That had been hours ago. Since then they'd held each
other, talked—again without mentioning what was most on
their minds—eaten, and now were preparing for bed. He
had showered—an honest-to-God real shower!—while
Elizabeth was still soaking in the old-fashioned porcelain
tub, bubbles almost up to her pretty little nose. Her head
rested against the back of the tub; her eyes were closed.

What was she thinking?

What was he doing?

Wiping the last of the lather from his face, he silently
crossed the room, squatted before the tub and, scooping a
bubble onto his finger, plopped it onto the end of her nose.
Lazily she opened her eyes.

They stared at each other.

Her hair was piled atop her head and held in place with
the ivory comb he felt a mysterious kinship with. Her cheeks
were flushed a dusty-rose color; her face glistened with a
thin film of perspiration. Her eyes... God, her eyes drove
him crazy! They were wistful, melancholy eyes, the eyes of
a woman, the eyes of a child. They were the pensive eyes of
a dreamer, the sensual eyes of a lover, eyes that wanted
something he wasn't even sure she could define. All he knew
was that when he made love to her, those eyes shone with
satisfaction.

He was different, she thought. Subtly, but nonetheless
different. The lines of his face were still harsh, rugged,
stony—they would forever be—but the severity mellowed at
odd, unexpected moments. Even so, there remained a restlessness about him, as if no place were home, though sometimes when he kissed her, the restlessness seemed to

dissipate. Just as his eyes, ever watchful, ever brooding, seemed to relax their eternally anxious vigil.

"Ready?" he said.

She nodded.

He picked up the fluffy towel and held it wide. She stood and stepped out of the tub and into the bath sheet. He folded it about her and moved back to the bathroom mirror to comb his damp hair. After drying herself, she fastened the towel above her breasts as she had the night before. The act produced the same frown from Cougar, but, as then, he said nothing.

"Want a clean bandage?" she asked.

He watched the sway of her hips beneath the terry fabric as she automatically sought out the dressing material.

"Yeah. Please," he said, his throat suddenly tight—both from the sight he'd been taking in and from the fact that this would be the last time she changed the bandage. He abandoned the latter thought for the more pleasant former.

The procedure had become so routine that each well knew his part. Periodically their eyes grazed. Occasionally his breath fanned against the top of her head, and her breath warmed his arm. Cougar's knuckles did not brush her breasts. Which only accentuated their awareness.

"It looks good," she said, struggling to keep her mind on what she was doing.

"It'll be all right soon."

"Have you finished the antibiotics?"

"One more."

She glanced up. His eyes were a deep coffee-brown—and intently watching her. "There," she said breathlessly, indicating that she'd finished. "That should do—"

Cougar reached up and ripped away her towel. She gasped as it fell to her feet, and a soft pink color stole into her cheeks. He stepped closer and smiled.

"We're gonna have to work on that blush. But then, only a little bit. I'm growing kinda fond of it." Too fond, dangerously fond, a little voice told him. He ignored the intrusive remark.

"Are you?" she asked, the words only wisps of sound.

"I am." His voice was as thick as the mist steaming up the bathroom.

She flattened her palms against his hair-matted chest and stared up at him with a patently sensual look. "Why is it that I can't wear a towel and you can?"

Cougar's eyes darkened, while his heart found a very masculine beat. "If you want it off, take it off," he dared.

Slowly her fingers crawled down his chest and slipped inside the fabric. She tugged. His towel joined hers. The same hands that had released the towel now slid, palms down, along his thighs, feeling his warm skin and the springy coils of hair. She loved the way he felt—hard, powerful, all male.

Cougar felt nothing beyond the pleasure of her first aggressive act.

Her hands raked back up his thighs, across a hair-dusted patch of stomach, and down. They stopped, however, as they had the night before, just short of intimately touching him. Time likewise seemed to have stopped.

His eyes begged, as did his ragged breath.

She eased her hand lower.

"Ah, Lizzie," he whispered as her fingers tentatively, then more surely, closed around him. He leaned his forehead against hers and willingly gave himself up to her caress, musically chanting her name all the while.

Finally he could withstand no more of her sweet torture. Scooping her up and starting for the bedroom, he reminded himself that there was a limit to how often the male body could sexually perform. He wondered, as he had once before, if the lady in his arms was driving him into *The Guinness Book of World Records*.

A long while later, enveloped in the night and enfolded in each other's embrace, Cougar asked, "Has anybody expressed an interest in buying the plantation?" In their earlier talk, Elizabeth had mentioned that she and her aunt were thinking of selling. At that point, neither she nor he had wanted to pursue the subject of Rose Haven.

Elizabeth still would have liked to postpone it. She wanted to drift blissfully on their idyllic cloud that had no past, no future. But she sensed the idyll was heading for an end.

"Everyone, it seems," she answered. "Actually, I've had four offers." She recounted from whom.

"How well do you know these people?"

"Why?"

With her back leaning against his chest, his shrug rumbled through her body. "If someone's interested in permanent access to the plantation, it might mean he's involved in the gunrunning. On the other hand, it might mean he simply wants to own the plantation."

Elizabeth explained that she'd known these people for years—all her life, really. "Aside from Leland Webster's always appearing dissatisfied with a small practice in a small town, Dr. Haywood's infatuation for sports cars, and Ruth Dixon's snobbishness, there's nothing outstanding about any of them. Certainly nothing to indicate criminal behavior. And I can't come up with anything even the slightest bit negative about Ben Adams."

"He's the sheriff with the football injury?"

Elizabeth nodded.

"Maybe he feels life cheated him and he intends to even the score. And maybe this Webster character blames everyone but himself for not making a change. Or maybe this Ruth Dixon isn't as socially proper as she appears. With the clash of your families, she might feel that using Rose Haven was poetic justice. And everyone knows that sports cars cost money. Maybe the good old doc can't make enough prescribing antibiotics to patients who lie about having tonsillitis.''

Elizabeth grinned and tweaked the hair on the arm draped across her stomach. ''You're a very suspicious man. To say nothing of ungrateful.''

''I am grateful. And I'm paid to be suspicious.'' *That's how I stay alive.*

He resisted the last thought, unable to reconcile his harsh existence with the soft woman in his arms. An existence he had to go back to all too soon. He concentrated on the feel of that soft woman. Kissing the wrist that now bore only faint yellow evidence of his fingerprints, he raised her arm and, shifting her body slightly, slipped her palm behind his neck. Her back still to him, she sinuously curved in his arms, and his hands traced her corded ribs.

''Have any of them tried to alter their relationship with you?'' At what he sensed was going to be her question, he qualified, ''Tried to get friendlier . . . you know, socialize in a way they haven't before?''

''No,'' she said, nuzzling her cheek against his shoulder. Abruptly she righted her head. ''Wait. Ben Adams did call and ask me out for next week.''

Cougar's hands stopped. ''On a date?''

''I guess you'd call it that,'' she said, wondering if the man beside her would care in the least if she went out with another man. She suddenly wanted him to care a great deal.

Years of training enabled Cougar not to flinch a muscle in reaction. It was none of his business if she went out with Ben Adams, he told himself. He had no right to ask her not to. Yet it surprised him that that was precisely what he wanted to ask of her. Where had this possessive feeling come from?

"I see," he said, seeing far too much in his mind's eye. He visualized another man kissing Elizabeth, saw him making love to her, saw him holding her afterward the way he himself was now holding her. Stay out of it, Collins, he warned himself. It's none of your business. Not even if she prettily blushes for him? No. She doesn't belong to you. Just keep your mouth shut. Just keep... "Are you going out with him?" he heard himself say, hardly recognizing the throaty voice as his own.

She held her breath. "Would it matter to you?"

Cupping her chin in his hand, he angled her head back over her shoulder. Not roughly, but then, not altogether tenderly. In the dim moonlight, their eyes met. "Are you?" he repeated with a rasp.

She swallowed and shook her head against his chest. "No," she whispered.

Long heated moments passed before his mouth claimed hers. When flesh connected with flesh, he groaned, turned her in his arms and, pulling her belly to belly, chest to breasts, held her tightly. Elizabeth hugged close the knowledge that he *had* cared. Cougar, on the other hand, damned himself for his lack of control. And for feeling so relieved that she wasn't going to accept a date that shouldn't have meant anything to him.

The night passed in great lapses of silence. During these, they simply held each other, touching, caressing, exchanging sweet kisses. Slowly, however, like the building cadence of a storm, tension grew. Their touches became more turbulent, their caresses more urgent, their kisses deep and long and desperate. They both knew what was coming. What had to come.

It was a few minutes after two o'clock, in the innocent hours of the morning, when he delivered the blow.

"I have to leave."

They lay on their sides, facing each other, his hand on her hip, her hand on his chest. Her fingertips, rubbing his nipple, hesitated.

She had known the moment was coming, had sensed it all evening, yet now that it was here she felt as if she'd had no time to prepare for it.

"When?" she asked, willing her voice to be strong but hearing it only as a weak whisper.

"Tomorrow."

She raised her face to his, spraying her hair about her in a black shadow. "That soon?"

Irresistibly drawn to her ebony silhouette, he tenderly touched her hair, lightly combing his fingers through it again and again before finally crushing it in a gentle fist.

"I've been here too long already, Lizzie," he said, knowing that he'd stayed beyond what the injury had demanded. He knew, too, why he'd stayed. The reason could be summed up in one word: *her*. He knew one other thing as well. His staying because of her was the most perilous path he'd ever walked. However, he'd seemingly had no choice but to follow that path. "Promise me something," he said, trying to get the words past the knot in his throat.

"What?" she asked, having similar problems talking.

"Stay away from the back of the plantation."

She hesitated.

He insisted. "Swear it."

Finally she nodded.

"Say it."

"I swear."

Her face was tauntingly close to his. So close that neither could catch a full breath.

Please don't go!
Don't beg me to stay. Please.

To keep from pleading, Elizabeth turned her head and kissed the wrist so near her mouth. Cougar lowered his lips to her forehead. Dipping her head, Elizabeth found the hollow of his throat, kissed it, then inched lower onto his chest, leaving kisses everywhere her mouth worshiped. Cougar sighed and ran his hands down her spine and onto her hips, as if trying to memorize every curve, every indentation, of her body. She, too, moved her hand to his buttocks, where she kneaded and stroked as she planted kisses lower and lower. As she kissed him, he kissed her—her shoulder, her hair, any part of her his mouth could reach. A new tension began to build with each touch of skin to skin. It was a frenetic, tangible thing that blossomed into a frantic flowering. Suddenly, frenziedly, it was as if neither could touch or taste enough of the other.

She kissed his stomach; his hand caressed her thigh.

She kissed his navel; his hand stroked the back of her knee.

She kissed his hip, bit, kissed again; he growled and hauled her the length of his body until her mouth was only inches from his own.

Breath mated with breath.

"Cougar—" she started to say, willing to shed her pride and beg him to stay.

"Don't!" he whispered. "Don't ask me to stay!"

His mouth slammed into hers, and at the same time he pressed her to her back and covered her body with his. Without preliminaries, his body entered hers. Their lovemaking was desperate. All through it Elizabeth felt that blinding flash of emotion she'd first felt that morning in the shack. It was still hot, burning, and too bright to look at too closely. Cougar, on the other hand, thought of nothing beyond stamping the woman beneath him as his. And of saying something with his body that he couldn't even verbalize to himself.

The end came fast and furiously and appeased little. He was still going away, she still wanted to ask him to stay, and neither had spoken of whether he'd ever return.

When she awoke, he was gone.

Intuitively Elizabeth knew that he was gone not only from her bed, but also from Rose Haven. Though his absence hurt, she was relieved that she wouldn't have to say goodbye. That was something she wasn't at all certain she could have done.

After a lame attempt at breakfast, she allowed her emotions to rule and walked to the cabin where Cougar had holed up. Just as she had suspected, he wasn't there, nor was there any sign of his ever having been. Unless you counted the red rose that lay on the weathered mattress—testimony to his knowing that she'd come—and the empty brown pill bottle sitting on the mantel.

Empty.

It was exactly how she felt. Empty, yet curiously filled with tears that needed shedding. Crying, however, was a luxury she would not permit herself.

Somehow, the red rose almost constantly in her hand, she got through the day. And the long days that followed. On Tuesday she checked Aunt Siddie out of the nursing home and took her for lunch and an afternoon ride in the country. The white-haired woman, evidently sensing that more than sighting a ghost was troubling her niece, had asked no private, personal questions about why she vacillated between long stretches of silence and sudden flashes of unnaturally energetic conversation. The older woman had simply clasped the younger woman's hands tightly during their farewells and reminded her that Jarrett woman were traditionally strong.

Two days later, on a July evening so hot that it couldn't help reminding Elizabeth of the swelteringly hot evenings she'd spent in Cougar's arms, she had dinner with Pamela Shaw and her family. The children had been delightful, but seeing Pamela and her husband together, a couple truly in love, only seemed to deepen her ache. Pamela, loyal as always, didn't press for explanations to her friend's quiet mood; she'd simply made it known that she was there if and when Elizabeth needed her.

Need.

What she needed more than another heartbeat was to see Cougar again. Would she ever? The question was a harsh one, the answer even harsher. She didn't know. She knew that something, a bust of some kind, was going down—Cougar had told her that much. What she didn't know was whether he'd be part of it. And even if he was, would he make the effort to see her again? Or was their time together simply some surreal slice of history that was never to be explained or repeated?

The following Sunday evening, exactly a week to the day since he'd left, she made the realization. It stole softly into her heart as she stood on the gallery at sunset staring at the oak tree. She loved him. It was the only explanation for the heartache she felt. And yet, the realization, the feeling, surprised her. She'd loved before, in an innocent, youthful way, but this love was different, deeper, fuller, the product of maturity. It was that burning, blinding light she'd sensed before, but it was also more. The light had now burst into millions of warm, glittery, quiet feelings—a starstorm—that silently seeped into her soul.

But would she ever have the chance to tell him of her love? Would he care to hear of it?

And where, dear God, was this man who'd so thoroughly stolen her heart?

Thousands of miles away, in Central America, a jeep jostled its way along a primitive path cut through the dense, overgrown jungle. The driver, a man notoriously called El Puma, dodged a low, overhanging branch, the leaves of which fluttered across his worn face and ruffled his unruly blond hair.

It was sunset, that time of evening when the sun seeks shelter for the night and the jungle moon, eager to prowl, awakens, stretches and claws its lunar path skyward. The man at the wheel was thinking of other sunsets, pastel sunsets that heralded a softer, vastly different kind of night, a night not filled with hungry eyes and stalking sounds.

Ahead, El Puma spotted his destination: a squalid, thatched hut sitting in the middle of nowhere. Drawing the jeep to an abrupt halt, he cut the engine. He was immediately accosted by the noisy silence of the jungle—birds chattered, monkeys screeched, unidentifiable animals cawed and called. He was also accosted by a dark-skinned, sloppily dressed man who appeared out of the shadows carrying an M16 rifle. As El Puma lazily spilled from the jeep, discarding a pair of sunglasses in the process, he cast quiet disdain at both the man and the weapon.

The man, attempting a show of power, jerked the gun toward the door. El Puma, gunless and at the wrong end of a rifle, looked far more the man in command. It had something to do with the expressionless set of his face, the coldness in his dark eyes, the rigid, unyielding posture of his wide shoulders. It had something to do with an I've-got-nothing-to-lose attitude.

The barrel of the gun found the middle of El Puma's back and nudged him inside the rustic hut. El Puma didn't flinch;

he merely found the eyes of the man seated at the crude metal desk perched on the dirt floor. For a moment the two men, chieftains in the encounter, stared.

"Call off your goon, Eduardo," the man named El Puma drawled softly but as though the words had been cast in steel.

The other man, heavyset, black-haired, blacker-eyed, let his eyes drift over the tall man dressed in jungle fatigues. Slowly he nodded for the guard to step back. Without invitation, El Puma took the chair opposite the desk and sprawled out his long legs. He let his gaze wander about the room. Another armed guard, as disreputable-looking as the first, stood at the hut's far end. Plastic packages of a white powder lay piled in a corner. Cocaine. Drug of the rich. Plaything for the bored. Illegal tender for the gun buy that was going down if everything could be satisfactorily arranged.

In a far back corner, unnoticeable at first in the shadows, was a man strung from the rafters by a rope tied to both wrists. He hung limply, his head sagging in blissful unconsciousness, his back bearing the lash marks of a strap. El Puma seemed in no way moved by the grim sight. It was as if he'd seen it a thousand times before. His eyes, frigid, blank, again found those of the man he'd come to see.

"A little disagreement as to where his loyalty lay," Eduardo explained.

"Dead men display loyalty to no one."

"He's not dead," Eduardo said. "He just wishes he were." Bending forward, the man, with short, thick fingers, cordially offered a cigar, which El Puma refused with a negligible shake of his head. Lighting one for himself and flicking the match to the floor, Eduardo leaned back in his chair. White, acrid smoke curled about him. "I don't like the delay," he announced at length.

El Puma shrugged. "There's a problem."

"What kind of problem?"

"Seems as though a body was found in an abandoned well. It's spooked our boys."

"Whose body?"

"The caretaker's. He was apparently working for them."

"Know anything about who killed him?"

El Puma looked as if the question bored him. "It's an ugly world out there. Lots of crime. Lots of violence. Lots of people with loyalty problems."

Through a haze of smoke, the man called Eduardo studied the man before him. El Puma had steadily emerged over the past year and a half as the powerful kingpin of a Central American gun-trading cartel. It was his job, for a cut of the profits, to act as a broker, to bring those men who wanted to buy guns into contact with those who wanted to sell them. El Puma had quickly developed the reputation of being efficient, ruthlessly efficient. He was respected, he was feared, he wasn't above doing what had to be done. Which might even mean eliminating a troublesome character, like a caretaker, who threatened to jeopardize a well-planned, profitable buy? While it was true that both ends of the gun-running spectrum, the seller and the buyer, had to trust the broker, it was also true that in such a shady business no one really trusted anyone else. Not even one's own mother.

"Yeah," Eduardo commented. "The world, she is a mess."

The man hanging from the rafters moaned.

"Wednesday," Eduardo said. "I want it wrapped up Wednesday."

"I'll see what I can do."

"Wednesday. Or not at all."

"I'll relay the message," El Puma said, pulling to his feet and starting for the door.

"Tell them that the delay's already cost them. The way I figure it, the guns are only worth eighty thousand now."

El Puma halted, then turned slowly, letting his cold, granite-hard eyes slide into those of the man sitting at the desk. "The way I figure it, it's the hundred thousand agreed upon or I'll call the deal off myself."

The room grew silent, motionless.

"What makes you think I need a go-between at this stage?" Eduardo asked around an arrogant swirl of smoke.

"Because you're nothing but a two-bit hood who couldn't find his ass with both hands without my help," El Puma drawled.

Anger jumped into the black eyes; the anger inspired the sound of rifle rounds being chambered. Suddenly, unexpectedly, Eduardo's laughter bounded about the shabby room. The two guards finally laughed also, not out of understanding of what had been said, but because their boss laughed. Without even a smile, El Puma turned and stalked out of the hut. The last thing he heard was a moan mixing with the merriment.

The nearest Guatemalan town, if it could be called that, was five miles away. It was actually nothing more than a few shanties and a cantina, which had an oscillating fan, a bar and the only phone in town. Without delay, he deposited the coins he needed for the long-distance call and dialed the number of his Louisiana contact.

"Hello?" came the familiar voice of the subordinate with whom he'd been forced to deal.

"They want Wednesday."

Hesitation. "I'm not sure that's possible."

"It is if you want the action."

"But the well incident—"

"Don't give me that spooked crap. I'm taking as big a chance as you."

"I'll see what I can do."

"Yeah, well, while you're at it, tell your boss that I'll deal only with him."

Another hesitation. "He isn't gonna like that."

"My heart's bleeding for him." He switched ears. "It's the head honcho or the deal's off. It's Wednesday or the deal's off. Got that?"

"I'll get back to you."

El Puma gave him the cantina number, hung up and ordered a bourbon without a trace of water. Taking the table nearest the phone, he slouched down in a chair and embraced the liquor. Overhead the fan slowly spun, whirling the hot air around aimlessly. The cantina was empty except for him, the bartender, another customer, who was already inebriated into a stupor, and the bar's token whore, who looked more tired than lusty. As he always did when working, El Puma emptied his mind of all thoughts except those pertinent to the moment. His ability to do so was the secret of his success. It was the reason he'd lived long enough to be sitting in a hot bar, drinking hot bourbon, on a hot-as-Hades summer night.

As he knew she would, the woman slipped from the bar stool and started toward him. Wearing an old gaudy dress that visibly displayed her ample wares, she slid into the seat beside him and smiled. She was as worn as the dress, though pretty in a raw kind of way. El Puma noted that a cross incongruously hung around her neck and nestled in the valley of her pendulous breasts. He wondered if he looked as worn as she. And if there was any chance that a whore's god would understand, embrace, forgive a man who'd never set foot in a church, never prayed a prayer. Could her god care for a man whom no one else had ever cared for—not even the man himself?

"*Señor?*" Her voice was husky, persuasive.

El Puma knew what she was offering. *"Non. Por favor."*

"But I am good . . ."

"I'm sure you are."

". . . and I could take a loong time." She leaned forward, giving him an unrestricted view of her breasts.

"That's just it. I don't have a long time."

"Then I will be queek," she said, teasingly trailing her hand up his leg.

"Non," he said, stopping her hand before she intimately touched him. Abruptly the phone behind him rang, and he was out of his chair before the ring had even been completed. "Yeah?"

"Wednesday."

The phone went dead, and El Puma recradled it. Stepping back to the table, he downed the last of the bourbon before starting from the room. He'd taken only a few steps, however, when he turned and fished some bills from his pocket. These he threw onto the table.

"A drink for the lady," he called to the bartender.

The lady smiled, and for a moment El Puma broke his own emotional code. He thought of another ebony-haired woman, a woman with wistful, dreamy gray eyes and cheeks flushed with a delicious pink blush. A woman whose hand he wouldn't have stayed from an intimate mission. A woman who possessed an incredible softness, a softness that made him, and his life, seem bitterly hard. A woman who for just a moment he could imagine caring about him. A woman he could imagine making him care about himself.

Chapter Eleven

*For all that we shared, he never spoke of love. I think
it was a word he did not trust, a word he feared, and yet
I longed to hear him say it just once. So that I might
cherish it through the lonely nights, so that I might
cleave to it if the day came when he never returned.*

Elizabeth heard the plane go over Wednesday evening just
as the sun was sinking below the horizon. The sound
brought an instant rush of adrenaline, along with the instant recollection that she'd promised, sworn, to stay away
from the back of the plantation.

Stepping out the back door of the house, she watched the
plane descend, lower and lower like a swooping bird. It
really would be so very simple to follow it . . . and not at all
dangerous if she kept to the woods and out of view. But she
had promised, hadn't she? Yes. Yes, she had. And she'd
honor her vow. Because if Cougar found out she'd dis-

obeyed, there'd be the devil to pay. Of course, if he weren't here, he couldn't very well catch her in an act of disobedience, could he? And if he were here, well, wasn't the possibility of getting a glimpse of him worth risking his anger? One too many lonely nights, one too many uncertainties as to whether she'd ever see him again, tipped the scales in favor of breaking her promise.

The approaching night would be a hot one, Elizabeth knew, for already its warm, humid fingers curled around her shorts and bare legs. Ignoring the heat, however, and her better judgment, she started walking toward the dilapidated slave quarters. Upon reaching them, she spared them only a glance, then kept walking, hurrying through the taller weeds, hastening past the silver-surfaced pond, and finally slipping into the shaded woods that would take her to the clearing at the far reaches of the property.

The plane had alighted on the grassy ribbon of land. The propellers, whirling and whining, slowed before stopping altogether. A silence rushed forward, a silence in which Elizabeth heard birds chirping, leaves and undergrowth rustling as animals scurried—slithered?—through them, and the incessant drone of eager insects. She also heard the sound of the plane doors opening; two men and muffled voices spilled from the small aircraft. Elizabeth crouched behind the screen of a full bush, the sound of her thick, hard heartbeat momentarily deafening her to all else.

The taller of the two men snapped out an order Elizabeth couldn't understand. His companion obviously did, though, for he quickly moved to help drag a long crate out of the plane's interior. From the way the men were grimacing, from the way their arm muscles were bulging, the box was clearly heavy. So heavy that the subordinate man lost his grip, the crate thudded to the ground, and the top fell open. Amid angry swearing, guns whammed into the ground.

Guns!

Somehow, in that moment, the gunrunning seemed real in a way it never had before. Cougar had told her what was happening on her property, and after her initial shock at the idea, she had believed him. Now she realized that it had seemed like some fictional fantasy, like something shown on television or a movie screen, something far removed from reality. But it was reality. Strange men were unloading a crate of guns at the back of Rose Haven.

Elizabeth might have panicked at the thought had she had the luxury of time. But she did not. At that moment, from seemingly out of nowhere, in a cloud of dust, a car arrived. Where had it come from? The only road to the back of the property had been closed years before. Long before she'd entered high school. Prior to that, while Rose Haven was still producing cotton, the road had been used to transport farm machinery. Once closed, it had become a favorite parking lane for youthful lovers. Obviously, if the road was in use again, someone had had prior knowledge of its existence. Someone like Ben Adams? Or Leland Webster? Or Dr. Haywood? Or perhaps Ruth Dixon?

The car came to a stop, and four men got out, two from the front, two from the back. Taking orders from the man who'd issued them before, the men trooped off in the direction of the mill. From her hiding place, Elizabeth watched for the next fifteen minutes as one after another crate was brought from the cotton mill to the clearing. A dozen and one in all. Unlucky thirteen. Waiting to be picked up and transported to Central America.

Who was behind the operation at this end? The unknown man giving all the orders? And who was in charge at the Central American end? And did Cougar know that the buy was going down now?

Suddenly another swirl of dust appeared, and in its midst tooled a white sports car—a Maserati. Even before it stopped, Elizabeth could sense the driver's impatience. Perhaps even the driver's anger. It had something to do with the arrogant sway of the car, the way it ground to an abrupt halt, the way the door was slung open but not closed behind the emerging figure.

The last dying rays of the sun glanced off the man's head—the man's bald head. Wearing an expensively cut suit, he irritably jerked loose the tie that was knotted beneath his salt-and-pepper beard.

No, Elizabeth's mind denied, even as another quadrant of it insisted that the man was Dr. Haywood. There had to be some logical reason that Grover Haywood, the family physician of lo, these many years, was in a clearing at Rose Haven walking toward a man who'd just stockpiled thirteen crates of guns. Probably stolen guns. Most certainly guns that were being smuggled illegally. The only logical reason was, unfortunately, the obvious and unpleasant one: Dr. Haywood was involved in the gunrunning. No, heading the gunrunning, Elizabeth amended, anger suddenly flooding her at this man's betrayal of her family. The anger made her bold, and she scurried, her bare knees biting into the dirt, to a fallen tree, where she lay flat on her stomach. The ground was hard, earthy-smelling and strewn with twigs and decaying leaves.

"Where the hell is he?" Elizabeth heard Grover Haywood bark.

"Should be here any minute," the man Elizabeth had once thought in charge replied. "We're ready for him."

"Yeah, well, I don't like the feel of this." As he spoke, Dr. Haywood looked around, as if trying to flush out any danger lurking in the shadows.

Elizabeth scrunched lower, feeling the coolness of the ground against her exposed legs. She also felt something creeping up the back of her calf. As noiselessly as possible, she swiped at the unidentifiable bug with the toe of her tennis shoe. She refused to think of what else might be crawling nearby, though she couldn't help remembering that woods were the home of things that slithered.

"I shouldn't be here," Grover Haywood insisted.

"But El Puma said he'd deal only with you."

"To hell with El Puma!"

El Puma. The strange name settled about Elizabeth. He had to be the Central American connection. And the fact that Grover Haywood was here when he didn't want to be, simply because this El Puma had demanded it, told her a lot about El Puma. Whoever he was, he was powerful. Further conversation, much of it garbled because Grover Haywood continuously paced, revealed that El Puma was the infamous, dangerous kingpin of a gun-trading cartel. Elizabeth was just wondering if Cougar knew of this man when suddenly another plane, this one larger, older, noisier than the first, dropped out of the sunset-streaked sky.

And at that precise moment she saw the snake. It coiled at the end of the rotted log she lay hidden behind. Its eyes were dark and beady and staring right at her; its tongue flicked the air quickly, ominously. While she knew little about snakes, except that she was deathly afraid of them, she knew this one was poisonous. Its color and bands told her it was a copperhead; its pose told her it was about to strike. With a muffled cry she rolled to her side, sat up and scooted backward.

The men awaiting the second plane whirled.

"What the hell!"

"Who is she?"

For a brief moment, her eyes locked with those of Dr. Haywood. By comparison, the snake's eyes looked friendly. "Get her!" he ordered.

She scrambled, stumbled—once more her knee dug into the unrelenting earth—then scrambled again. She started to run. The branch of a tree struck her at midchest, its leaves fluttering across her face. She scraped it aside and ran on. Instinct caused her to look back.. One of the men—the largest, she would have sworn—was close behind. Too close. When Elizabeth turned back, and before she could stop herself, she plowed into a bush. Crying out as thorns lacerated her legs, she circumvented the briers as best she could. She raced on, hearing nothing beyond her breath roaring in her ears.

Abruptly a brawny arm slid around her waist and yanked her off the ground.

"Let go of me!" she shrieked as her nails dug into the arm. Her feet kicked and thrashed. The arm tightened, painfully squeezing the air from her lungs. Elizabeth gasped, succumbing to the superior strength.

"That's it, sweetheart," the panting voice thundered near her ear, "just give it up like a good girl."

At this patronizing remark, Elizabeth gave another wriggled protest, which was met by an even more forceful ramming of the arm into her diaphragm. Totally breathless now, she collapsed against the sweaty chest. Vaguely she noted that someone had killed the snake. Dimly she heard the plane sink into a landing. She felt the ground once more beneath her as she was unceremoniously dumped at the doctor's feet. She struggled to stand up. When she finally managed the feat, her gray eyes, haughty with disdain, slid into those of the man before her.

"Ah, Elizabeth," he said with deceptive calm, "why couldn't you have minded your own business?"

"I'd say—" She gasped from the oxygen gushing into her lungs. "I'd say what happens at Rose Haven is *my* business."

"And I'd say, unfortunately, that it's now my business to make you sorry you made it yours." Grover Haywood looked at the man who'd chased her down. "Tie her." Almost before the order was fully out of his mouth, Elizabeth felt her arms whipped behind her and rope chained about her wrists. She struggled, but the rope cut too deeply to keep up the frenzied movement.

"Damn you, Grover Haywood, who do you think you are? And what's going on—"

"Gag her."

"Don't you dare! Don't you—" The words sputtered against the handkerchief drawn across her mouth. Elizabeth tossed her head from side to side, dislodging the cloth. "Don't—"

Elizabeth heard the sharp crack of Grover Haywood's palm across her cheek before she felt it. When the delayed feeling started, it tingled like numbing ice, then burned like a searing fire. Tears glazed her eyes. Both fear and anger fought for expression.

"We can do it the hard way or the easy way," Dr. Haywood said. "It's entirely up to you." When Elizabeth said nothing, he motioned for the man to secure the gag.

This time she didn't protest. Grimacing as the man carelessly tied her hair into the knot at the back of her head, it crossed her mind to wonder why she hadn't obeyed Cougar. If he found out, he'd kill her. No, she admitted ruefully, there probably wouldn't be enough left of her to kill.

"He's here," one of the men said, and all attention, even Elizabeth's, turned to the outdated C47 that had just rolled to a rough stop.

"Keep your eye on her," the doctor told the man who'd captured her.

Despite her personal circumstances, Elizabeth sensed the tension that suddenly crackled in the air. The atmosphere reeked not only of expectancy, but of fear as well.

In minutes, a tall, lean man, his face hidden behind sunglasses despite the increasing darkness, emerged from the plane. Though he was accompanied by three other men, no one paid them any heed. All eyes were fixed on this man. All eyes including Elizabeth's. She watched as his long legs, encased in jungle fatigues and boots, arrogantly ate up the distance. El Puma. Elizabeth instinctively knew the man was El Puma. For just an instant instinct told her one other thing—that there was something vaguely familiar about his stride, the sweep of his shoulders, the tawny gold of his hair. The thought was lost, however, as she saw Grover Haywood discreetly check what she assumed to be a gun beneath his suit jacket. He stepped forward.

El Puma stopped directly before him. Neither spoke, as though it were a test of wills, of strength.

Finally Grover Haywood said, "You got the stuff?"

Still the man named El Puma didn't speak. Instead, as if sensing that something wasn't quite right, he raised his eyes and spanned the assembly of people. When he spotted the woman in the shadow of a tree, he stopped, froze. Then, stepping past the doctor, he started for her. Curiously, no one said anything.

The closer he got, the more sure Elizabeth became of who he was. That identity was confirmed when, with a cocky flick of his wrist, he yanked the sunglasses from his eyes.

Cougar.

Relief, profound enough to sway her knees, swamped Elizabeth. Relief, however, slipped away bit by brittle bit as his eyes, once warm with passion but now cold and hard, raked over her. They took in her tied hands, her gagged mouth, the still-red imprint of a man's hand on her cheek, the cuts and abrasions and dirt on her bare legs and knees, the fear in her eyes. At no time did the coldness in his own eyes melt. At no time did the hardness soften.

Why doesn't he say something? Why doesn't he do something? Why doesn't he help me?

Her eyes pleading, Elizabeth took a step toward him, but the man at her side restrained her. Roughly. A fact that seemed to move Cougar not at all.

Finally his dark voice rumbled, "What the hell's she doing here?"

"Never mind her," Grover Haywood said. "She owns the plantation and just got a little too curious. I'll deal with her."

If there was something unsettling about having the man she loved view her with such cold dispassion, it was nothing compared to how she felt when he dismissed her with nothing more than a flicker of his eyes. Turning, he strode away, just as if she didn't exist . . . just as if she'd never lain in his arms . . . just as if the two of them had never been breathless lovers.

Elizabeth whimpered around the cloth in her mouth. Cougar kept walking.

Her hands painfully tied behind her, her heart painfully tied inside her, she watched as the crates of guns were hastily loaded onto the C47. Cougar, totally oblivious to her presence, motioned for an attaché case to be brought to him. It quickly was. As he snapped open the latches, Elizabeth could see neat little rows of plastic bags containing a white powder. Cocaine? Heroin? She assumed the drugs were barter for the guns. Hadn't she seen this whole sordid scene on *Miami Vice*? She again had that strange feeling that she was living fiction, not reality.

Fiction.

Reality.

Cougar had told her he was a federal agent, but wasn't it possible that that, too, was fiction? A plausible story to account for her having found him out? A lie, bold and plain and hurtful? He had shown her no credentials, nothing to substantiate his claim of working for the Bureau of Alcohol, Tobacco and Firearms. Why, then, had she believed him so easily, with no reservations? *Maybe because you wanted to believe him, stupid. Maybe because when he took you in his arms, you would have believed anything he'd said.*

Looking at him now, so coolly efficient, so apparently experienced in carrying out the buy, Elizabeth had to admit that maybe the reality was that he was this El Puma character. Couldn't he just as easily have killed the caretaker because Joshua found him nosing around the property? Or maybe Joshua was involved and it was nothing more than fraternal infighting. And how was she to know whether there ever was a Jake Jennings, and, if there was, couldn't he have been Cou—El Puma's operative, whose death he would have been equally interested in avenging?

A big fat yes to everything, Elizabeth admitted. Maybe El Puma was the man in the middle who supported himself by living off the greed of other men. She'd long sensed his desperate life-style. She even remembered his once telling her that it would be better, for her, for him, if she didn't know who he was. She'd once believed that he might be a criminal. Maybe that's what he was after all.

But her heart wanted to believe otherwise. Oh, how it wanted to believe! Wasn't it possible that this was all an act, some sort of setup? Wouldn't admitting he knew her, cared about her, not only jeopardize the sting, but also endanger her life? And his? She allowed herself this faint glimmer of hope.

In minutes, too few to even be believable, the buy was completed. The last crate of guns had been loaded aboard the aircraft, the drugs had been tested for purity, the attaché case had been slammed shut. Elizabeth's heart began to pound. Would Cougar, El Puma, whoever he was, leave her here to face heaven only knew what?

The two leaders—Cougar and Dr. Haywood—exchanged words. They were low, monosyllabic. Elizabeth could still sense each man's wariness of the other. The others had clustered into two uneasy factions.

Slowly, as if drawn there by Elizabeth's fierce concentration, Cougar's eyes once more found hers. His were still stone-cold, granite-hard. They still held no memory of the passion they'd shared. The faint glimmer of hope that had surfaced now hung on for dear life. Suddenly that lifeline was cruelly cut.

"Kill her," Cougar said, his voice as atonal as if he'd just demanded the demise of an irritating bug. He then turned, and with legs she could clearly remember entwined with her own, resolutely strode for the plane.

Kill her.

The words rained about Elizabeth like flecks of fire that burned away all feeling, seared all senses. She felt nothing. Nothing. The very words had been lethal enough to accomplish what he had ordered. She felt herself dying, from the inside out.

Suddenly a shot was fired, its sound exploding around Elizabeth. So dead was she that she didn't even flinch. Had she been shot? Had someone immediately carried out the grim order? All she knew was that she felt nothing, no physical pain. But then, would she in the overwhelming face of her emotional pain?

The instant the shot rang out, all was frenetic activity, though in Elizabeth's eyes, the world had slowed to a crawl. As if in slow motion she saw Cougar spin, saw his eyes immediately seek her—had the coldness thawed, or did she only need to believe so in these last few moments of life?—saw him break into a run that looked almost comical in its unhurriedness. He was then sailing through the air, still with an uncanny slowness, reaching toward his leg for a gun and hitting her with the full impact of his considerable weight. In one whoosh of air from her lungs, he toppled her to the ground.

As she fell, she peripherally noted that Grover Haywood's compatriots were scurrying, they, too, slowly, as they were chased by the men who had accompanied Cougar. She saw unfamiliar men, six to eight of them, charging from the woods. She noted also that other shots were popping—here, there, all around. One zinged dangerously near, chipping the bark on the tree. And then she knew nothing except Cougar's body smothering hers—darkness, a delicious weight that both shielded her and restricted her breath, the damp smell of perspiration. Her hands, anchored behind her, ached from the awkward position. His gun fired, once, twice, three times, each time leaving a loud ringing in her ears. Instinctively she burrowed deep into his chest.

And then it was over, almost as fast as it had begun, and gunshots were replaced by shouts.

"Got the bastards!"

"Need to call an ambulance. Three're down."

"Now ain't that a shame. The Maserati has a shattered window. Did you do that, Cummings?"

"Hell, no," the man named Cummings drawled. "I shot out the tires."

"Too bad about the car, Doc," another federal agent said, "but by the time you get outta stir, it'll be outta style, anyway."

"Let's go, boys. We gotta little party to attend."

"You have the right to remain silent, you have the right..."

Cougar rolled from Elizabeth and stared down into her dirt-streaked face. "Are you all right?" His voice was taut.

She nodded, sucking as much air as she could past the handkerchief still clogging her mouth. Cougar didn't remove it. Instead, discarding his gun, he pushed her to her side and began to jerk her wrists untied.

"I thought I told you to stay away from here," he began, his fear giving way to a relieved anger. "Dammit, you scared the living hell out of me! Don't you know you could have gotten yourself killed?"

He yanked the ropes from her hands and threw them aside. He then turned his attention to the gag tied at the back of her head and ripped the knot undone. It hurt as much to take the handkerchief off as it had to put it on. Elizabeth, however, relished this pain... and the fact that Cougar was there and that he cared enough to be angry.

"I oughta kill you myself," he fussed, urging her onto her back once more. The gag fell away, air danced into her lungs, blood sang through her cramped arms. "If you ever pull this kind of stunt again, Elizabeth Noel Jarrett—" their eyes met, his sparkling with emotion, hers dewy with it "—I swear I'll kill you. I swear I'll... I'll..." He groaned and, bracketing her jaw with his hand, crushed her lips with his.

The kiss was brutal. On another low, guttural sound, he sent his tongue deep inside her mouth, staking her as his, defying the death that had hovered briefly, yet menacingly, about her. His leg had eased between hers, his chest once more covering hers, while his arms shifted to form a brace for her head. Her hands, chafed at the wrists from the tight ropes, folded themselves around his neck. She greedily clasped him to her. The kiss ended only when both needed to breathe.

"I thought—" she began.

"I know. I know," he interrupted, his lips rapaciously rolling back onto hers.

Seconds later, the sound of someone discreetly clearing his throat brought the interlude to a close. "Excuse me, sir," the local agent named Cummings said, "but we, uh...we need you."

Pulling away from Elizabeth, Cougar once more drew his eyes into hers. "Right," he said, coming to his feet and, reaching down, assisting her to hers. He then slipped the gun into the waistband of his pants. "Would you see that Ms. Jarrett gets back to the house?"

"Yes, sir."

Without another look, without another word, Cougar turned.

"Cougar?" Elizabeth called out.

He stopped and looked back. He read the question etched in her gray eyes. "I'll be there in a little bit."

Nodding, she watched him walk away, back toward the men huddled around the wounded sports car. She had a brief view of an unhappy, handcuffed Grover Haywood. Three men lay sprawled on the ground. Fiction. It all still seemed like fiction. Shouldn't some producer call out, "Cut! That's a wrap"?

"Ready, ma'am?" the man named Cummings asked.

"Yes," Elizabeth replied, suddenly very glad to have the stranger's supportive hand at her elbow. The aftershock of the ordeal had left her legs the consistency of pudding.

"Are you all right?" Cougar asked, his voice sifting through the silence twenty minutes later. In the background, cicadas strummed their artful songs, while the night finally opened wide its ebony arms.

Standing before the latticed railing of the gallery, illuminated in the golden glow of the porch light, Elizabeth turned, and for long, unguarded moments the two soaked in the sight of each other. Cougar's hair was disheveled, his brow was popping with perspiration, his gun was still tucked into his waistband, while his shirt was partially untucked. He looked hard, tough, like what he was—a man whose job description read deception and violence.

Elizabeth, on the other hand, looked guileless, vulnerable, as open as the roses blooming nearby, as feminine as the richest, most delicate tatted lace. The image was accentuated by the tangle of her hair, the mistiness of her eyes, her slightly trembling lower lip, the cuts and scrapes covering her legs. Her bare feet, at least to Cougar's mind, enhanced the vision.

Slowly, his boots thudding against the wood, he mounted the steps, walked across the porch and stopped in front of her. She angled her head up.

His eyes wandered closely over her face before his crooked finger caressed the cheek that was still tender from Grover Haywood's slap.

"Did they hurt you?" The question was so darkly heated with emotion that it might just have been telegraphed from hell.

"They just . . . They just scared me." His nearness, the gentleness of his touch, persuaded her to finally let go of the control she had so fiercely been holding on to. "Oh, God, I was so scared," she said, the tears beginning.

Wordlessly Cougar hugged her to him. She banded her arms about his waist, buried her face in his chest and cried, heedless of the gun subtly separating them.

"It's all right," he whispered. "It's all over. You're safe. Nothing's going to hurt you now."

Over and over he stroked the back of her head with his large hand, over and over he offered soothing words, over and over he loaned her the strength of his body, the power of his will. Slowly the tears abated.

She wiped her nose with the back of her wrist, which still bore a red crease from the rope. "I thought..." She couldn't say the hateful words.

But she didn't have to. He did it for her. "...that I'd lied to you about being a federal agent." She nodded. Sniffed. Pushed back the pain she'd felt looking into his hard, cold eyes, eyes that were now blanketing her in warmth. "I had to make you believe that," he said, brushing back a wisp of hair from her cheek. His voice had lowered when he added, "Your life depended on it."

"I know. I should have listened to you."

"Why didn't you?" His caring anger was back.

She disarmed the anger with the truth. "I wanted to see you."

He swore and once more hauled her into his arms, but this time his lips swept down to capture hers, slicking in sensual circles that instantly caused spirals of heat to coil in her belly.

"Ah, Lizzie," he groaned, eating, biting, teasing her mouth with his, "you feel so good. So damned good." Her tongue met his; her body pressed closer, her breasts flattening against the hard wall of his chest. *Too good,* he warned himself, *the kind of good that can't be stopped once it's reached a certain point.* Reluctantly, breathlessly, he pushed her from him. She went unwillingly, surprised. Threading his fingers through the hair at her temples—he felt her pulse beneath the pads of his thumbs—his eyes locked with hers. Rapid heartbeats—his and hers—filled the silence. Finally he said, "Lizzie, I have to go back."

Fear jumped into her eyes. "No!"

"Now. They're waiting for me."

"No!" she repeated, manacling his wrists, which were still at her temples, in an effort to restrain him.

"Please try to understand—"

"Don't leave me again." She knew that what she was asking was unfair, but the hollowness his announcement had carved inside her demanded the plea.

"Lizzie, don't—"

Long-taut emotions snapped, and she tore from his embrace. Tears gathered again. "What do you want from me, Cougar? I'm just a simple woman living a simple life. I don't understand all these cops and robbers games. I don't understand agents and undercover work and gunrunning and plastic bags of dope in attaché cases. And I sure as hell don't understand getting your rear shot off. My God, those were real bullets being fired out there!" Her voice had risen to almost a scream.

By contrast, Cougar's voice was calm when he said, "Right now what I want from you is for you to try to understand why I have to go back."

Rather than let him see the tears threatening to spill forth, she turned her back to him and focused on the sporadic beacons of lightning bugs.

She looks so fragile, he thought, *with her shoulders already stooped in defeat*. He hardened himself to what he had to do.

"Elizabeth, listen to me. I have to go back to finish out this assignment as El Puma. Too many people's lives are depending on me." He took a step closer but stopped. He didn't want to crowd her. Well, actually he did, but he knew better. "I can't run from my responsibility—as much as I'd like to. I am who I am, and at this moment, I'm under deep cover. I'm El Puma. Right now this identity is who I am, not just what I do for a living. Can you understand that? Even a little bit?"

It crossed his mind that what he was asking might border on the impossible. How did you ask an emotionally honest individual to understand a life of fraud—legalized fraud, but fraud nonetheless? Moreover, how did you explain that being someone else, anyone else, was often less painful than being yourself?

El Puma? Cougar? The words juxtaposed themselves in Elizabeth's mind. Why was she just now getting the connection between the names? Probably because getting slapped around and getting shot at weren't conducive to logical thought. And why, dammit, did she understand what he was trying to say?

"Yes," she whispered, "I understand. Though I wish to God I didn't."

Cougar took another step. "I know. I wish I didn't have to go back." He suddenly realized that he'd spoken the truth. For the first time in his life he wished he had a dull, nine-to-five job that would allow him to rock away the lazy summer nights...with Elizabeth beside him. The realization was startling and a little frightening. He mentally stepped back from the issue. "Deep cover—that's what it's called when you go underground like this and assume a persona. It usually doesn't last long. The chances of being found out are too great. Besides tonight's, we've already made another small bust using El Puma. One more is planned."

"And then?" The question trembled on Elizabeth's lips.

Cougar closed the distance between them. She could feel him standing behind her.

"And then I'll be back," he said, the words low, throaty, filled with the same heavy sweetness as the rose-scented night air.

She turned, her eyes meshing with his. "Swear it." It was what he'd repeatedly asked of her.

His eyes darkened to the shade of a moonless midnight. "I swear."

She swallowed. "When? When will you be back?"

"I don't know. Two months, three, four..."

The open-endedness of his statement gutted Elizabeth's stomach, though in reality she'd expected his answer. To survive, she had to fill the gutted hole with something. That something was love, a love that mellowed her eyes, softened her expression.

"Don't," he rasped, sensing, seeing, what was coming. "Don't say it. Wait until I come back."

It was she who now begged him. "Please try to understand. I have to. I can't let you go without telling you."

"Please, Lizzie—"

"I don't know how it's possible," she began, defying him. "I mean, I haven't known you long, but—" she smiled "—sometimes it seems I've known you forever."

"Lizzie, don't—"

"I don't know how or when it happened, but I—" she reached up and caressed a strand of blond hair from his sweat-dotted forehead "—I love you, Cougar Collins, El Puma, whoever you are. More than I ever thought it possible to love anything or anybody."

Silence. Stillness. The swell of the night around them.

Cougar knew that he'd remember this moment for the rest of his life. Because it was the happiest, saddest moment of his life. He knew what she expected to hear in return. It was something he couldn't say. It was something he couldn't even admit to himself. He knew his feelings for her ran deep, but he couldn't, at this point, use the word *love*. Love was an emotion he couldn't afford ... not with what lay ahead of him. But, oh God, how could he tell her this?

"Lizzie—"

The sound of summer-dry grass being crushed beneath boots interrupted whatever he would have said. Both Cougar and Elizabeth glanced toward the man who apologetically reappeared. Cougar stepped back from his intimate proximity to Elizabeth.

"I'm sorry," the man named Cummings said, "but you said to tell you when everything was wrapped up."

"Have the injured men been taken to the hospital?"

"Yeah. Everything's ready."

"I'll be right there."

Elizabeth's heart began to pound. It doubled its rhythm when Cougar once more faced her. Time stood perfectly, if impatiently, still.

Say it, she begged silently. *Tell me you love me.*

Understand, he begged. *Please understand that my job demands a sterility of emotion.*

"I ..." he began. He stopped. Then offered her all he could. "I'll be back," he said hoarsely.

It wasn't what she wanted to hear, but if it was all he could give her, she'd cherish it. She nodded. And suddenly felt tears forming again. Once more she turned away. She heard him step toward her, felt the warming shelter of his body behind her, felt his hands as they reached out to grasp her upper arms.

"No," she whispered before his hands reached her. "Don't touch me. Just go. While I have the courage to let you."

Long, long moments passed before his hands lowered. Even longer moments passed before he stepped back and, with a whispered "I'll be back," resolutely, hastily, fled across the porch and down the steps. Elizabeth deliberately looked away so she couldn't see him leave.

She would never know how long she stood where he'd left her, nor would she ever know how long she cried, but through it all she desperately clung to his promise that he'd be back. What he hadn't said, however, but what she knew, was that his return was conditional. He'd return...if he lived to do so.

Chapter Twelve

I carry his child. The realization fills me with a gentle awe. That the stranger's sweet kisses, that his sweet caresses, could leave me—I who never thought to hold a child in my arms—with a babe is the sweetest of all miracles. Already I feel the child kicking against my belly, and I whisper to it to grow strong and brave, for there will be those ready to shame us. But I shall never be ashamed. I shall never regret. Whatever the future might hold.

"Grover Haywood ought to be hanged from the nearest tree!" Pamela Shaw said, her Southern voice dripping with anger.

She sat at the table in Rose Haven's dining room, *The Shreveport Times* spread before her, a cup of coffee steaming at her elbow. When she'd opened the paper that morning and seen its headlines, she'd quickly called her friend.

When no one had answered, she'd made a mad dash to Rose Haven, where she'd found a haggard-looking Elizabeth who was deliberately avoiding phone calls. Though the newspaper had not mentioned Elizabeth personally, the report on what had happened the evening before at Rose Haven had brought endless calls, beginning even before daybreak, ranging all the way from genuinely concerned to nosy. Elizabeth had finally stopped answering the incessantly ringing phone.

"Would you listen to this?" Pamela continued. "The guns were stolen from an arsenal in Huntsville, Alabama. Now, how do you suppose ol' Grover pulled that off? Oh, and listen to this! The guns were paid for with cocaine. My Gawd, whatever happened to Visa and American Express?"

Her question met with no reply. Pamela read on, sometimes silently and sometimes aloud, thoroughly engaged in the newspaper's report of the event.

"The Guatemalan government arrested seventeen people at their end—the buyers, who were also charged with trafficking in drugs and a list of other violations as long as your arm." She quickly flipped to where the front-page article was continued. "Wonder how federal agents found out about it all. The paper seems a little vague about that, don't you think?"

Once more there was no answer to the question.

"I still think Grover Haywood ought to be strung up. Or maybe that's too good for him. Maybe I ought to turn Carol and Casey loose on him. They could slime—" Pamela stopped. "Elizabeth?"

The woman seated across the table silently stared down into her untouched coffee cup.

"Elizabeth?"

Elizabeth jumped, raising her eyes to the source of the intrusive sound. "What?"

"Are you okay?"

She managed a smile she was far from feeling. "Of course," she lied, uncoiling her bare feet from beneath her, rising and walking to the window.

Outside, a summer sky blazed in a brilliant shade of blue. She wished she could work up the same enthusiasm, the same optimism, that the day evinced. But she couldn't. She'd been upset by the drama of the evening before and by Cougar's departure, upset to the point of not sleeping one wink all night. But she hadn't understood the real meaning of the word *upset* until she'd read the morning paper. Though it had been purposefully vague, though she herself was not sophisticated in the workings of the shadowy undercover world, she was nonetheless intelligent enough to put two and two together. If people were arrested in Louisiana and also in Central America, didn't that mean that as soon as the bust went down, Cougar's cover as El Puma had been blown? At least to the people he'd been working with? And their nefarious associates? And to whatever far ears listened at the grapevine? He had said something about the difficulty of maintaining deep cover for a long period of time, but what he'd failed to say was that it was damned near impossible. And grew riskier with each venture.

The blood in Elizabeth's veins turned ice-cold at the thought of the danger he was placing himself in. She hugged her arms about her at the sudden chill.

"What's wrong?" At her friend's gently asked question, Elizabeth glanced over her shoulder. "I mean, what's really wrong?" Pam said. "Forget that Grover Haywood betrayed you, forget that he was running guns off your property, forget everything except what's been bothering you for the last couple of weeks—ever since someone put bruises on your wrist."

Elizabeth considered evading the subject the way she had evaded it before. But right now, and maybe for a long time to come, the only link she had with Cougar was remembering him, and admitting his existence might help her hold him in her heart if she couldn't hold him in her arms.

"I've met this man," she began. "He showed up on my doorstep, shot..." Minutes later, the entire story told, the uncanny coincidence between present and past duly noted, Elizabeth concluded with, "I love him." Her eyes grew glassy. "And I'm not certain that he's not walking into something he won't walk away from."

Pam jumped from the chair at her friend's distress. "Hey, are you crazy? Agents are trained to survive. That's their job. He'll be fine." What she lacked in solid argument, she made up for in conviction.

But Elizabeth saw his position only from the vantage—or disadvantage—point of a loving heart. "If anything happens to him..." she whispered, tears once more clustering in her eyes.

Pam pulled her into her arms. Elizabeth cried softly, the phone rang loudly, her friend consoled gently, while both remembered clearly that the first Elizabeth's lover had never returned.

Somehow, borrowing a strength that seemed genetically instilled, Elizabeth made it through the rest of July. August, too, passed, except for its last day. It was then that her mother's possessions, those promised by her British husband, the penultimate spouse in a long list of spouses, arrived in the mail. Elizabeth, who'd heard nothing from Cougar, and who'd given up on sleep and food—the very thought of the latter brought a wave of nausea—was pleased to have anything to divert her mind. To add to her stress, September first was the date set aside for her and Aunt Siddie to make some decision concerning the sale of Rose Haven. And to be honest, she didn't know what she wanted to do. She told herself over and over that Cougar could find her wherever she was, that he knew she taught at Bryn Mawr, that he wouldn't expect her to sit around waiting for him, but somehow or other she seemed disinclined to leave. And it didn't have to do entirely with Cougar's return. Rose Haven had seeped into her blood in a way it never had before.

The letter accompanying her mother's possessions apologized for the delay, not only for the delay since he'd spoken with Elizabeth, but for keeping the things the last year and a half since the divorce. Lord Worthington-Smythe had only recently found them stored in the attic.

Sitting cross-legged on the floor, Elizabeth rummaged through her mother's things, an eclectic accumulation of her personal belongings. An exquisite silver perfume decanter, still half-full of an amber, heavy scent. A glove leather date book richly scrawled in red reminders of upcoming appointments, all in a signature Elizabeth had seen far too little of. An ornate gold key chain, a collection of Hermes scarves, an alligator purse. Elizabeth opened the purse, which Lord Worthington-Smythe evidently hadn't. In it she found the enormous receipt in British pounds for python shoes. An outdated wallet calendar. A roll of Tums—changing husbands like one normally changed clothes had obviously taken its toll. A... Elizabeth reached for the folded piece of paper. She'd recognized it at once as an article on Rose Haven that had appeared in *Louisiana Life Magazine*, a copy of which Aunt Siddie had sent her a couple of years ago. She'd obviously sent Regan one as well. And Regan had kept it.

Why? Why had she bothered?

But then, why had she wanted to hang on to Rose Haven even though she never visited it? A puzzled frown creased Elizabeth's forehead. And why had she never realized until now that Regan had always retained her maiden name, that she'd never once taken the name of any of her harem of husbands? She'd also made certain her daughter had the name, even though it would have been more appropriate had she given her her father's name. Elizabeth's frown deepened. Hadn't she herself acted similarly when she'd married Brad? Hadn't she just naturally assumed the hyphenation of Jarrett-Gilford? Did both her and her mother's actions suggest family pride?

Pride, Elizabeth thought. She'd been so busy running from the family's notoriety that she hadn't considered the possibility of being proud of the Jarrett women. And wasn't it possible that Regan had chosen to run from that notoriety as well? Wasn't it possible that she and her mother had simply chosen different paths to run down, she sedately, her mother flamboyantly?

As Elizabeth pondered the answer to this question, her hand closed around a large oval locket. Popping it open, she focused on the picture inside. It was a picture of herself. A grade-school picture. With a wide, innocent smile that spotlighted where her two front teeth had once been. Elizabeth smiled, running her fingertip around the frame. It was the kind of picture that only a mother could love.

That only a mother could love. The words were like a soothing balm to an old wound. Was it possible that Regan, in her own eccentric way, had loved her after all?

The question, along with those concerning her ties and loyalty to Rose Haven, danced through her mind that night as she was once again unable to sleep. Curiously, Cougar's words about responsibility and identity haunted her, too.

Maybe she did have a responsibility to the plantation. And the truth was, no matter how far she ran, no matter how fast she ran, she was a Jarrett woman. She always had been; she always would be.

As morning streaked the sky in sunrise, Elizabeth made the decision of what to do with Rose Haven. She made one other decision as well.

"I don't want to sell Rose Haven," Elizabeth said the next day as she sat in her aunt's room at the nursing home.

Siddie Jarrett's age-spotted hand hesitated over the piece of the puzzle she was just fitting into place. The Big Chief tablet, containing its usual scathing letter, lay off to the side.

"When did you decide?" she asked.

"Last night." Elizabeth grinned. "None too soon, I'd say, since today is the first of September." *And five weeks exactly since I've seen Cougar.* This latter thought diminished her grin.

"Why? Why did you change your mind?"

Elizabeth discarded a piece of the puzzle she couldn't fit in. "I'm not sure I understand myself. It's just that I... that I can't chop away a part of me. Rose Haven's in my blood. It always has been, I guess, but I've been running so hard and fast from it that I never had time to notice it before."

"Sometimes what we run from is what we most want to run to," Aunt Siddie said, repeating what she'd said on another occasion.

"Yeah, maybe," Elizabeth agreed, rising from the chair and approaching the window. The afternoon was sunny and hot, just the way most of September would be. The dog days of summer, they were called, and everyone who'd spent ten minutes in the South knew that they could be the most miserable days of the year.

Miserable. God, she felt so miserable! Her heart ached, her body ached, until she was beginning to wonder if either would survive. If only she could sleep, if only she could eat, if only she could shake her fear. "I, uh...I've decided something else as well."

"Oh?"

"I'm not returning to Bryn Mawr this fall." She glanced over her shoulder. "I'm going to stay on at Rose Haven. I called the school this morning and talked with the president." Elizabeth smiled. "It helps that the president is a close friend when you break a contract at the last minute."

"I imagine it is most helpful," the older woman acknowledged with teasing lights in her eyes. Those lights slowly faded. "And what will you do at Rose Haven?"

"I, uh...I'm thinking of writing a book. On the Jarrett women."

"I think that's an excellent idea."

"Do you?" Elizabeth asked in a burst of enthusiasm that defied her misery. She crossed the room and reseated herself in the chair opposite her aunt. "Do you really think it's a good idea?"

"I do."

"Do you think I can do it?"

"A Jarrett woman can do anything she sets her mind to." The two women smiled. Aunt Siddie's smile eased into one that was soothing, consoling. "He'll be back, child," she said, brushing a wisp of black hair from Elizabeth's cheek.

Typically Elizabeth had finally shared her heart with the woman who'd been both mother and friend. Just as typically, Siddie hadn't been surprised at Cougar's resemblance to Rose Haven's ghost. It was as if in her world such things happened all the time.

"Do you believe that?" Elizabeth asked, desperately needing reassurance.

"I believe it. For a Jarrett woman, a man will defy heaven or hell, life or death." The older woman tilted her niece's chin. "By the way, have I told you you look awful?" she asked softly.

"No, I don't think you have this visit."

"I must be slipping. You look awful."

"I'm fine," Elizabeth lied.

"You're pale and much too thin."

"I'm fine. Truly."

"See a doctor."

"Grover Haywood?" Elizabeth said with a harsh laugh.

"Another doctor," her aunt chided.

"What could he tell me? That I'm miserable?"

"A physician could tell you whether you're all right physically."

"But I'm—"

"Think about it."

"But I don't need—"

"Just promise me you'll think about it."

Elizabeth sighed. "I promise to think about it."

And she did think about it. At odd moments during the next week, when she suddenly felt completely exhausted or when she had to stop eating the food she was forcing down because of nausea. At all other times, she ignored the idea of seeing a doctor. On September fifteenth, however, she could ignore her health no longer.

Tired, exhausted, feeling that she could sleep a lifetime if only she could put her mind at ease regarding Cougar, she slipped into a nightgown and sat down on the stool before her vanity. She drew the ivory-handled brush through her thick hair, then stood to make her way to the bed. She was only inches away from it when the lightheadedness struck her. Her head seemed to empty of everything, especially blood, which seemed to rush everywhere else in her body, while a darkness swiftly descended.

Was this what it was like to faint? she wondered seconds before she crumpled to the floor.

She came to quickly. Dazed, she crawled to the bed and climbed into it. Once more, she didn't sleep. This time she was afraid not only for Cougar, but also for herself. What was happening to her?

Three days later, the doctor she'd traveled to Shreveport to see told her.

"You're pregnant, Ms. Jarrett."

Pregnant.

Why had it never crossed her mind that she might be pregnant? Why had a reasonably intelligent woman overlooked all the signs? *Probably,* she defended herself, *because you've had only one thing on your mind: Cougar.*

"Are you... Are you certain?"

"Yes. Quite certain. I'd say you're about two months along." The doctor tactfully glanced down at Elizabeth's ringless finger. "Is the pregnancy going to be a problem?"

"No," she answered, a crazy smile at her lips, a song in her heart. "Absolutely none. I couldn't be happier."

Elizabeth drove home through a glaze of joyous tears. Once back at Rose Haven, though only late afternoon, she changed into a nightgown and went to bed. She simply wanted to be alone with the news. Alone with her baby. Cougar's baby. *Their* baby. She was going to have a baby! Running her hand along her stomach, she could hardly believe that a life grew just beyond her palm. What she could believe was that Cougar's beautiful kisses, his beautiful touches, his body loving hers with such sensual perfection, could create something this beautiful, this perfect. Only that kind of beauty could breed beauty; only that kind of perfection could spawn its equal.

Dear God, how she missed him! How she longed to share this moment with him! Strangely, for the first night since he'd been away, she slept. Deep in her heart she allowed herself to believe that he'd be all right now. He simply had to be—even if it meant defying history. Because he had to come back to her and their child.

Something was wrong.

Cougar could feel it, could taste its sinisterness on the steamy jungle mist, could smell its prowling darkness in the warm November air. Every precaution, he knew, had been taken to preserve the safety of the sting, and yet it just didn't feel right.

The operation had been moved from Central America to South America, hoping to leave behind any gossip of the last bust. The gun sellers were out of California, which planners hoped was a safe enough distance from Louisiana that no connection could be easily made to the recent arrests there. A discreet amount of time had also passed, allowing the gun buyer's and the gun seller's caution to succumb to greed. While Cougar had known the passage of time was necessary, it was this that he'd hated the most. Every day he spent waiting for the deal to be made, for the bust to go down, was one more day spent away from ...

He chased Elizabeth's image away. Now wasn't the time to clutter his mind with soft remembrances.

"What d'you think?" the federal agent at his side asked.

Clamping his hands at his waist, Cougar looked around him at the makeshift landing strip, at the dense, strangling forest that choked the strip's edge, at his men, all federal agents, waiting in various stages of nervous readiness. Nothing ever changed. It was always the same. It was always the same dirty job.

"I don't like it," Cougar said, his voice giving away none of his own personal anxiety. "Last-minute changes always make me leery."

Until twenty-four hours before, the bust had been planned for southern California, but at the eleventh hour their contact there had insisted that the locale be changed to the Colombian jungle. The guns were being brought to Cougar rather than his having to go after them. The only problem with that was now he couldn't utilize the support system of local Californian authorities. He and his men were going to have to wing it alone.

"So what do you want to do? Call it off?"

Did he? Did he want to call the whole thing off? As the senior figure in charge, he had the power to. Was his wariness justified, or had he simply become paranoid because he wanted the damned thing over so badly so he could return to...

Again he banished thoughts of the gray-eyed, black-haired woman who waited a world away.

"No, let's go with it," he said finally, unsure that the government wouldn't suggest another El Puma assignment if this one had to be forfeited. And he didn't want to be detained any longer than was absolutely necessary. "But tighten the ranks," he cautioned. "And tell everyone to watch his ass. And the man's next to him."

The agent nodded. "Right."

"Oh, and Thornton, you handle the cocaine."

What Cougar didn't have to say was that would leave him free to keep the situation assessed more closely.

The man nodded again, and Cougar watched him step away. Henry—Hank—Thornton and he were polar opposites. A husband and father of four, Hank was warm, a man who gave and received friendship easily, a man who had a face so open and honest he could have sold a used car to even the most cynical of buyers. On the other hand, he himself was cold. Clinically cold. Capable of fencing in all his feelings. It was a defense mechanism he'd learned early in life. With no father and with only an occasional mother, he had learned to survive by not caring for anything. And that specifically included himself. When no one cared about you, you didn't care about yourself. Partly because you figured you obviously weren't worth caring about and partly because you had no caring feelings to emulate.

A vision of his elderly, gray haired grandmother flashed through his mind. She was the only person who'd ever given him an ounce of love, but she'd been so broken-spirited, so disappointed with her daughter's useless life, so ridden with health problems, that she'd been of limited help. When she'd died when he was just shy of twelve, he typically hadn't grieved. The fences around his feelings were already securely in place.

He'd bounced from foster home to foster home, never trying to fit in anywhere. Except with a gang that roamed the Detroit streets. The day he became sixteen, he'd quit school. By then he'd had a police record of petty crimes a mile long; it was a list that promised to grow longer and graduate from petty crimes to the real thing. He had seemed dedicated to achieving both.

Then one day when he was eighteen, and purely on a dare, he'd joined the Marines. They hadn't been the slightest impressed with his tough-man act. In fact, the drill sergeant had taken a special delight in breaking him. But—and here was the first real chance he'd ever gotten—the man had cared enough to discipline him. Cougar knew that he hadn't cared about him personally, only the fact that he was a Marine. As one of the few, the proud, the Marines, he had something positive to live up to.

It was funny, Cougar mused almost a dozen and a half years later as he waited for a plane to land in the Colombian forest, what a little pride could do.

As a Marine he'd received a chestful of medals, then quit after his third tour in a war-hot Vietnam. He'd gotten his high-school diploma, gone to college, then joined government service as an agent, first in the Federal Drug Enforcement Administration, followed by the Bureau of Alcohol, Tobacco and Firearms. In both departments he'd quickly gained the reputation of volunteering for the most impossible, most dangerous jobs. And of pulling them off. There was no way of knowing how many men had looked into his cold eyes, had believed him to be the role he was playing and, as a result, had gone to prison.

Everyone said he was good at what he did, that he was a natural. Only he knew why he was so good, why he was that natural. Only he knew that he'd never learned to care about himself. Only he knew that death held no terror for him. That he'd never really lived, not with any joy inside him, and, consequently, he'd had nothing to lose. It was the man who had nothing to live for who had the clearest head, the steadiest hand.

Which was what scared him spitless. Because now he wanted to live. God, how he wanted to live!

And it didn't matter that he'd deliberately refrained from saying he loved the woman with the soft gray eyes, the woman with the black satin hair, the woman whose caress could cure him of a lifetime of not caring or being cared about, because the emotion was still there. He loved her. Dammit, he loved her! And if that caused his mind to be muddied, his reflexes to be slowed, then he'd have to die knowing that for once in his miserable and lonely life he'd loved . . . and been loved.

"Here it comes!" someone shouted.

Cougar turned his attention skyward. In a whirl of noise, a silver C47 approached and ultimately began its descent.

One more time, Cougar told himself. One more time he'd play the perilous game of seduction. Subtly testing the automatic pistol under his pant leg, he stepped forward as the plane rumbled to a halt.

"Keep your eyes open," he warned the eight agents who stood ready to transfer guns for cocaine before making the arrest. "And let's wrap it up quickly. The Colombian government has promised to start extradition procedures to the States as soon as we bring them in."

In minutes, Cougar was staring into the face of his counterpart, a suntanned Californian named Arnie Levine, a man whose life-style needs had outgrown his legitimate job.

"You got the guns?" Cougar asked.

"That's why we made the trip," the suave Californian dressed in white said.

Impatient, Cougar motioned for his men to begin unloading the plane.

"No!"

Cougar's eyes lowered to those of the man before him.

"The coke first."

Cougar hesitated. The feeling that things weren't right drifted about him again. He felt his stomach muscles tighten.

"How else will I know it's pure?" the Californian inserted into the pause.

Slowly, wordlessly, Cougar nodded for Hank Thornton to step forward.

The Californian's drug tester, a man so feature-perfect he looked as if he should be starring on a soap opera instead of standing in the middle of a Colombian forest testing the grade of cocaine, stepped forward as well.

Silent, tense minutes passed as everyone watched. Cougar, in a show of power, spent the time with his eyes trained on his rival, just as that man spent his time watching Cougar. He'd been right to think that nothing changed, Cougar mused. He'd looked into this man's eyes a hundred times. As always, he saw reckless greed. But was he really unlike this man? Weren't cop and criminal merely different sides of the same coin? Didn't they both commit the same acts, live on the same sharp edge, but simply for different reasons? Weren't they in reality equally hard men? Was it fair of him to ask a soft Elizabeth to—

The tester vouched for the drug's purity.

His boss reached for the attaché case containing the cocaine.

Cougar nodded for his men, who were already positioned at the plane's closed door, to unload the crates.

Levine motioned for the door to be opened.

Slowly it swung wide...and from the dark hole came the loud, repeated shots of an Uzi machine gun. Two of the federal agents went down even as Cougar watched. Then instinct and training prevailed. Throwing himself to the ground, he rolled over and over, reaching as he did so for his gun. Before he stopped tumbling, he shot, bringing down the feature-perfect, suddenly gun-toting drug tester. Cougar's body splayed to the earth, he shot again and again, but his firepower and that of his agents was nullified by the constant roar of the machine gun.

"Stop the Uzi!"

"Can't get near it!"

"Christ, Thornton's hit!"

Cougar crawled through the grass toward the plane, heedless of the burrs and twigs eating through his fatigues. He fired rapidly, carefully, killing one man, then another.

"Cover Collins! He's going for the Uzi!"

Shots thundered all around him.

He fired again, this time wounding one of the men standing near the plane. So close was he now that he heard Levine, who'd already boarded the craft, shouting for the pilot to take off. Engines immediately revved to life. The plane started to roll, changing the arc of the Uzi's fire. Another federal agent went down. Cougar reared and, steadying his right hand with his left, fired two rounds. Both went into the chest of the man holding the blazing Uzi. The barrage of bullets stopped abruptly, the silence now punctuated with solitary shots.

One...

Two...

The third, coming from Levine's gun, struck Cougar. He dropped where he stood, blood instantly gushing from his chest. He'd been shot, he thought dazedly, unable to accept his lying in the grass as reality. Adding to his disbelief was the fact that he felt nothing. Absolutely nothing. Why was getting shot always that way? Why nothing now and all-hell-to-pay pain later? Was he hurt bad? He ran his hand down his chest...to the hole widely gaping open. Ah, crap, he thought, thinking that the blood on his fingers looked like a liquid rose. It was bad...bad...bad.... Consciousness began to fade, but he zealously clung to it.

"Jesus!" someone shouted as he scrambled to his side. "Easy, Collins. Just take it easy, man."

Two thoughts simultaneously crossed Cougar's mind. This was twice he'd been shot in six months. *Sloppy, Collins. You're getting damned sloppy.* And he wasn't going to see Elizabeth again. He was never going to kiss her, hold her, tell her he loved her. And for that he was more sorry than he'd ever be able to say.

Suddenly he groaned as poker-hot pain tore through him. His breathing shallowed, his heartbeat grew irregular and darkness closed itself around him. The last word he whispered before his head lolled to the side was "Lizzie..."

Three days later, on a cold November morn, Elizabeth read the newspaper article. It was a small article, probably included only because of the gunrunning incident that had occurred in Natchitoches that July. The same federal agents, the paper reported, had been involved in a California-Colombia buy and three of the agents had been killed, three more wounded. Among the dead was an undercover agent known as El Puma.

Elizabeth's heart stopped. Shock, numbing and total, shrouded her. Methodically she cut the article from the paper and started to fold it, over and over and over, until it was the size of a coin, which she clutched in her palm. Tightening her fist around it, she went back upstairs to her unmade bed, where she crawled once more beneath the sheets.

She lay there all day, all night, neither sleeping nor eating nor crying. She simply existed. Come sunrise, she rose and ate for the sake of her child, but all the while she held the article tightly in her hand. She then went back to bed.

It was there Pamela found her that afternoon.

"Elizabeth?" the woman called softly into the drape-shaded room. She stepped toward the still mound in the bed, then eased herself to the bedside. When Elizabeth didn't acknowledge her presence, she touched her lightly on the shoulder. Elizabeth slowly rolled toward her and stared with blank eyes.

Finally, simply, she said, "He's dead."

"I know. Oh, Elizabeth, I'm so sorry."

Elizabeth, the article still clutched in her now-aching fist, allowed herself to be gathered into her friend's arms. Pamela cried. Elizabeth did not. She longed to but could not. Except for the child alive in her womb, she was dead. Dead like the man she loved. Dead like their dream. Dead to all the lonely tomorrows that she would know.

Chapter Thirteen

The child is born. I have called her Rosemary and long most desperately for her father to see her. She is pink and plump and as perfect as the union that produced her.

The weeks pass since Rosemary's birth—three tomorrow. Where can the stranger be? He promised to return to be by my side.

I am trying not to worry, but . . .

He is dead. His friend told me. But my heart cannot believe it. His friend, his hat crushed in his hands, sat with me for an hour; we said nothing. There was nothing to say. As he was leaving, I asked, "What was his name?" The man, sitting astride a roan, replied, "He said to tell you only that he was a stranger . . . a stranger that heaven, in its kindness, once blessed."

I have ceased to live. I breathe now only for my child, eat only for her sake. I try to sleep but do so only when exhaustion overcomes me...and then I dream of warm lips, strong arms, tender words... and a rush of tears overtakes me, pinning me beneath its moist and leaden weight. And always in my dreams I hear him say he loves me. How barren shall be my soul that I never heard the words from his sweet lips!

The nights are long, like endless dark swells on an angry black sea.

Is God punishing me? Or is it only that something as perfect as our love could not live in this imperfect world?

Sometimes I hear voices...then realize they are naught but my own.

Merciful God, be with me, for I am most surely lost.

I saw him today! Standing beneath the oak tree! I thought myself mad—perhaps I am—for when I approached him, he disappeared, vanished like a tempting vapor, but not before I felt the brush of his lips against mine, not before I heard my name whispered on the wind, not before he could lay a red rose at my feet. I pray he will return—I care not in what form as long as my eyes may feast upon him, as long as I may feel life once more flow through my lifeless body, as long as I may once more find my lost soul.

November wintered into December.

The live oak trees lining the long drive of Rose Haven, and the single one standing a lone watch in its front yard, stalwartly guarded their evergreen leaves. By contrast, the rose garden lay dead and dormant, the blossoms, the sweet fragrance, only memories in the minds of those who cared to remember.

Elizabeth remembered. Vividly. Everything from scent-laden rose petals drawn across the aching summit of her breast to rough hands that left tender messages in their tactile wake. She remembered hot lips and hotter eyes... and the newspaper article that said she'd never see either again. The article, creased into dozens of tiny squares by the sorrowful pressure of her fist, now lay on the mantel. She would save it for their child.

Their child.

It grew strong and sure, swelling and stretching her womb with its gentle presence. Sometimes Elizabeth would sing to it; sometimes she would read to it from her great-grandmother's journal. Increasingly, she talked to it... and to herself. The frequency of the latter made her wonder if she, perhaps like her great-grandmother before her, was going just a little bit mad.

"Please, God," she'd whisper as she lay awake in the black of the night, "let me go mad if it would help to ease the pain."

She also prayed for tears. But they wouldn't come. Not once had she been able to cry since reading of Cougar's death. For a moment she'd thought that she would cry when she'd finally, after interminable red tape snipping, reached the federal office of the Bureau of Alcohol, Tobacco and Firearms. She'd wanted to get some background on Cougar, how he'd died, where he was buried, if he had family and where they were. He'd never talked of family beyond the negative comments about his mother and the gentler comments about his grandmother, but perhaps there was someone out there who'd want to know that she was carrying his child. She herself longed for some contact, any contact, with someone who could share her memories of Cougar. But not even that much was destined to be hers. The Bureau, though polite, could give her—or, more to the point, chose to give her—no information at all. It was as though he'd never existed. Had his child not been growing in her belly, she might have questioned her own memories.

That night, tears had been close, as close as rain on a cloudy day, but still they hadn't come. But then, how could they when her heart felt dry, parched? How could they when her spirit felt withered and worn?

And so, tearless, Elizabeth plumbed the depths of her being simply to survive one day at a time, one fragile, friable day at a time. In her heart she knew she would survive—her survival was ordained in her great-grandmother's journal, though why Fate had duplicated history, she would never understand.

In the end, it was a brown plastic bottle of antibiotics that finally ended the drought.

On the first Saturday of December, the way it did the first Saturday of every December, Natchitoches held its Festival of Lights. In honor of the Christmas season, people from all over the area gathered for parades, fireworks, food, entertainment and a fairyland showing of Christmas lights. Pamela had not asked Elizabeth if she wanted to go; she'd simply shown up on her friend's doorstep, forced her to get dressed, then pushed her out the door.

What am I doing here? Elizabeth thought an hour later as she watched Pamela's husband lovingly slip his arm around his wife's waist, as she listened to their children shout in glee when the sparkling fireworks burst in the night sky. The fireworks, and the lights draped on the two bridges, reflected their glitter across the surface of the still waters of Cane River Lake, leaving behind the sad message that what she was doing there was hurting. Amid the crowd, she'd never felt more alone. Amid the gaiety, she'd never felt more miserable.

Two days later she came down with a cold. It would have been easy to blame the chilled night she'd spent at the Festival of Lights—indeed, it had probably been the straw that had broken the camel's back—but she also knew she was physically worn down from emotional stress. Her body had to pay for the abuse—too little food, too little sleep—she'd put it through. Twenty-four hours after the cold developed, a sore throat started, which was immediately followed by an acute flare-up of tonsillitis. Her obstetrician prescribed the appropriate and safe antibiotics.

They came in a brown plastic bottle. A brown plastic bottle that looked exactly like another brown plastic bottle, which she hadn't been able to bring herself to throw away.

She'd worked so hard to keep infection at bay after he'd been shot. And for what? she thought, a hot wash of anger consuming her. He'd died anyway. Died God-only-knew-where, from God-only-knew-what. A bullet in the head? The heart? Had the end been quick? Or had he suffered agonizing pain? And, amid that pain, had he thought of her? Had he cried out her name? Why, dammit to hell, if he'd had to die, couldn't he at least have done so in her arms?

And why—the tears, impatient from their wait, jumped to her eyes and coursed down her cheeks—why couldn't he have told her he loved her? Just once...just once...just one lousy once? The tears, which for weeks wouldn't start, now wouldn't stop. And so, huddled in bed, her hand splayed across her stomach, she cried, sobbed, until the blessed oblivion of sleep descended.

If she'd hoped that crying would purge her, would raise her to a plateau closer to emotional recovery, she'd been sorely mistaken. If anything, she felt worse. She'd cried;

ow there was nothing else to do. Nothing else that she could hope would help. All she could do now was live with he vast emptiness in her heart.

And that was what she was doing three days before Christmas, when the rest of the world seemed disgustingly oyous. Rose Haven was bare of any decorations proclaiming the holiday. Next year, she promised the baby. Next year he'd feel like celebrating; next year she'd start on the book he wanted to write about the Jarrett women. Next year. Anytime but now. Now was reserved for simply surviving.

A storm had been predicted, and already the late-afternoon sky was brimming with murky streaks that ranged rom gray to lavender to purple. The night promised rain hat would turn into sleet and ice before the innocent, unsuspecting morning came.

Retiring early to her bedroom, Elizabeth stoked the fire n the cast-iron Franklin stove, sending waves of warmth unneling into the denim of her jeans and the wool of her lack sweater. The jeans, old, comfortable and oft-washed, vere unzipped and unsnapped to accommodate her bulging stomach, while the sweater riding over them was a aggy, floppy affair that suited her condition perfectly. Her air was haphazardly gathered atop her head with the ivory omb, and on her feet snuggled thick socks and a pair of uzzy house shoes.

"We'll be warm tonight," she said to the child, returning he poker to its stand.

Almost in challenge, the wind keened around the corners f the house, a mournful dirge that pierced Elizabeth's soul nd drew her to the window. She raked back the lacy curtain and stared out. Darkness hovered, ready to pounce like nocturnal beast. Out of habit, her eyes found the ancient ld oak. The wind stalked through its mighty limbs, bending them in cold acrobatics, while the leaves shivered a chilled plea for mercy. Even the navy shadows beneath the tree seemed to writhe in the sudden, vigorous charge of air. They swayed, flickered, and, in the span of a heartbeat, one stepped forward.

Elizabeth's eyes blinked; her heart quickened.

No. She had simply *thought* the shadow had separated itself from the tree's massive trunk. There was no way... It couldn't have possibly... Elizabeth crossed to the door, opened it and, hugging her arms about her in defense against the cold, walked onto the tiny porch that linked the bedroom with the outside stairway. A breathless emotion clutching at her heart, she peered down...willing the shadow back into its normal place.

It didn't return. Instead, it took another step, then another before slowly ambling its way to the gallery porch. In the darkling light she could tell it was the silhouette of a man, a man with broad shoulders, lean hips, long legs. A man who had his eyes trained on the woman who stood waiting at the bedroom door.

It was a man she recognized. And with the recognition, her heart now mercilessly banged against her ribs. Dear God, was she dreaming? Hallucinating? Had she longed so desperately for Cougar that she'd forced him to materialize? Or—this thought she didn't even find surprising—was she simply viewing his ghost? Would two lost lovers now haunt the halls of Rose Haven? Or were they one and the same?

His measured footfalls rang against the gallery steps, across the length of the porch, up the stairway to where Elizabeth stood. As Cougar's figure drew nearer, nearer, ever nearer, Elizabeth's heart thudded until her head swirled from the too-fast beat. She reached for the newel post of the railing as an anchor.

Her eyes, insatiably greedy for the sight of him, roved from his wind-tousled hair to his booted toes. A lock of pale blond hair slanted across his creased forehead, while a paler froth of chilled breath escaped lips so familiar that their every curve and line and taste was indelibly etched in her memory. He wore a fur-lined jacket, below which jeans tightly encased his legs, legs that bent at the knees as he climbed step after step to bring him to stand before her.

Her eyes slid deeply, drowningly, into his, just as his plunged into the winter-gray depths of hers. The emotions scoring her were myriad. Hope—dare she even hope that he was alive? Dread—what if she reached out and her hand met only thin air? Fear—what if hope were too fragile a thing to keep him before her? What if he disappeared, never again to return to her? The myriad emotions were also painful. What if her heart simply couldn't stand this savage racing?

Slowly she reached out a hand to his cheek but hesitated before making contact. Never had so much rested on so very little.

Are you real? her eyes begged.

Yes. Yes, the figure assured her. *Just touch me and see.*

The hand near his face trembled as she worked up the necessary courage. Finally, praying as she never had before, she settled her palm on the clean-shaven cheek. The flesh was warm, solid, real. So warm, so solid, so real, that tears instantly sprang to Elizabeth's eyes. She thought that she would surely faint.

As it never failed to do, her simple touch ripped through Cougar with the power of lightning. He felt his skin branded by her caress, felt his heart heated with love. He smothered her hand with his, urging her palm closer. When it proved anatomically impossible to push her hand into his very being, he roughly drew her palm to his mouth, where he planted desperate but tender kisses. Warm kisses that radiated completely to her soul. Warm kisses that spilled tears onto her wind-chafed cheeks.

Finding her eyes above her fingertips, he saw the tears. She was close to breaking, from confusion, from emotions that were flooding her too quickly. Her tears were his undoing. All the plans he'd made while lying in the hospital bed, the plans to slowly, logically explain what had happened, what he hoped would happen, went sailing out the proverbial window. All that mattered was holding her, comforting her.

"Oh, God, Lizzie!" he growled, hauling her into his arms and burying his face in the delicate curve of her neck.

Her tears fell, hard and harsh and without restraint. Restraint was something she was no longer capable of. The tears were too primitive, too basic, coming from too deep in her heart. Her hands dug into the nape of his neck, his back, urgently drawing, even clawing, him to her.

"I love you, I love you, I love you," he chanted, as if the words were the glue holding both him and his world together in that fractured moment.

I love you.

Elizabeth heard his fevered recitation and thought that if she never heard another word, those would be quite enough to make up for the loss. Could she ever ask to hear anything sweeter? Even as the longed-for words rained about her, warm spatters of his breath against her skin, they began to take their emotional toll. So desperately had she wished to hear them that they started tremors pulsing across and through her body.

Cougar felt her trembling. Opening his jacket, he pulled her flush against him. Her tears moistened the column of his neck, her breath fanned his throat, her breasts caressed his chest, her stomach mated with his. Tighter, tighter, he pulled her . . . until she became he, he, her. Every shade, every nuance of her body began to slowly register on his starved senses. Her tears were wet, her breath warm, her breasts full—were they fuller?—her stomach round and bulging. Round and bulging. Round as in gained weight. Bulging as in preg—

Slowly he pushed her from him. His questing eyes found hers before immediately dropping to her waist. As hesitantly as she'd laid her palm to his cheek, he now splayed both hands across her stomach. Her swollen stomach. His eyes, stunned and disbelieving, sped back to hers.

"Our child," she whispered at his silent question.

Our child. He had his hands on the swell of their child. If he had died—and God alone knew why he hadn't—he would have died without knowing that his child grew in her womb. His child. Sweet and glorious heaven, *his* child!

For a man who had faced everything—deception, danger, death—and had faced it without a trace of fear, he suddenly had the most monumental case of fright. The kind of fright that comes from learning what a near miss you've had. His breathing shallowed, his heart pounded, his hands tightened, balling her sweater into his fists.

"Tell me . . . tell me you're pleased," she begged.

He struggled for words, but nothing could pass the knot tied in his throat. He swallowed, slowed his breath, eased the pressure of his hands until they again rested flat on the curve of her stomach. On the evidence of his child. *His* child!

Pulling her once more to him, he searched for her mouth, found it and gave her an answer with the beauty of his kiss. He cherished her, worshiped her, loved her with his lips, his tongue, the cupping of her face with his hands. Until they both trembled from passion. And from the cold. Inching his mouth from hers, he stared down into her face. He brushed the pads of his thumbs across the tears streaming down her cheeks, tears that threatened to freeze in the rimy breath of the wind.

"You're cold," he growled, protectively swinging her up into his arms and moving into the bedroom. Warmth greeted them, and he closed the winter behind them with a swing of his hip. He walked unerringly, purposefully, toward the canopied bed.

"I thought you were d-dead," she said, clinging tightly to his neck, staring up into his face. "The paper said... I called the Bureau ... I—"

His lips claimed hers. "Later," he whispered into the hallowed sweetness of her mouth. "We'll talk later. Right now just love me." He gently released the arm beneath her knees and allowed her to slide the length of him. "Please," he begged, shrugging from his jacket, throwing it to the floor and recapturing her mouth all in one swift movement, "love me."

This time the kiss was like instant combustion. With two souls eager to be burned in the conflagration. His mouth was hard, masterful, passionate. Hers met his with the same fierce need. His lips parted over hers, making the perfect bridge for the foraging entrance of his tongue. Twisting her lips beneath his, she took the velvet invader deep, twining her own tongue with his. Her hands curled into his back.

"Ah, Lizzie," he rasped, spearing his fingers through her hair and sending the comb flying to the floor. Feverishly his mouth tore from hers, trailed along the length of her arched neck, dropped to the breast rounded beneath the black sweater. Even through the heavy fabric, she could feel his hot breath; he could feel her nipple harden.

She moaned.

Yanking the sweater up and over her head, deliciously tangling her hair in the process, he tossed it to the floor.

"They're so full," he whispered, drawing the backs of his hands across her breasts. "So... full," he repeated, his mouth loving one, then another, through the sheerness of her bra. Slipping his hands behind her, he unfastened the lacy garment. When it fell away and his mouth moved over the aching peak of her bare breast, she bit her lip, then cried out as he gently sucked. At the shattered sound of his name on her lips, he took her in his arms once more and laid her in the middle of the bed. He lowered his eyes to her stomach peeking through the V of the unsnapped, unzipped jeans.

"I... I don't have any maternity pants," she explained, her look begging him to think she was still pretty despite five months of pregnancy. The feel of his lips—his trembling lips—on her stomach effectively stilled all doubts.

The next few minutes were filled with the sound of rustling denim as he slipped the jeans from her legs, the sound of the subtle shifting of her body as she raised her hips to aid him, the airy, brazen sound of lacy panties dropping to the floor. All this was followed by the sounds of intimacy kisses, caresses, muffled words and sweet, sweet sighs. Increasingly, the sighs became moans, groans, then cries, urgent and clear.

Elizabeth reached for the buttons of his shirt as if her survival depended on the sight of his bare chest. Wrenching the shirt from his jeans, she fought at the buttons with unsteady fingers. Ultimately, as impatient as she, he helped her. It was when he drew the shirt from his wide shoulders that she first saw the scar—still red from its newness, still tender-looking around its edges.

Shot. He'd been shot. Her brain interpreted what she saw, then rejected it even as her fingers gingerly touched what she was denying.

"What—"

"I'm all right, Lizzie."

Her eyes rose to his. "You were...shot?"

"Yes, but—"

"Oh, my God," she whispered, panic racing across the gray landscape of her eyes. "Oh, my God," she repeated.

"I'm all right. It's over. It's—"

"No," she said, tears welling once more as she caressed the scar running along his breastbone. "No...no...no..."

Her words were incoherent, her thoughts a jumble. She kept telling herself she ought to be happy that he was alive, that the scar was simply confirmation of what she'd suspected all along. What she felt, however, was that she'd almost lost him, and, in some mysterious way, that was more frightening than actually having done so. With him beside her, she now knew the flesh-and-blood dimensions of that loss.

Cougar heard the desperation in her voice, saw the havoc the scar was wreaking on her nerves. She was close to hysteria. He responded to it by making love to her. Slipping out of his remaining clothes, he eased his body atop hers, his lips delivering kisses and vows of "I'm all right" while he positioned himself between her legs.

They made love intensely, quickly—it was what both wanted, needed. Together they climbed the sensual spiral. Together they cried out their release. When he rolled to his side, taking her with him, he could still feel, however, the tension in her taut body.

"Don't leave me again," she pleaded, her eyes imploring him, her fingers digging into his upper arm. "Please, don't go back. Please—"

"I'm not going back."

"...don't leave me. Don't—"

"I'm not going back, Lizzie. I'm never going to leave you again."

"Please—"

He cupped her chin in his hand. "I'm...not...going...back."

She took a deep, uneven breath as she tried to focus on what he'd said. Finally she whispered, "Swear it."

"I swear it."

"Again."

"I swear it, I swear it, I swear—" His lips melded with hers. Tenderly, repeatedly, he kissed her until he could feel her body relaxing. "I swear it," he said one last time, drawing her cheek to his chest and enfolding her in his arms.

An eternity passed before either spoke, and when Elizabeth did, it was with her fingertips, which she drew across the jagged scar.

He felt her question. "It was a bad bust," he said, his voice rumbling deep within his chest. "My cover had been blown."

He deliberately left the details for another time, a time when she'd be stronger, better able to cope. Maybe even a time when he was stronger, more capable of coping. He'd tell her then about how her name had been on his lips as he'd slipped into unconsciousness, how he'd later died on the operating table, how bright lights and peace had beckoned from the end of a long tunnel, but how he'd fought to return to her—and had, to the tune of a miracle. Maybe he'd even tell her of the award the government had given him for bravery beyond the call of duty.

"Why didn't you let me know you were all right?" Her eyes teared again. "I almost died thinking you were..." She tried to say the word but couldn't.

"I know, I know, baby," he whispered, pulling her close. "In the beginning no one in the department knew to call you. Then, after we hatched the plan to make it appear I'd died, we had to make it believable. There couldn't be any leaks. The department wanted to make certain that if anyone was watching you, you'd appear grief-stricken.''

Again, he didn't tell her that some disgruntled South Americans had put out a contract on him, a contract reputedly in excess of $200,000, within hours of the shooting, just in case luck had been on his side. And luck had. Luck and love. He'd allowed her to suffer only because their future, her safety, had depended on it. He hadn't known he'd also been protecting the safety of his child.

This realization made his voice husky when he asked, "How do you feel about living in New York?''

She angled her head upward. "New York?''

"Yeah. I'm going to have a nice, quiet, safe desk job training other agents for the field. Just the kind of job for a man with a wife and family." Just the kind of job, he thought, for a man who no longer needed to substitute adrenaline for emotion. Brushing a tangle of hair back from her face, he asked softly, hoarsely, "Will you marry me, Lizzie?''

She longed to answer him, even tried to, but she couldn't for the knot in her throat. Instead, she wrapped her arms about him and kissed him with all the love in her heart. Visions of matching gold wedding bands, an apartment-with-a-view in New York, taking their child, their children, to Central Park, long vacations back at Rose Haven danced in her head. They were visions sweeter than any seasonal sugarplums.

"Is that a yes?'' he asked when their mouths parted.

"Yes," she whispered. Suddenly the beauty of life shone like a bright sun breaking through thick gray clouds. "You're alive. You're really alive!'' she shouted, elation filling her heart, happiness filling her eyes. "You're really, really alive!''

"Yes. Yes. God, yes!" he shouted, too, rolling her to her back and thinking that for the first time in his life, his barren life, he *was* alive! Really alive! Bona fide, go-for-broke, all-the-way alive!

This time they made love slowly, gently—it was what they both wanted, needed. And when it was over, they quietly held each other. A long while later, as the wind wailed outside the window, as the fire battled the winter night, Cougar's hand slipped from the fullness of her breast to the fullness of her stomach. He'd touched their child a hundred times now, but each time he did, it was more humbling than the last.

"Are you all right? I mean, have you been feeling well?"

She placed his hand atop his. "Yes. Except for a cold and tonsillitis."

"Tonsillitis?"

"Yeah. The real thing. No wounded stranger on my doorstep."

For a moment each thought back to that summer night that seemed so long ago, yet curiously not so long ago at all.

"What about the baby? Is she healthy?" he pressed, automatically assuming a future "Jarrett woman."

Elizabeth responded in kind. "She's fine."

A thought occurred to him, rumpling his brow. "We didn't hurt her, did we? I mean, making love . . ."

"It didn't hurt her." Cougar could feel Elizabeth's smile. "Besides, it did her mother a world of good."

Cougar grinned, a lopsided, irresistible slashing of his mouth. "It did her father a world of good, too."

They kissed, and she turned in his arms, bringing her stomach flush against his. She could feel the hair that swirled near his navel; he could feel a faint fluttering. The hand at the small of her back stopped in mid-caress. His eyes rushed to hers.

She smiled. "Did you feel it?"

"Yes," he said, awe in his voice. "What was she doing?"

"Kicking. Maybe she was getting even for waking her."

Cougar's impish grin returned. "Vindictive, huh? Well, she'd better get used to her father making love to her mother. In fact, he's gonna make love to her a dozen times a day, in a dozen different ways." His body hardened to prove the capability of his silken threat. "Lizzie, are you blushing again?"

"No," she denied, ducking her head.

"You are," he said, trying to raise her chin.

"I'm not."

"You are."

"I'm—" His lips captured hers.

Sighs later, she said, "Cougar, do you understand any of what's happened? I mean, everything duplicating itself?"

Silence. "No. I don't understand. But maybe it isn't important to."

"My aunt says that you miss half the beauty of life if you limit yourself only to those things you understand."

"I say maybe she's right."

Another silence followed as Elizabeth tunneled her fingers through the golden hair on his chest. "What if they found a way to be together?" she asked, raising her eyes to his, hoping she didn't sound like a lunatic for what she was suggesting. There was no need to qualify that "they" referred to her great-grandmother and her lover.

"You mean, through us?"

Elizabeth nodded, spraying dark hair over their shoulders.

"Maybe," he said. Brushing back a wisp of hair from her cheek, he added in a voice that trembled slightly, "That would be all right with me. I'll love you enough for two men, for two lifetimes, for two eternities."

They simply stared at each other; any other word, all other words, would have been superfluous. Slowly, predictably, their mouths merged.

This time they made love like old, familiar lovers—it was what they felt they were. They touched in ways they knew would please, in places they knew would please, with laughter and giggles and hearts wide open. And when it was over, they did what all lucky lovers do: they fell asleep in each other's arms.

But just before sleep enveloped them, Elizabeth snuggled close and whispered, "I love you."

"I love you."

"Swear it," she said, her voice dreamy and vague.

"I swear it," he whispered, knowing that he did so by the stars, by the moon, by the life she'd given him, by the child she carried for him. "I swear it, Lizzie. For always."

They slept. And as they slept, the wind howled, the sleet plummeted against the house, the old oak swayed and dipped. The warmth of the stove, the contentment of hearts, filled the room, while lingering whispers and sighs bounced from wall to wall, splashing down on the entwined lovers. None could have said just when, but sometime between the mid of night and the dawn of morn a single, perfect red rose appeared at the foot of the love-rumpled bed. And a voice, as light and airy as the heart's fondest dreams, teased the silvery silence.

"Ah, Lizzie, my love," the stranger whispered, "we chose well...."

* * * * *

Silhouette Intimate Moments

WHEN OPPOSITES ATTRACT

Roberta Malcolm had spent her life on the Mescalero ranch. Then Hollywood—and Jed Pulaski—came to Mescalero, and suddenly everything changed.

Jed Pulaski had never met anyone like Rob Malcolm. Her forthright manner hid a woman who was beautiful, vibrant—and completely fascinating. But Jed knew their lives were as far apart as night from day, and only an all-consuming love could bring them together, forever, in the glory of dawn.

Look for Jed and Roberta's story in *That Malcolm Girl*, IM #253, Book Two of Parris Afton Bonds's Mescalero Trilogy, available next month only from Silhouette Intimate Moments. Then watch for Book Three, *That Mescalero Man* (December 1988), to complete the trilogy.

Silhouette Intimate Moments

SET SAIL FOR THE SOUTH SEAS
with
BESTSELLING AUTHOR
EMILIE RICHARDS

This month Silhouette Intimate Moments begins a very special miniseries by a very special author. *Tales of the Pacific*, by Emilie Richards, will take you to Hawaii, New Zealand and Australia and introduce you to a group of men and women you will never forget.

In Book One, FROM GLOWING EMBERS, share laughter and tears with Julianna Mason and Gray Sheridan as they overcome the pain of the past and rekindle the love that had brought them together in marriage ten years ago and now, amidst the destructive force of a tropical storm, drives them once more into an embrace without end.

FROM GLOWING EMBERS (Intimate Moments #249) is available now. And in coming months look for the rest of the series: SMOKESCREEN (November 1988), RAINBOW FIRE (February 1989) and OUT OF THE ASHES (May 1989). They're all coming your way—only in Silhouette Intimate Moments.

IM249-R

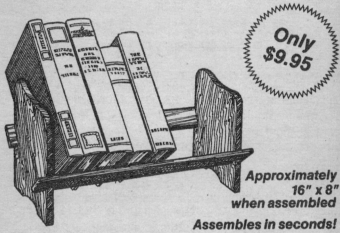

Silhouette Special Edition

COMING NEXT MONTH

#475 SKIN DEEP—Nora Roberts
In book three of THE O'HURLEYS!, private eye Quinn Doran stakes out
Chantel O'Hurley's too-avid, threatening ''fan.'' But his tougher case is
uncovering the warmth beneath Chantel's icy exterior.

#476 TENDER IS THE KNIGHT—Jennifer West
A spell had been cast that Juliet meet a man worthy of her tenderness.
And poof! armor-clad Rocco Marriani appeared. But could simple
conjuring conquer Juliet's private demons?

#477 SUMMER LIGHT—Jude O'Neill
A match between bohemian Wiley Ranahan and conservative Molly
Proctor couldn't possibly last forever. But after spending August basking
in his affection, Molly began wondering if summer love could linger....

#478 REMEMBER THE DAFFODILS—Jennifer Mikels
Knowing whimsical, unpredictable Ariel Hammond would eventually let
him down, sensible Pete Turner had left before she broke his heart. Now
he wanted her back, but had his practicality compromised their passion?

#479 IT MUST BE MAGIC—Maggi Charles
Upon meeting her volatile new client, Alex Grant, Josephine suspected her
rule about business and pleasure was about to be broken. But could the
magic of love make her deepest fears vanish?

#480 THE EVOLUTION OF ADAM—Pat Warren
For self-made Adam Kinkaid, to-the-manor-born Danielle Ames held the
key to high society. He thought he wanted in...until rebellious Dani made
him long for so much more.

AVAILABLE THIS MONTH: